THEN CAME EDGAR

MORGAN CROSSROADS SERIES - BOOK 1

TOM BUFORD

THEN CAME EDGAR
A Morgan Crossroads novel

Copyright © 2018 by Tom Buford

ISBN 978-0-9708103-5-9

All rights reserved. No part of this book may be reproduced or transmitted in any form or by any means, electronic or mechanical, including photocopying, recording, or by any information storage and retrieval system without the written permission of the author, except where permitted by law.

This is a work of fiction. The characters, incidents and dialogue are drawn from the author's imagination and are not to be construed as real. Morgan Crossroads and Whipper County, Alabama exist only in the mind of the author and in the pages of *Then Came Edgar* and other books in The Morgan Crossroads series of fun fiction.

Any similarity between places or characters in this book and places or people, living or dead, that may exist somewhere in the world is purely coincidental. If the places and characters in this story remind you of a place you've wished you lived or a person you've wished you'd known, that's good. That means the author did his job.

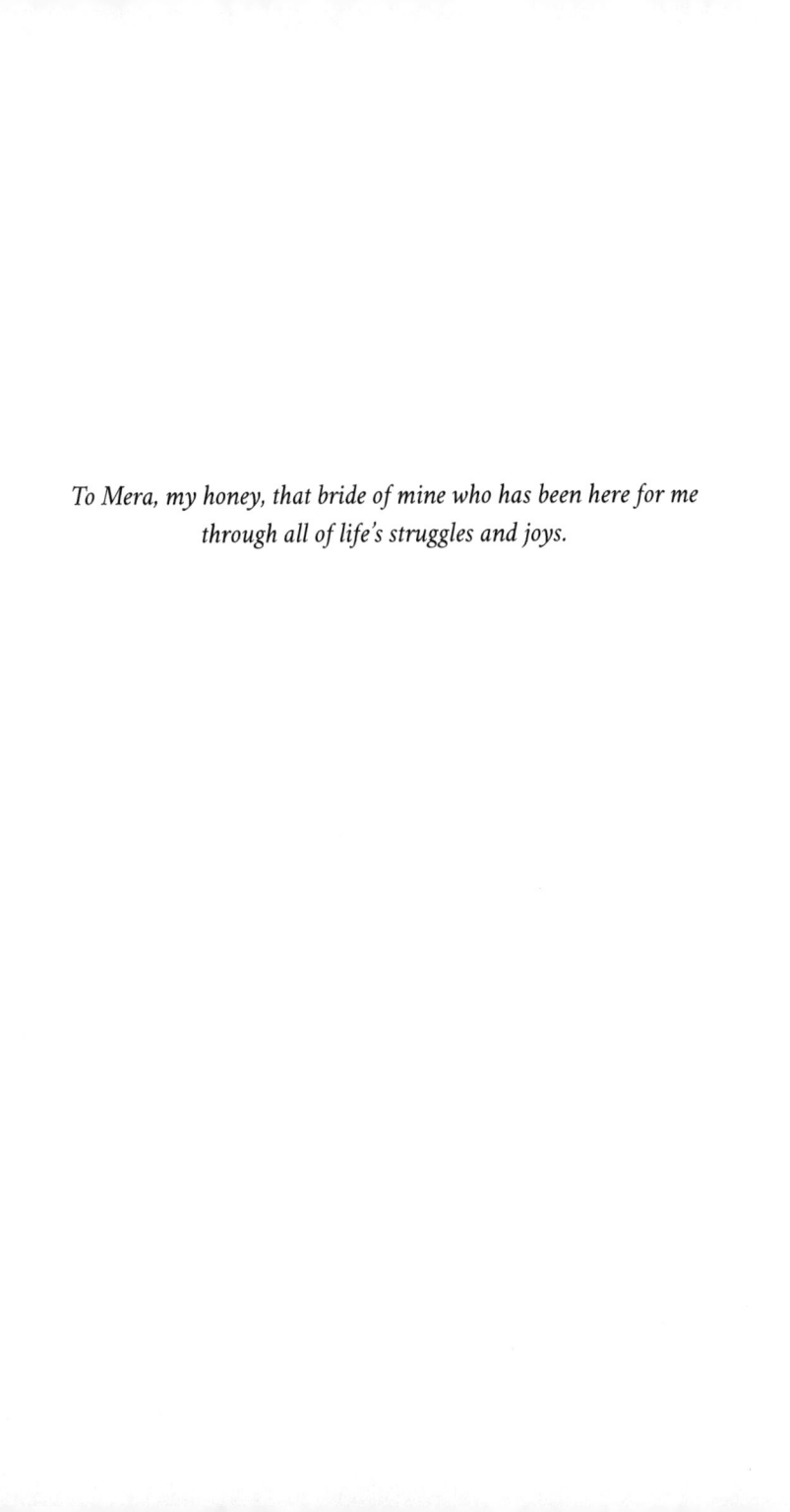

To Mera, my honey, that bride of mine who has been here for me through all of life's struggles and joys.

PREFACE

Here's your chance to visit a place that's big enough to notice (if you were to ever drive through and happen to catch the light on red), but not large enough to need full-time police or a Walmart.

Don't forget to stop by Lucy's Cafe. Stella will make sure you're treated like royalty. If you decide to try the best burger this side of the Mississippi, be sure to leave room for a slice of homemade pie and a glass of sweet tea.

At Brown's General Store, you'd be forgiven for thinking you'd somehow stepped back in time. Henry's idea of a cash register is a pocket on his bib overalls and an old coffee can under the counter. By the way, you might think twice about trying to use your credit cards there. (Hint: Henry doesn't trust them.)

ACKNOWLEDGMENTS

I thank Pat and Cindy for your eyes and comments early on in this project. I love you.

Jeanette, your comments and critique helped to make this book better.

Doyle, you'll never know how much I appreciate having you as a writing partner and friend, someone to bounce ideas and mistakes off of. I feel certain that you must have parts of this book committed to memory by now.

CHAPTER 1

Marcella Peabody wedged her sixty year-old Chevy between the no parking sign and the concrete porch at Lucy's Cafe.

By the time she had gathered her stack of freshly cleaned lace doilies and linen napkins from the passenger side of the front seat, Eva Jo Clomper, her lifelong friend, was standing on the porch with a cup half full of coffee.

"Well, Honey, that was a bit close, don't you think?" Eva Jo said.

Marcella smiled. "Do you think Papa's car is larger than my old car? I think so."

"I'm not sure they make cars bigger than your old Cadillac. Driving that thing was like trying to drive a barn down the street," Eva Jo said. "I'm pretty sure I could park my old truck twice in the space it'd take you to park that thing."

Marcella joined Eva Jo on the porch and bent over the edge to see just how close she came to scratching the car. "I'll have to work on that. It's that hood ornament that throws me off. It's too big, I think. Don't you?"

"Could be. I can't say I've ever thought too much about my hood ornament."

Marcella held the napkins out. "Can you take these? Thank you. Is everyone here?"

"Most of them are."

Marcella turned toward the open door. "Don't you smell that delicious coffee? I think we have a new blend today."

The Rosebud Circle, as the women called themselves, had gathered around the rear corner table in Lucy's Cafe for more than thirty years. Gertrude Gleaves was there along with five or six others. Over time, members had come and gone, the latter usually because they died.

Stella, the bent-over owner of Lucy's Cafe, stopped by to top off the coffee cups. "Ooh, look at the pretty new doilies," she said. "Marcella, did I see you bring those in?"

"I found these in my linen closet," Marcella said. "Aren't they beautiful?"

Gertrude and the twins chimed in together. "They're beautiful."

The Rosebud Circle was so named because every time they met, they drank coffee and ate breakfast on Rosebud china that for several years had been tucked safely away between meetings in a cupboard behind the counter. The dinnerware became a fixture at the meetings after Eva Jo's sister brought it to the first meeting. Two years later, she succumbed to cancer and left the china to the group in her will.

"Anything else for you?" Stella asked. "I've got some real nice cantaloupe back there. Jewell Crabtree picked them just yesterday."

One of the Pearle twins said, "I'd love some, please," holding her coffee cup in such a way that her pinky finger pointed directly at Stella.

THEN CAME EDGAR

Dora Mae Crawford stared at Marcella much like a calf might stare at a new gate.

Marcella opened her mouth to ask Dora Mae a question, but was promptly cut off.

"Oh nothing. I was just wondering what you call that lipstick shade," Dora Mae said.

"Oh, it's called hushed red," Marcella said. "I can tell you where to order some if you think you'd like it."

Dora Mae nodded.

Whipper Countians who knew Marcella dearly loved her. When her name came up in conversations, there were always the comments about her kindness, her four decades as a teacher in the Morgan Crossroads public school, or the vivid colors she was so fond of wearing.

Marcella always found pleasure in learning new ways to compliment her features whether with a dress from Saks, a brand of foundation that she ordered from Macy's, or a particularly pretty belt from Neiman Marcus. Mama would've dressed this way, she'd always told herself.

Dora Mae sat transfixed and as quiet as a stone. She was motionless except for the involuntary twitch that sometimes sent her own overly glossed lips into a motion that might vaguely remind one of a blinding red hula hoop wobbling wildly around a small white center. She had lived in Morgan Crossroads since she was five years old and legend said that she had worn the same shade of red lipstick since she was nine.

When she and Henry Brown were ten, Henry snuck up on her next to the slide in the school yard and tried to wipe the red from her face but came away convinced that she had somehow dyed them. Six decades later he was just as convinced that she was still wearing that same red.

Polly Brown snapped her fingers in front of Dora Mae's face. "Dora Mae, are you in there?"

Dora Mae shook her head. "What?" she said, looking around as if totally surprised that anyone else was present.

"Surely Marcella's lipstick didn't send you flying off the planet, did it, Dora Mae?" Eva Jo asked.

Marcella asked, "Who brought the coffee cake?"

"Okay. I'll admit, it's mine," Eva Jo said, grinning. "Dig in."

Gertrude asked no one in particular if they had heard about the new preacher at the Baptist church in Porterville. "Now I wasn't there, but I heard he didn't let those poor people out of there until after one o'clock."

Eva Jo asked, "Did he lock the door?"

"Well, no, I don't suppose he did, but it would've been awfully rude to just get up and walk out on the poor old man," Gertrude said.

After several minutes of forks clinking against china, Jewell said, "We need to get together and take some food out to the Johnsons. Bessie's been sick for more than a week and I imagine those boys are about to drive her nuts."

"Somebody said she could be in bed for another week or two," Eva Jo said.

After an hour of deciding who would prepare what and who else would deliver it, the Rosebud Circle broke up for the week. Stella gathered the china, washed it, and stored it away for next Tuesday. Marcella took the linens to launder them.

When Marcella left Lucy's Cafe, she laid out in her mind the chores that she would get done. It was her habit on Tuesdays to buy groceries at Haley's as soon as the Rosebud Circle meeting was over. And today she would do her grocery shopping, but first she would stop in at Crossroads Pharmacy and pick up her monthly ration of laxatives and fiber supplement. Doctor Sue Crofton over in Porterville had told her they might make life easier in that department.

She considered the route she would take, pulled out onto the brick pavement and half a block away stopped at the light. She looked left and right, then left. Just as she released the clutch, Dora Mae Crawford's Pomeranian dog, which made its rounds through Morgan Crossroads every morning, decided it was his turn to cross as well. Fortunately for the dog, Marcella saw him. But, in the process of avoiding a collision with the hairy little resident, she stalled the engine.

There she sat, square in the middle of the intersection directly under the only working traffic light in Morgan Crossroads. At one time, before all the hosiery mills and thread factories in Whipper County shut down, the light had been a kind of referee allowing traffic to flow through with a minimum of improper contact. Now, it was little more than a multi-colored ornament dangling over the intersection.

Main street was paved with brick in a herringbone pattern of red from the light south to the block past Haley's Grocery. Gothic style finials topped the black iron fence that surrounded the freshly painted white church at the corner across from Lucy's Cafe. From there south toward the Dairy Bar, almost every home owner along those blocks had a fence, some of pickets and a few of decoratively designed metal. Small flower beds, tended by Abe, the unofficial town gardener, were strategically scattered along both sides of the street. People stopped to chat on ornamental benches in the shade of sycamores, gingkoes, and sugar maples.

Except for an occasional walk down Main to enjoy the flowerbeds, Marcella insisted on driving wherever she went even if it was a block down to the church on cleaning day. She had just hauled the old Chevy that she inherited from her father out of storage after Johnny Mack Durant sideswiped and consequently totaled the boat of a Cadillac that she had bought new in 1973. He had just driven his tractor, which was towing a hay baler and a four-wheeled flatbed wagon, around the corner across from Lassiter's Laundromat. The tractor got away from him when he jerked the wheel to avoid a boy on a red bicycle with a pair of white earbuds stuffed into his ears.

Grumpy at the garage behind the Post Office had gone over the old Chevy from end to end and within a week made it road-worthy. Since Marcella began driving Papa's car some of her friends wondered if she'd given up trying to tell it what to do and pretty much just started the engine and let it go wherever it wanted. The car had a manual shift transmission with the shifter on the steering column. She had owned it for forty-three years but had not driven it until recently. After five decades of driving cars with automatic transmissions, the idea of having to use both hands and both feet at the same time just to get the car rolling still hadn't quite settled in. Thanks to her cousin Henry Brown's instructions, she had become adept enough at driving it that she could manage her trips to Haley's for a quart of milk or to Polly's House of Beauty for her weekly hairdo.

Most of the time she selected the correct gear, depending on whether she wanted to back across the street for her mail, or drive to Lucy's Cafe around the corner and down the street at the light as she had on this morning. The brake pedal seemed harder to press than the one she'd been accustomed to. If she managed to get the car stopped before it did anything unruly, she considered it a good day. Her ability to handle the old car was improving with every trip, and so far she hadn't suffered the embarrassment of driving through anyone's flowerbed.

Marcella looked out the corner of her eye, hoping no one

was laughing. She said to the car, "I wish you would just behave and go on now. You're holding these people up."

Eva Jo, whose rusty old pickup truck was the first vehicle behind her, tried not to laugh, but found it difficult to hold it in. She steeled herself, threw her shoulders back and walked to the center of the intersection.

"Slide over," she said to Marcella. "Let's get this thing out of the road."

Once on the other side of the light, Eva Jo returned to her truck and Marcella rolled along to the drug store.

"Good morning, Marcella," Linda Cruz said. Linda was a young woman, short and thin with coal black shoulder length hair and eyes that seemed almost as dark. She was a recent graduate from the School of Pharmacy at Samford University in Birmingham and had received her license as a pharmacist. She came to Morgan Crossroads after her uncle announced that he would soon retire and would like her to take over the store.

Marcella went to the section where she normally looked for digestive aids, but did not find them. She asked, "Linda, can you tell me ...?"

"I'm sorry, Marcella. They're up here on the counter, waiting for you. I knew you'd be coming in."

Marcella paid for her purchase. "How is your uncle?"

"He's fine. I imagine he's having the time of his life."

"He didn't go off on another vacation, did he?"

Linda looked at her watch. "Right about now, he should be on a cruise ship pulling out of Miami."

"Miami," Marcella shrieked. "I didn't think he could find his way to Porterville. How did he manage a trip like that?"

Linda laughed. "He had plenty of help. He's with a group of people his age."

"You mean old people," Marcella said, laughing.

"They're senior citizens from Huntsville. They flew down there yesterday. I'm sure he won't get lost."

Marcella gathered her purchase and her purse. "I'll see you in a month or so."

Linda said, "Okay, but there's no need to make yourself so scarce."

CHAPTER 2

Brown's General Store, which in an earlier incarnation had been a one room school house, had two rusting orange and blue fuel pumps — one for diesel and one for regular grade gasoline. Both pumps were several decades outdated. The price per gallon displays could not display any price greater than ninety-nine cents so the owner, Henry Brown, painted over the price window. He set his gas prices in easy to calculate amounts — $1.90, $2.00, etc. — and did the calculations using his favorite calculator, a pad of paper and a yellow number two pencil. He rounded his totals downward to avoid having to give change in any increment smaller than a nickel. Life was simpler that way, he said.

Brown's wasn't the only place in Morgan Crossroads to buy gas, but it was the only place within several blocks of the light. Out front, a car with a Georgia license plate parked at the pump. A fortyish man in a business suit got out and after looking the pump over, went inside.

"Morning," Henry said. "What can I do for you?"

The man held a credit card toward Henry. "I need to fill up with regular."

Henry pointed to the sign above the counter that said, "We don't take plastic money." He then turned himself around to the nail-keg-turned-game-table where he sat and continued his game of dominoes with a whiskered old man from the other side of Scottsboro who seldom communicated with anything more than a grunt. Henry did not trust the banking system enough to be a part of the plastic money trail. It scared him. Cash it was. He insisted on paying cash to every supplier whose goods he sold and he presumed his preference upon every customer who graced his counter.

"I need gas. I'm on empty," business suit said.

"You got any cash?"

After digging in his pockets for what seemed like too long, business suit came up with some bills. "Twelve dollars. That's all the cash I have."

Henry retrieved the pad of paper from the bib of his overalls, scribbled for a few seconds, and told the man how many gallons he should pump. "Just put the money on the counter," he said, returning to his dominoes. "And don't forget to clear the meter if you want to get what you paid for."

"Clear the meter," the man said in a lost sort of tone. "How do I do that?"

Without looking up, Henry said, "The little crank on the side. Turn it a few rounds."

The man wobbled back to his car, wondering how, on such a beautiful sunny day, he had found himself in the middle of a time warp.

Morgan Crossroads had once been the commercial center of the valley. That was the very reason the light existed at the intersection of Main and the Porterville highway. Whipper County had paid to have it installed so that there would be some way to referee the traffic, especially when it was shift change time at the mills.

In Henry's way of thinking there were limits to how much new technology people around there should accept, though.

Cotton gins were considered high tech when Eli Whitney first came up with the idea and every cotton farmer in the valley was excited when the new gin opened on the highway south of Morgan Crossroads. And when half the female population in America was wearing panty hose, Whipper County had been right there reaping the benefits.

In fact, the first job Grumpy had after graduating from high school was working nights overseeing machines that made the single legs that his mother sewed into panty hose during the next day shift.

But now, the cotton gin south of town was little more than a big square chunk of rust in a giant bed of Johnson grass and the stocking factory existed only in memories.

Still, something new would occasionally sneak up the valley, but only after it had existed in most other areas for a year or two. Higher population areas attracted technological advances first, but the entire population of Whipper County would not have qualified as high enough for first shots at anything.

Ollie Smith had refused to buy into the satellite dish craze, in spite of his wife's insistence that he buy one so she could keep up with her favorite television evangelist. "These rabbit ears have been working for forty years. I suspect they'll work for another forty. Find yourself a low-tech preacher to listen to."

In the immediate Morgan Crossroads community most residents still had wall or desk telephones since cell phone service was still so spotty as to be unreliable. For one person her phone would work in one spot; for another, the good spot might be around the corner. Some had reception in one end of the house, but not in the other.

Eva Jo failed to see the importance of a phone she could carry in her purse. That is, on the rare occasion when she actually bothered with a purse. "If I can't get to the phone before it stops ringing, I figure whoever it was didn't need to talk all that bad."

Porterville, a few miles west, had top notch cell phone service. Morgan Crossroads residents held on to the promise of improved service by early next year.

Except for a few holdouts, the residents of Morgan Crossroads had been excited twenty years earlier to tap into the new public water lines, or running water as they called it. Ollie Smith balked, as did Henry Brown, but only because they had seen a television report of a municipal water system somewhere in another state whose water smelled of sulfur.

"What if some of that gets into our water? What are we going to do then?" Ollie had asked.

The state paid to install water lines all the way up Mount Olivet Road from the Huntsville highway. Public sewer facilities had accompanied the water lines to Morgan Crossroads, but only along the Porterville Highway and Mount Olivet Road, or Main Street as it was called when it passed through Morgan Crossroads. That left the majority of homes without public sewer lines. Consequently, the septic tank business in Whipper County hummed right along.

Along with the sewers came garbage pickup service. Trucks began weekly pickups to stop Grumpy and every other resident having to burn their garbage.

Dora Mae Crawford had pounced on that development with a headline story in *The Whipper County Gazette*. "Pollution Cloud No Longer Hanging Over Morgan Crossroads," the headline said. Then she followed up with, "Whipper county residents can breathe better now that Los Angeles has taken back its pollution."

After half the town's residents threatened to cut off her paper supply, Dora Mae picked up all fifteen copies of the paper and destroyed them.

Henry Brown balked at anything more than the basics when it came to modern technology, though. After the county health department had paid him an unscheduled visit, he had sealed his water well and tapped into the public water supply. This, to satisfy the state's health regulations governing establishments that sold bologna sandwiches, saltine crackers with hand-sliced cheese, and Spam. He refused any semblance of an electric slicer, too. Whether it was for slab bacon, pimento loaf, or longhorn cheese, to Henry, it was his sixty-year-old butcher block and knife or nothing. No electronic scales either since the equally old white porcelain mechanical scales still satisfied the locals.

If it was not falling off the building, Henry refused to go to the unnecessary expense of updating his store. That included covering the wood floor and its attendant cigarette burns, warped boards, and hundred-year-old finish. In the back of the building, past the Double Cola, the roofing nails, and the chicken feed, sat a potbelly wood burning stove. The local men often gathered around the stove to do their lying, spitting, and whittling when the weather was too cool or stormy to do it on the front porch. From the looks of the floor surrounding the stove, there had been plenty of cool or stormy weather.

Strangers were rare at Brown's General Store. Seldom was it that an unfamiliar person crossed the front line of whittlers and spitters on the front porch and walked through the squeaking screen door. Most who did elicited little more than a nod or maybe a half-hearted wave. Once in a while, though, one would stop by that just about made them swallow instead of spit.

In Whipper County, Alabama, one can stumble upon any of a hundred different species of critters if he stays long enough. Sometimes they crawl around on a dozen or more legs. Sometimes they stand on two and are six feet, eight inches tall with muscles such as the average person has never seen. Sometimes they bring with them pets that appear to have fallen off the assembly line before all their final adjustments had been made.

That variety can show up without invitation and hang around long enough that you can't figure out how to live with them or without them. Sometimes they come carrying the seeds of change.

When the brass bell over the door rang, Henry glanced toward it, and then gave Johnny Mack Durant the rest of his change for the Vienna sausage, saltine crackers, and Red Man chewing tobacco he had bought. "See you tomorrow about this time," Henry said. "Remember, homemade sausage and sourdough biscuits tomorrow morning."

Johnny Mack stuffed his Red Man into the bib pocket on his overalls. "Okay, I'll try to get by here before that Johnson bunch."

"What can I do for you, young man?" Henry asked the stranger standing at the door.

"Stay there," the visitor told his canine sidekick. After a minute of convincing the dog to follow his command, the man ducked through the screen door and looked around for a few seconds.

"How about a bottled water?" he asked, noting the conspicuous absence of any reach-in coolers.

Henry Brown answered, "No bottles, but I can give you a cup and there's a faucet right back there."

"That'd be great."

Henry gave the man a cup and pointed in the general direction of the sink faucet.

The man returned with the filled cup and set it on the counter. "Wow. Look at that." He traced a finger along the intricate metalwork on the old ornamental brass cash register. "It's huge. How old is this thing?" he asked, noticing the hand crank on its side.

"Don't know for sure. It's at least a hundred years old, though," Henry said. "It hasn't worked for the past fifteen or twenty years." Henry handled all financial transactions from the cash he carried in his pockets. If his pockets ever felt too full and heavy to suit him, there was always the coffee can under the counter.

"Why don't you sell it? I'd bet there are people who'd pay good money for a register like that," the man said.

"Can't do that. It holds the counter top in place." Henry said, patting the timeworn wood on the counter.

"Okay, that sounds like a valid reason. Well, it's beautiful." The man said. He took a sip from the cup Henry had given him and asked, "What do I owe you for the water?"

"It's on the house, fellow," Brown said, wondering why a man would want both arms tattooed from his wrists to his shoulders. "You just passing through Morgan Crossroads?"

"I'm on my way to New England."

"New England? Seems to me that you might be just a tad lost if you're aiming for that part of the country."

"I'm not lost, or at least I don't think I am. I'm looking for Miss Marcella Peabody. Do you know her?"

Henry hesitated. "Depends on who's asking—and why he's asking."

"She and my dad used to be friends. He's always talked about her, so I thought I'd see if I could find her. I'd like to know who this lady is."

"What did this lady that your dad knew look like?"

"I've never seen a photo of her, but Dad says that when he knew her she was petite and had red hair. And he said she always had an energetic way of walking."

"The years have been good to her, but she's not as young as your dad remembers her being. She's a few years north of seventy, but she's still a classy lady. There are lot of people in this county who love her like they were kin to her." Henry's right eyebrow hitched up a notch.

"I'm sure she's as classy as you say. I promise you, Sir, I'm here for no other reason than to meet her. That's all. Now, can you give me an idea where she lives?"

"When you step off the porch, turn right. Go through the intersection, walk past the church and keep an eye out for a house on your right with a huge garden in the side yard. Turn right beside that garden and Marcella's is the third house on the left, straight across from the Post Office. Big white house with red shutters and two huge cedar trees in the front yard. If she's not home, try the church. Bingo should be over soon."

The stranger said, "Thanks. I should be able to find that from here." He walked toward the front door.

"Young man," Henry said.

The stranger stopped with his hand still on the screen door. "Yes, Sir?"

"Nothing," Henry said, waving the man through the door. *What is this guy up to?*

The screen door creaked and popped, wood slapping against wood. The tallest man ever to grace Brown's General

Store disappeared through the intersection, his dog on his heels.

Henry picked up the receiver from the old black desk phone. The cord dangled, disconnected at the other end. "When am I going to get that fixed?"

CHAPTER 3

Marcella woke later than usual to the sound of tree limbs tapping gently on her bedroom window. She slid her feet into her house shoes and shuffled to the window. She pulled the cord to open the drapes. "What a splendid day." The sky was blue without a cloud in sight.

After a shower, she took a leisurely hour or two to dress, read the Huntsville paper, and ate a breakfast of oatmeal and yogurt. She washed her cereal bowl and and hung the towel to dry. She poured a cup of coffee and had just taken the first sip when she heard odd noises coming from the front porch. As quietly as she could, she stepped to the window, pulled the curtains back and looked out, but saw nothing. Cautiously, she turned the lock and opened the door. There, staring at her through the screen door, was the source.

Sitting before her, as still as if he had won first prize in his obedience class, was a medium size black and white dog with a face that seemed to be smiling. Had it not been for his tail sweeping back and forth on the porch, she might have checked to see if he was real. "Are you lost?"

TOM BUFORD

∽

Jewell Crabtree's car bumper had missed the fire hydrant on the corner by inches when her eyes locked onto the stranger walking past the church. What in the world?

She gave the gas pedal a little extra punch and roared to a stop outside Polly's House of Beauty.

Inside, Gertrude Gleaves sat under a dryer and Dora Mae Crawford had a head full of shampoo.

"Jewell, Honey, are you all right?" Polly asked.

"You people just don't know what I saw going down the sidewalk."

"Where?" Gertrude asked.

"Over on Main Street by the church."

"Well, are you going to tell us?" Polly asked.

Jewell straightened her shoulders and took a deep breath."

"It was a man. And a dog."

"A man and a dog. Let's see. That could've been Grumpy and that mongrel of his. It wouldn't be Ollie. He never brings his dog into town," Polly said.

"No, it wasn't them. I've never seen anything like this," Jewell said.

"Like the man or the dog?" Gertrude asked.

"The dog was just some kind of mutt. But that was the tallest man I've ever seen. I know he had to be seven feet tall. Maybe more. And ...."

Dora Mae slung suds in Polly's face when she flew up out of the shampoo sink. "Where is this man? I'll need to put this in the *Gazette*."

Polly grabbed Dora Mae on both shoulders and pressed her back into the chair. "You can't go looking like that, Dora Mae."

Dora Mae touched her hair and looked at the shampoo

THEN CAME EDGAR

on her hand. "Oh, I guess not. Well, hurry. I can't let a story like this get past me."

For more years than anyone cared to count Dora Mae had put out, or as she called it, published, *The Whipper County Gazette*. Most issues contained two or three pages of gossip and a paragraph or two of actual news, although by the time she published the story, everyone in town had already known or forgotten about it.

"Are you sure he was that tall?" Gertrude asked. "That would be one big man, you know."

"Well, I didn't stop to measure him, but he was huge. It could've been all those muscles that made him look so tall."

"You've seen tall men before. Do you remember that boy in the eighth grade that you went all syrupy over?" Polly asked.

"David what's-his-name? He wasn't that tall. He was just skinny," Jewell said. "This guy had tattoos. Lots of them."

"What do tattoos have to do with how tall somebody is?" Gertrude asked.

"Look at Henry. He has a tattoo and he's been the same height since he was in the tenth grade," Polly said.

"Henry has a tattoo? Why have I never seen it?" Jewell asked.

"Probably because you're not married to him," Gertrude said.

Dora Mae squirmed. "Can you hurry a bit? We've got news happening and I'm missing it as sure as the world."

∽

Marcella stepped out on the porch and stroked the dog's long wavy coat. "What's your name? A good looking dog like you must have a name."

"It's Spotlight."

Marcella spun around and found a muscular tower of a man standing at the end of the porch. She slapped herself in the chest. "My Lord, you startled me. Is there something I can do for you?"

"I'm sorry and I didn't mean to startle you. This is the correct house, I hope. Are you Marcella Peabody?"

"Yes, I'm Marcella," she said with a furrowed brow. "How may I help you?" She stepped back behind the screen door and quietly latched it.

"Ma'am, I apologize for coming unannounced. I've looked forward to meeting you because I believe you may be the lady that my dad talks about often."

Marcella asked, "What is your name?"

"I'm Jesse."

"Is that your only name?"

"No, but I doubt you'd believe my real name."

"Try me."

"My birth name is Jesus."

"Surely your mother didn't ...."

"She did." Jesse took his wallet from his pocket and flipped it open to his driver license. "See?"

Marcella stretched her neck for a good view. *J.e.s.u.s.* "I see." Her focus moved to the photo of a bare-chested Jesse beside the license, then quickly away. She patted her cheeks. *I hope my face isn't red as it feels.*

Jesse flipped the wallet shut. "She thought it would be cool with all the Hispanic kids that lived in our neighborhood. She never used the Hispanic spelling or pronunciation and her friends gave her a hard time about it. So, she unofficially changed my name to Jesse before I learned to talk."

"Well, I'd prefer we go with Jesse," Marcella said. "We'll drop it right there. Do you have a last name?"

Jesse took a step toward the porch swing.

Marcella twitched, and when she did, her lips tightened. "No, you don't. You're not sitting on my porch until you explain yourself." She scanned Jesse from his ponytail to his sandaled feet, squinting to better make out the detail in the tattoos that covered everything she could see other than his face, hands, and feet. "You're standing in my yard looking like something that, quite frankly, we're not accustomed to around here and you expect me to warm up to you right away? Now who are you?"

Footsteps crunched the gravel in the driveway. "Is everything okay, Marcella?"

"Hi, Henry."

Jesse said, "Hello again. I'm sorry, but I didn't catch your name."

"I'm Henry Brown."

Marcella looked first at Jesse, then at Henry. "You two've met?"

Jesse said, "Yes, we met at the general store."

Henry stepped on to the porch and noticed that Marcella still had her hand on the screen door latch. "Who are you, young man?" Henry asked.

"I'm Edgar Garrison's son."

Marcella opened the screen door and inched onto the porch beside Henry. "Who did you say your father is?"

Jesse said, "Edgar Garrison. But, he's my adoptive father."

Marcella's legs faltered. Her breathing halted for a moment.

"Are you okay? Here, sit down," Henry said, steadying a large white wicker chair for her.

Jesse stepped as near the porch as he dared. "Mr. Brown, I told you earlier that I'm not here to cause any harm to anyone. I came here to meet the lady I've heard about for most of my life. That's all."

Henry and Marcella looked at each other. "I'll be okay, Henry. I'll call if I need you."

"You sure, Marcella? I can stay if you want me to."

"No, you go on back to the store. I'm fine."

Henry glared at Jesse for a second or two, then walked away.

Jesse said, "Wow, that man keeps a serious eye out for you."

"Cousins can be like that."

"Oh," he said, thinking back to his encounter with Henry at the store.

"Did Edgar and your mother marry?"

Jesse said with a look of surprise, "No. He's my mother's oldest brother. My mother divorced when I was two years old. But she raised me until a month or so before my twelfth birthday."

"What happened then?" Marcella asked.

Jesse looked away, toward the cedar trees, and slowly returned his gaze to Marcella. "She died in a car accident. I was with her, in the back seat. I got some cuts and bruises but she ... she died."

"I'm so sorry, Jesse," Marcella said, barely above a whisper.

"It's okay. Sometimes I remember it as if it happened this morning." He scratched Spotlight behind the ears. "I'm okay. Promise."

Marcella said, "I knew an Edgar Garrison long ago, back in college. But I'm not sure your dad is the same Edgar. The one I knew would be old enough by now to be your grandfather."

"Dad is twenty years older than my mother."

Marcella's eyebrow hiked up a tad. She knitted the fingers of both hands together in her lap.

Jesse said, "I can tell you this much. If you were a teacher in a one room school somewhere around here; if you're redheaded, which I can see you are; and if you were real pretty when you were young-I mean younger-then you must be the one he talks about all the time."

He raised an apologetic hand toward her. "I'm not saying you're not pretty now."

"You might want to stop before you step in any deeper," Marcella said, smiling. "Do you have any sisters?"

"One a year older than I. Gloria. Dad adopted her, too. But I'm the only boy. Mama said having me was all she could take, so she wasn't going to put herself through that aggravation again."

"What was your birth father's name?"

"I have no idea. To Mom, it was as though he was nameless."

"Could he have been Hispanic? That might account for her trying to name you Jesús."

"She was married for a while, but not to my father. She never discussed him, whoever he was."

"Edgar would know who your birth father was, wouldn't he?" Marcella asked.

"I asked him before he adopted Gloria and me. It seems we're both products of one-night stands. Dad never saw or met either of our birth fathers."

Jesse paused. "What about your family?"

Marcella pointed to the porch swing. "Have a seat if you want to."

"Thank you. I think I've over-worked my feet."

"Jesse, I've tried, but I just cannot imagine how you found me. It's been fifty years or longer since your father and I've seen or spoken to each other. I've lived right here in this house ever since I graduated from The University of Texas. I have no brothers or sisters. By the way, how old are you?"

"I'll be thirty-one week after next."

Marcella chuckled. "You're still just a puppy." She spread her floral skirt across her lap, being careful to cover her knees.

Jesse leaned back in the swing and laid his legs straight so that the heels of his sandals rested on the floor.

Marcella cleared her throat. "Jesse, I'm not sure how to say this, but ...."

"You wonder what Dad thinks of me and the way I look," Jesse said.

"Well, yes I guess I do. How did you know?" Marcella said nothing for several seconds. "I've lived a conservative life here in Whipper County. To be honest with you, I can't say I've ever seen ...." She waved her hand between her and him.

"Tattoos?" Jesse asked.

"Oh, I've seen tattoos. Henry has one he got when he was in the Navy," she said. "Not a very nice one, either. But yours are .... They're a lot bigger."

"Miss Peabody," Jesse said.

"Call me Aunt Marcella," she said. "That has a nice ring to it, don't you think?"

Jesse said, "Dad has always taught me to never judge a person by what I see on the outside. I've never heard him say a disparaging word about any person he didn't know on a personal level, and when he did, it was as a cautionary statement to protect us from a fraudulent act or something like that."

"Really?" Marcella asked. "He was that way when we were classmates. It never mattered how people treated him or talked about him, he never responded in an ugly way. I'm sorry if I seem judgmental."

"Apology accepted. People often do that when they meet someone different from whatever they're accustomed to."

"How did you find me?" Marcella asked. "I must know how you did that after all these years."

"Dad has mentioned Morgan Crossroads, Alabama a hundred times or more. I couldn't find anything significant in the library about it, but I found it on an online map."

Marcella wrung her hands and rubbed her swollen knuckles. "Why couldn't he've come before now?"

"There is an imaginary line that Dad won't cross when it comes to talking about you. And I guess that answer is one thing he keeps hidden behind that line."

"So he never told you why?"

"Aunt Marcella, you need to ask Dad. I wish I could help you, but I simply don't know that answer."

Marcella said nothing for a moment, then jumped up and opened the screen door. "Sit right there for a minute. I think my telephone is ringing."

Jesse asked Spotlight, "Did you hear a phone ringing?" Spotlight cocked his head to one side. "No, you say? Neither did I."

Marcella spoke into the phone with a yelling whisper. "Eva Jo, get yourself over here. Right now! There is something on my porch such as you've never seen."

"Marcella, I can't come right now. I'm in the middle of canning okra."

"Don't worry about that okra. Come on!"

Marcella hung up the phone and on the way to the porch, stopped by the hall mirror to check her lipstick and to be sure her skirt was straight. She gave her hair a little extra attention. A pick here and a pat there should hold it in place.

Through the screen door Marcella asked, "Jesse, would you like a glass of sweet tea?"

"No, thank you. I've heard about Alabama sweet tea and I'm not sure I could handle the sugar rush."

Marcella waved at him, as if to say it wasn't that sweet.

"A glass of water would be nice though," Jesse said.

Marcella returned to the porch with tea for herself and water for Jesse, who was on the lawn playing catch with Spotlight.

"Does Spotlight need a bowl of water?" Marcella asked.

"He might like that. Thank you."

Marcella returned a minute or two later with a large blue bowl of water.

Jesse tossed a well-chewed rubber ball. Spotlight did the catching and the slobbery return. "Who was on the phone? Anyone Dad might have mentioned?"

"I doubt it. Just a friend I've known for much longer than you've been alive."

"What's her name?"

"Her name is Eva Jo Clomper, and she's one of the finest examples of femininity I've ever known."

Jesse winked at Spotlight and asked, "What did she want?"

"My, you sure are nosy, considering you wouldn't know her if she walked up and sat next to you."

Marcella, Spotlight, and Jesse turned toward the rattling sound to see who was coming up the driveway.

"There she is now," Marcella said, leaving the porch to meet Eva Jo.

CHAPTER 4

Eva Jo caught her apron in the door of the rusty old pickup truck when it slammed shut. She retrieved the apron and after straightening it and adjusting her bra, walked straight to Spotlight. He smiled at her. She smiled at him and stepped back with her hands rolled up on her hips. "What have you done to this dog's eyes, Marcella?"

"Nothing. I don't own a dog. Remember?"

"Well, whose dog is it?"

Marcella pitched her head toward Jesse.

"Good morning, Eva Jo," Jesse said without moving.

Eva Jo looked back and forth between Marcella and Jesse's neck and arms. "Where did you find this, Marcella?"

"I didn't find him. He found me. His father is a long-lost friend." Marcella, for the first time, ventured a pat on his back. "I'll call him my nephew for now."

"What's your name, long-lost distant nephew?" Eva Jo said.

Marcella interrupted. "Just call him Jesse, Eva Jo. He likes that name."

Eva Jo asked, "Okay, Jesse, what's your real name."

Marcella inhaled quickly and before she could do any advance damage control, Jesse came out with it.

"Dewayne Garrison."

Marcella let out a short sigh.

Eva Jo plopped down on the porch steps. "How do you get Jesse out of Dewayne?"

She looked at Marcella. "What did he say his name was?"

Jesse brought his wallet out and produced his driver's license.

Eva Jo glanced first at the photo next to his license, then at the name on the license and said, "Jesus. Dewayne. Garrison."

Before he folded the wallet, Eva Jo stopped him and peered at the photo again. She chuckled. "Marcella, did you see that? He's got a little lady like the one Henry's got."

"Put that away, Jesse," Marcella ordered. She waved toward his wallet. "Just put it back wherever you got it."

"Lord knows what she'd have named you if she could have shot out into the future and seen that picture. What does all that artwork mean?"

"The part across my chest is for the people that society forgets," Jesse said. "The left arm is about the men and women who went away to war and never came back. The right one is referencing some of my favorite artists."

"That's good," Eva Jo said. "I can't see anybody sitting still long enough for all that ink to dry unless it means something. By the way, what'd you weigh when you were born, fifteen pounds?"

"I don't know, but when I was little, she sometimes called me her ten-pound pain. Never figured out what she meant by that."

Eva Jo bumped Marcella on the arm. "I knew it, Marcella. I knew it." She laughed. "His mama must have come up with that right in the middle of giving birth to him. Any woman that laid a ten-pound egg could let just about anything out of her mouth. My Lord, and can you imagine if that egg takes a while to make the trip?"

Jesse, who had been sitting on the grass, stood. As his body unfolded, it reminded them of his size. Both women's laughter simmered to a stifled chuckle.

"Spotlight." Jesse patted his leg. "Come here."

Eva Jo asked again, "What happened to that dog's eyes?"

Marcella said, "Nothing. I see nothing abnormal about them."

Spotlight turned toward Marcella.

"Look again, Marcella!" Eva Jo said in a high-pitched voice that might peel bark from a tree.

Spotlight glanced at Marcella, and then Jesse stole his attention long enough that Spotlight looked toward him. At least he turned the left eye toward Jesse. The right one turned the other direction, toward Eva Jo. Marcella jerked.

"Did you see that, Eva Jo?" Marcella yelled, covering her mouth at the same time.

Jesse walked over to Spotlight and snapped his fingers over the dog's head. Spotlight looked up with his right eye and down with his left. When the left one turned upward, the right one looked downward.

Together, Marcella and Eva Jo yelled out to Jesse. "What did you do to that dog's eyes?"

Jesse folded himself up again and sat on the grass with his arm around Spotlight. "He was that way when we met. I doubt he's ever had normal vision."

"Why'd you name him Spotlight?" Eva Jo asked.

"I enjoy watching old black and white movies. Sometimes in a scene, huge spotlights point every which direction in the air, moving from side to side and in circles. His eyes reminded me of those lights, so I named him Spotlight. The name fits, don't you think?"

Both women nodded, trying to keep their laughter under control.

"Where did you two come from?" Eva Jo asked.

"Austin. Austin, Texas."

"Texas!" Marcella squealed. "That's a long way from here, Eva Jo."

Eva Jo said, "I don't see a car anywhere. How'd you get here?"

"Hitchhiked."

"Oh," Eva Jo said. "Did the dog hitchhike, too?"

"Not all the way. We met in Louisiana, near Shreveport."

∽

Grit popped under Henry Brown's shoes as he walked across the general store porch. He joined Ollie Smith and plunked down in an old rocking chair next to the screen door.

Ollie Smith, a dairy farmer who lived four miles south, asked, "Who was that big old boy that just left with that dog?"

"He claims his dad is Edgar somebody and that Marcella's is supposed to know him."

Ollie removed a pouch of Prince Albert from the bib of his overalls and packed his pipe with fresh tobacco. "Edgar." He shook his head. "I can't think of any Edgars, can you?"

"No, I can't. Marcella's my cousin and I can tell you that the lady has lived right here in Morgan Crossroads her entire life, except for one short little stint she spent going to college. And I don't think that could have anything to do with it. She went to college fifty something years ago."

Henry said, "I walked over to Marcella's a while ago just to be sure everything was okay. I can't put my finger on it, but something in his story's not quite adding up." He opened the screen door. "You want a cup of coffee?"

Ollie said, "Sure. Toss four or five sugars in there if you don't mind."

Henry chuckled. "Having a little coffee with your sugar, then?" He disappeared into the store and soon returned with coffee and a honey bun for each of them.

Ollie said, "So you think something's fishy about his story."

"Maybe." Henry sipped his coffee. "Maybe not. You should have seen Marcella when that boy told her who his dad was. She looked like she'd seen somebody come back from the grave."

"What did she say?"

"Nothing, really. Nothing except that she'd be okay. She pretty much told me to leave."

"That don't sound quite right, does it?" Ollie said.

"I've got a real antsy feeling about that young man." Henry got up and reached for the screen door, pausing to peer down the road toward Marcella's street. "That's all I've got to say about it."

~

Jesse, Marcella, and Eva Jo kept Spotlight company on the front porch until the sun hid itself behind the hills in the west and stars gathered in the sky. Eva Jo told Jesse about her twelve children, all of them grown, and the thirty-one grandchildren that by themselves could fill a school bus. Among the three people present, she was the only one who had personal experience with marriage. She'd been through three husbands, including one whom she had out-lived, and two who had decided they had better things to do than their parts to make a marriage work. After them, she had decided there would never be a fourth.

Jesse asked Eva Jo, "Do you have any pets?"

"Depends what you want to call a pet. Hey You thinks I'm her servant. She my cat. There are always Chelsea and the other milk cows that act like they enjoy my presence, I guess."

"Spotlight is a good pet. He watches out for me and most of the time, he does what I tell him," Jesse said.

Marcella slapped herself on the knees. "Well, it's supper time. What would you like to eat, Jesse?"

"I'm not a picky eater. Whatever you cook will be fine with me. Or, if there's a restaurant around here, I'd be happy to buy dinner."

"That won't be necessary. Marcella's got a kitchen," Eva Jo said.

After a few minutes of discussion, Eva Jo left to retrieve a few vegetables from her garden. Marcella invited Jesse into the house to help her with fried chicken and table setting. Spotlight dozed off under the porch swing to the sound of crickets.

On his way through the living room, Jesse stopped to study several photographs that sat on end tables and the mantle over the fireplace. An old heavy framed photo of a young man standing in a field was on the table next to an antique Queen Anne wingback chair. He took the photo to the kitchen and asked Marcella, "Who is the man in this picture?"

"That's Papa when he was about your age," Marcella said.

"Your grandfather?"

Marcella pointed a flour-covered finger at the photo. "No, no. He was my father. Good looking man, too, if I say so myself."

"Where was this photo taken?" Jesse asked.

Marcella nodded toward the window over the kitchen sink. "Right out there. Years ago that was a cornfield. There was a man who lived across the road next to the post office and he had one of those old Brownie cameras. He was learning how to use it and took that picture of Papa right after he'd finished harvesting."

Jesse said, "Looks like a tall dude."

"I can't say I've ever thought of him as a dude, but he was tall, all right. Even taller than you. He had to duck under every door in this house," Marcella said, laughing. "Now, go put him back on the table and let's get these potatoes peeled."

After Jesse left the kitchen she added, "And be careful with him!"

Less than thirty minutes later Eva Jo returned, dressed in her Sunday best and carrying bags of fresh tomatoes, okra, and green onions. "Something smells good. That's not your cooking is it, Jesse?"

"Afraid not," he said. "I can't even get the flour to stick to the chicken long enough to put it in the oil."

"It's grease around here," Eva Jo said with a wink.

"Well, look at you, Eva Jo," said Marcella. "Are you going somewhere else when you leave here?"

Eva Jo said, "What makes you think I'm going anywhere? Can't a girl dress up a little now and then? What do you think, Jesse? Do you like this better, or that designer apron and that flour sack looking dress I had on earlier?"

"I think you look very nice, Eva Jo," Jesse said. "But what is a flour sack dress?"

"When I was little, flour came in big old cloth sacks." Eva Jo made hand motions indicating how large they were. "My mama made all of our dresses out of those sacks. Sometimes they'd be a floral pattern and sometimes they'd be plaid or something else. The trick was getting enough sacks that looked okay together. She could be creative with them though. Ask Marcella. She remembers those dresses Mama made."

"Her mother had a real talent for turning those sacks into pretty things. I remember them well," Marcella said.

"Well, it wouldn't matter if you'd come dressed in a flour sack dress," Jesse said. "Would you like to dance?"

Marcella laughed. "I doubt you've ever seen any of her favorite dances. That is unless you are old enough to remember the jitterbug or the Charleston."

"Don't you pay any attention to Marcella," Eva Jo said. "She's the one who taught me everything I know about dancing."

Jesse took Eva Jo's hand and broke into a fifteen second Perry Como impersonation of *Some Enchanted Evening*.

Eva Jo stepped back and asked, "Marcella, did you hear that?"

Jesse mustered up his best Fats Domino voice on two lines from *Blueberry Hill*.

Eva Jo and Marcella both stood with their jaws hanging, wondering who this man really was that had slid into their lives.

"Where did you learn those songs?" Marcella asked.

Eva Jo said, "He can't be just thirty. He's pulling our legs. I bet he's fifty or sixty under all that artwork." She scrunched her eyebrows. "You're not bionic or whatever they called that guy on TV, are you?"

Jesse asked, "What's that I smell?"

"Eva Jo, do you see what he made me do?" Marcella said, retrieving a pan of burned bread from the oven.

Jesse bent over the burnt offering. "Now that smells like my cooking."

The three of them laughed and after rescuing the remaining food from the stove, gathered around the table for dinner.

"Where did you learn those songs?" Marcella asked.

Eva Jo added, "And where did you learn to sing like that?"

"I've been imitating singers as long as I can remember," Jesse said. "I had to learn those songs in my popular music classes in college."

"Did you ever try imitating somebody that you just couldn't do?" Eva Jo asked.

"Michael Jackson. When I was little, maybe five or six years old, Mom bought the Jackson 5 Christmas Album. I tried so hard to imitate Michael singing *I Saw Mommy Kissing Santa Claus*. I almost wore that album out, I played it so often. Then one day she played a record of Tennessee Ernie Ford singing *Away in the Manger* and said I sounded more like him than Michael. I never tried another Michael Jackson impersonation."

"I can moon walk," Eva Jo said. "Watch this." Then she did something that more closely resembled a chimpanzee with a hula hoop.

Marcella said, "Honey, I don't think I'd let anyone else see that."

"Jesse, did you earn your music degree?" Marcella asked.

"No. No, I didn't." Jesse said. "Music was my minor for a year."

"I'm guessing that since you hitchhiked your way here from Texas, you must not have a job," Eva Jo said.

"I do have a job. I teach American literature at The University of Texas."

"You teach what?" Eva Jo asked.

"American literature. You know, Faulkner, Twain, Steinbeck—people like that."

"You sure don't look ...." Marcella said.

"Like a literature professor?" Jesse said. "How should one look?"

"I've never given it much thought," Marcella said. "It's been too many decades since I've been around a professor."

"Literature lovers and professors look like you. They look like Eva Jo's grandchildren. And some of them look like me," he said, pointing his thumbs toward his chest.

Eva Jo asked, "Did your mother enjoy reading literature?"

Jesse said, "No, unless you consider *TV Guide* or *National Enquirer* to be literature. Now Dad, he loves to read. I'd guess there could be two or three thousand volumes in his personal library."

The telephone in the living room rang once, twice, three times.

"I'd better get that. Lord only knows who might call at this hour," Marcella said on her way to the phone.

"It's probably somebody that wants to know how to do something," Eva Jo said. "Listen." She held a finger to her lips.

"Well, how many are you boiling? Just three? Put them in a pan of cold water and bring it to a boil," Marcella told the caller. "Yes, that's right. Put them in when the water is cold. Then start your timer. No, your timer. You do have a kitchen timer, don't you? Okay, your watch will do just fine. After ten minutes, take them off the stove, drain the water and run cold water over them."

"What did I tell you?" Eva Jo asked. "There's always somebody ringing her phone, wanting to know how to do something."

Jesse grinned.

"Who was that?" Eva Jo asked.

"That was Grumpy. He's playing bachelor this evening."

Eva Jo, Marcella, and Jesse sat around the table and talked

for hours after the subject of his occupation had come up. They talked about life, love, ambition, friendship, and a dozen other less important things. During the conversation, the women learned that Jesse had hitchhiked from Austin to Morgan Crossroads as a summer challenge to himself. An exclusive creative writing immersion program in the northeast had invited him to be a guest instructor for the session beginning in August. He had taken a leave of absence from his teaching position to pursue the opportunity.

"I'm sure you have a car," Eva Jo said. "Why in the world did you hitchhike here?"

"I've lived in central Texas my entire life and I've spent most of my time in Austin or San Antonio. I love it there, especially Austin. But when I find time to go out to Lake Travis and on west out of the city, I sometimes just want to stay out there. Dad lives on Lake Travis and when I was thirteen or fourteen, I'd just sleep out under the stars in the back yard."

"So you're taking this trip that way," Marcella said.

"I enjoy feeling as if I'm part of nature, not just a passerby." Jesse explained how he would make it from Austin to New England without a vehicle of his own, sleeping outdoors under the stars whenever he could and holding to no certain schedule other than to arrive at the program in New England on time. He stood and took a dirty plate from the table.

Eva Jo said, "Just sit back down. You are the visitor here. Guests don't do dishes in this neck of the woods."

"They do in Austin, though. It's in my genes, I think," Jesse said.

"Well, you are not in Austin, Jesse. Let us do that." Marcella took a plate and two forks from him and placed them in the sink.

"When are you leaving?" Marcella asked.

"Spotlight gets a little antsy if I stay put for too long. We should get back on the road tomorrow morning. We still have a long way to go."

"I don't know what you had in mind, but you are welcome to spend the night at my house," Eva Jo said. "There are four empty bedrooms in that big old house. You can take your pick."

"Papa's old room is upstairs," Marcella said. "It has a nice long feather bed that's just the right size for you. If you don't mind that, you can stay up there for the night."

"Thanks to both of you. I think I'd just like to snuggle up in my sleeping bag under the trees and stars. That's what I've done every night since I left Austin and I rather enjoy it," Jesse said.

"If you're sure you want to do that, there are several oak trees behind the house. The yard lights are bright though. If they'd bother you, you might like Eva Jo's farm better. It's up to you."

Jesse exchanged phone numbers and mailing addresses with Marcella and Eva Jo. Then, after a few minutes of goodbyes and a hug from Marcella, he and Spotlight rode to the farm in the back of Eva Jo's pickup truck.

"Good night, Jesse," Eva Jo said, sending her voice through the darkness.

Jesse returned the gesture and the traveling partners found a comfortable spot behind the main farmhouse. Jesse unrolled his sleeping bag near the pasture fence, then Spotlight found a comfortable spot to sit.

As Jesse turned his attention to the sky, Spotlight watched two Jersey cows that had bedded down ten or fifteen feet beyond the fence. Convinced the cows were no threat to him or his human, he curled up and went to sleep.

Jesse lay still with the sleeping bag pulled to his chin, determined to count all the stars he could see. He stared into the vast expanse of space. Except for the slow movement of the moon and the occasional falling star, the celestial dance that had been going on overhead for millions of years seemed imperceptible.

The heavens were Jesse's favorite examples of both change and consistency. He wondered why families could not be more like the nighttime sky—whether dark and gloomy or bright and cheerful, always there for you. The stormy nights never lasted for long and when they had moved on, the endless expanse of nothingness, made alive by millions of light beams racing at unimaginable speeds, was always and without fail there for you.

He counted the same group of stars again and again until the weight of his eyelids became greater than his will power. In the middle of nowhere on a clear summer night in north Alabama, both dog and companion had a sense of belonging.

CHAPTER 5

"I don't too much care what that old boy in that truck said." Ollie Smith looked around the table and across the room from the next table to another. "Where's the ketchup?"

Grumpy slid the half-full bottle so that it stopped just beside Ollie's plate. "Try this one."

Ollie upended the bottle and shook it until he had painted the top of his hash brown potatoes red. "I had that tractor plumb off the road when he come around me, blowing his horn like I was in his way. He didn't have to do that," Ollie said.

"Well, maybe he thought you were going to jump out in front of him," Henry said. "I'm pretty sure he didn't expect you to tear through old man Johnson's pasture fence."

"Well, neither did I," Ollie said. "Who in their right mind would've done any such thing? Do you know it took me a solid hour just to get that wad of barbed wire unwrapped from around my front axle?"

Stella sat a double stack of pancakes and a side of thick

sliced bacon in front of Grumpy and topped off Henry's coffee. "Anything else for you boys?"

"You might want to bring Ollie a new pair of glasses. He looked all over this room for a bottle of ketchup when there was one right here on the table," Grumpy said.

"Don't you believe everything he says, Stella. He had that ketchup hid somewhere. It doggone sure wasn't anywhere I could see it," Ollie said.

Stella patted Ollie on the back. "Don't worry, Ollie. It gets worse with age." She topped off the coffee at the next table.

"Where was I?" Ollie asked. "Oh, I know. That fellow and his horn scared the waddin' out of me. And now I've got to fix Johnson's fence and replace the heifer that got out and got itself hurt."

"Can you give him one of yours?" Grumpy asked.

"He won't hear of it. I tried to give him one of my Holsteins, but that heifer was a Jersey and nothing's going to replace it but another Jersey."

"Where are you going to get one?" Henry asked.

"Auction's next week over at Porterville. Somebody will have one on the block. Surely, that will satisfy him. You know, before his wife ran off with that door to door vacuum cleaner salesman he never used to be so ornery."

"That was a long time ago," Grumpy said. "Before I was born."

"He's been ornery a long time, then, ain't he?"

"Well, maybe he's just never had a tractor run through his fence before," Grumpy said just before he slid a fork load of pancake into his mouth. "That'd tend to fire up the ornery in just about anybody. Especially if it happens the day after he puts the fence up like you did his."

"New subject," Grumpy said. "Did you see a stranger strolling through town early this morning?"

"How early?"

"About a quarter 'til six. Maybe a little later."

"Don't reckon I did," Ollie said. "I'm guessing you did, though."

"I sure did. He was something else, too," Grumpy said.

"What's that supposed to mean?"

Grumpy stretched his arm straight up as far as he could. "Tall, real tall. Way taller than this."

"I don't reckon being tall makes a man special or something else, whatever it was that you said."

"This guy was big, and he had long hair tied up in a ponytail, and he had tattoos, acres of them," Grumpy said. "Oh, and he had an old Heinz 57 dog with him."

"Sounds like a fellow that was over at Henry's store yesterday," Ollie said. "Where'd you see him?"

"Out by Eva Jo's, walking eastbound. You say he was at Henry's?"

"I saw him leave the store yesterday, walking toward Marcella's house. That's where Henry told me he was going," Ollie said.

"Well, he was a long way from Marcella's when I saw him. You don't reckon he'd been out to Eva Jo's, too, do you?" Grumpy asked.

Henry Brown pulled out a chair beside Grumpy and waved at Stella, who gave him her "I'll be there in a minute" wave.

"What you got there?" Ollie asked.

"This morning's *Whipper County Gazette*," Henry said. "Dora Mae dropped them off early this morning."

"What kind of craziness is she putting out this time?" Ollie asked.

Henry tilted his head one way, then another. "I swear. If

she wants anybody over fifty to read this she needs to type it out big enough to see."

"Maybe you should write a letter to the editor and say that," Grumpy said.

"Listen to this," Henry said. "Giant Wanders Through Town. On Tuesday or Wednesday of this week a giant was seen walking south down Main with a black and white dog. However, the giant was in full color, according to my source who said he had what appeared to be tattoos covering every inch of his skin. While my source didn't personally measure the man, she assures me that he was at least seven feet tall and maybe taller than that. The dog appeared to be normal though. No one has reported seeing the man or his dog since then."

"Should I tell her?" Grumpy asked.

"Naw. Just let her think she knows a secret," Ollie said.

"Tell her what?" Henry asked.

"That I saw her giant walking down the highway early this morning."

"Where?"

"Out past Eva Jo's. Him and that dog. It pretty much had to be him except he shrunk overnight," Grumpy said.

"He's not seven feet tall. Close, but not quite," Henry said. "He must've spent the night somewhere around here. Last time I saw him, he was in Marcella's front yard and I'm pretty sure he didn't stay there. She wouldn't have that dog in the house."

∼

The bell over the pharmacy door announced Marcella's entrance a little more prominently than she wished. She'd never liked making a fuss or having one made over her, even if it wasn't intentional.

"You look happy," Linda Cruz, the pharmacist said. "I hear you had a visitor yesterday."

Marcella looked around, feigning an inspection of the adjoining aisles. "I am happy. Very happy, in fact. What visitor?"

"Does tall, dark, and handsome ring any bells?"

"Tall might, and handsome might; dark would be a matter of perspective, I think. Who told you I had a visitor?"

"Was no one supposed to know?"

"No, I wouldn't say that. Has Eva Jo been in here this morning?" Marcella asked. *I'm going to skin her.*

"If she came in, it must have been while I was in the back room. I haven't seen her."

"Henry. That's who it was. Henry Brown told you."

"I haven't seen Henry since last week. He usually comes in on Monday to pick up a Sunday Huntsville paper if I have any left. He missed this week though."

"Well, then. I suppose you'll have to tell me who told you."

"Oh, don't be too rough on him, Marcella. I doubt he told anyone else."

"Who is this he person?"

"Your gardener. Abe said he was going to stop by and trim your crepe myrtles but you and Eva Jo were talking to someone. When he saw how big the guy's dog was, he decided it could wait and left."

CHAPTER 6

Marcella laid her head against the chair back and tried to massage the pain from the swollen knuckles and joints in her fingers. Then she took the brown marble picture frame from the mahogany table beside her and dusted it. The frame surrounded and protected Papa's photo, the one that had forever captured the essence of a loving and supportive father, her only photo of him.

She spoke to Papa as she had every day since his death forty-three years earlier. "Papa, do you remember that time when I was seven, and I was crying because I had no playmates? You helped me pick out a little pink flowered dress with a white scalloped collar from my closet. I'm sure you'd remember it. It was my favorite. There was a tear in the lacy part at the bottom, but it was small and nobody ever saw it except you and I."

"We made sandwiches and loaded them in the picnic basket and the two of us carried it to your car," Marcella said. She closed her eyes and a smile crossed her face. "You and I had a picnic in Mason's meadow by the creek. And on the way, you stopped and bought me a baby doll with brown hair and dark brown eyes."

"'Here's a little girl who needs you to take care of her,' you said. Do you know I still have that doll? She's up in the attic. And she still has those little dresses that Grandmother Anna made for her."

When Marcella looked at the picture, the fading sepia tone of the once flawless photograph saddened her. A few more years and the image of her father might disappear completely.

She longed for the years when the two of them had lived together in this house. Papa had raised her. When she was old enough, she learned to cook his favorite dishes and to keep the house spotless. As Papa grieved the loss of his wife, so she sorrowed over the absence of a mother she'd never known, the mother who had died while giving birth to her.

Marcella returned the photo to its place on the table and wiped a tear from each cheek. "I wish we could go to the meadow again, Papa."

Marcella opened a small carved mahogany box that sat next to Papa and removed a skeleton key.

She braced herself on the chair's well-worn wooden arms and stood. For a moment she hesitated, then she walked down the hall to a narrow door with a glass knob. With a grimace she struggled to turn the key. Finally, with the strength of both hands, she unlocked and opened the door. Inside, she found the cotton string that hung from an old white porcelain light fixture high on the wall and tugged on it a time or two. The light crackled to life and lit the steep and narrow stairway.

Marcella gave the stairs a good long look, then took a deep breath of stale air and climbed to the attic. Twice she stopped and massaged her knees, coaxing them on. "It must have been ... thirty years ... since I've been up here," she said to herself.

In the attic there was one bare light bulb hanging from the rafters at the end of a wire. "Good, it still works," she said after finding the switch. The light was yellowed and dim, but with time, her eyes adjusted enough that she could find her way.

In a large cardboard box with black X's marked across the Camel cigarette brand, she found the doll that Papa had bought her and several report cards from school. "Marcella is an exemplary student. Would like to see her playing more with other students," her third grade teacher had written. On her fifth grade card, someone had written, "Eva Jo Clomper may be a bad influence on Marcella." Marcella smiled.

"I'm sure that trunk is here somewhere," she said in a hushed tone as she lifted paintings, deteriorated curtains and other household items. She pushed in vain against a box. "What could be so heavy?" she asked as she opened it.

"Papa's books," she said in a barely audible voice. She lifted a few books from the box, one at a time, and savored the memory of Papa's having loved English literature. "Here's *Pride and Prejudice*." She laid it to the side and picked up another. "*Great Expectations*. I'd forgotten that one."

"There is that trunk." The rounded top of the old steamer trunk stood above the smaller trunks and boxes around it.

In a slow deliberate way, Marcella rearranged boxes, bags with forgotten content, and more until she could open the trunk. She dug through legal documents and more of Papa's most prized possessions until she found a small metal box.

The box, one that Papa made with his hands, felt heavier than she remembered. On each end was a small handle. It had a hinged lid with a small unfastened lock on the front.

Inside the box, yellowed envelopes bulged out of a linen

napkin wrapped loosely around them. Marcella held the stack of letters on her lap and filed through them one by one. The words "My dearest Marcella" caught her attention. She held the envelope with both hands, first by its ends, then with both hands pressing it between them. She remembered the day Mrs. Stinson, the resident supervisor, delivered it to her college dorm room, accompanied by a bouquet of yellow and white flowers.

The fine stationery shook in her hand as she read the dignified cursive text, written there with a fountain pen.

> My dearest Marcella,
>
> I never imagined that you would fully understand my reasons for ending our relationship. Maybe I can better explain in this letter.
>
> Since the day we met in the library, you have been the only lady in my life. For two years, the sun has risen with me thinking of you, and it has gone down with me thinking of you.
>
> Tonight I am thinking of a future without you, how I will ever make it without you by my side. But I must. And so must you.
>
> A top Ivy League school has offered me the opportunity to do my graduate work there. I never told you that I had applied because I honestly never expected to be accepted. I anticipated that I would earn my PhD right here in Austin. This is a chance that I just can't pass up. If I were to refuse it, I fear that my

professional future might be dramatically and negatively affected.

I have not told you exactly where I'm going for I believe doing so would be unwise. If I am to finish my studies, I must be able to give my full attention to that goal. How can I do that when I know you are here waiting for me, when I am wishing that I were with you and you with me?

Perhaps it sounds selfish, but I don't believe I have the fortitude to carry on a long distance relationship.

My dear, you will earn your degree and go back to Morgan Crossroads where you will become the extraordinary teacher that no one forgets. You will be that teacher who draws students to her, not solely by charisma or personality, but because you have something to offer from inside you that your students will crave.

I hope that you will not try to find me. I would understand perfectly if you were to move on and marry someone who would take good care of you. But I have vowed there will never be another woman for me, no matter how long my life will be, in case fate should see fit to bring us together again.

If it is right that we come together in the future, we will. Nothing will be able to stop it happening.

Marcella, I love you more than I could ever hope to express. Go. Become that woman you are meant to be. I know you will.

> Love,
> Edgar Garrison

Marcella tried to keep up with the tears that flooded her cheeks. She had not seen or read the letter since the day she arrived home from college. She had gently laid it, and all those that had come before it, in the metal box and closed the lid on them.

After Papa died, she stored the box, without opening it, inside the steamer trunk that had been her mother's. For more than forty years, Edgar's promise lay safely stored away.

At the end of the attic a window overlooked a large yard and not far beyond that, a steep hill that ended in a wooded ridge. After she returned home from college, she and Papa would sit on the back porch and talk about things as if only they and the ridge could hear. Papa would talk to her about her mother—how special she was and how much Marcella reminded him of her. Marcella would tell Papa stories about things that had happened while she was away.

Today she wished she had told him about Edgar. There were so many stories to tell about the times they had shared. Papa would've liked Edgar, she thought. He would've liked Edgar's giving spirit, his willingness to help anyone he met who needed a lift out of a bad situation. But most of all, he would've liked the way Edgar treated her and protected her from anyone whom he thought might have been up to no good.

On the fourth of June following her sophomore year Edgar took her on a car ride beyond the western city limit of

Austin and parked in the grass off the edge of the road. He playfully blindfolded her then guided her down a trail to what he said was a secret place that only he knew about. Before he removed the blindfold, she guessed that the water she heard lapping nearby was a stream.

"No, guess again," he said as he untied the blindfold.

They were standing in a beautiful clearing surrounded by live oaks and willow trees on three sides, and Lake Travis in front of them. They sat on a blanket for over three hours, discussing everything from what species of trees those by the water's edge were to whether either of them thought there might ever be a truly effective treatment for polio. They ate sandwiches made with fresh tuna salad from a delicatessen that Edgar's mother frequented and apples that he had picked up at a fruit stand near the river in Austin. They wondered what had become of psychology Professor Smithson or Wally, the man who had kept the library hall floors shining last year.

"Don't you think we should be going back?" Marcella asked.

"Soon, but first I have ...," He reached into the picnic basket. "This." He brought out a miniature cake made for two. Across the top, a beautifully laid ribbon of frosting laced its way across a bed of cream cheese topping, in and out of sliced fresh strawberries, and spelled the words Happy Birthday.

"Edgar," Marcella said. "Where in the world did you get this cake? Did you bake it? You didn't, did you?"

"No. I can only wish I were that artistic." He brought out a small package from his pocket. "Happy birthday."

Marcella's eyes lit up her face. "What is this?"

"Open it," he said, pointing to the velvet box.

She eased the box open and froze, breathless. She held it in both hands and stared with narrowed eyes as if she were looking beyond the box somehow. "I don't know what to say."

"You don't have to say anything. Put it on. Let me see it on you."

Marcella's hands shook as she removed the brooch from the box. "Pin it on for me. Will you?" she said.

Edgar leaned toward Marcella and with a gentle touch, pinned it on her blouse. "It's beautiful on you. Just exactly as I pictured."

"What is it?"

"It's a brooch."

"And a beautiful one, but what are these stones?"

"Those in the center are diamonds. The stones around the outer edge are rubies," he said.

"I can't take this." She shook her head and started to remove the brooch. "It's far too expensive. You'll have to take it back, Edgar. Please."

Edgar stopped her. "No ma'am. I'll do no such thing. My grandmother gave that to me. It had been her mother's. When she gave it to me, she said that I'd know when I had met the lady who should wear it."

He took Marcella's hands in his. "You are the one, my dear. It's yours."

"Edgar ...."

He held a finger across her lips. "There's not a lady on earth who could wear that piece of jewelry more beautifully than you. I only ask that you keep it as long as you live. A little something to help you remember me."

"Edgar," she said in a whispered tone. When she could no longer continue staring into his eyes, she laid her head on his shoulder.

Together, without a word, they watched a lavender twilight slide below the horizon. Neither of them said a word until the lights across the lake replaced the sun with their fractured reflections across the water.

Marcella stood. "We should go now."

CHAPTER 7

*G*rumpy's Garage, the local tire and welding shop, was in the rear of the building that sat across the road from Marcella Peabody's home. Without the U. S. flag that flew out front, a stranger might never guess that the glass doors in front led to the local post office. Most residents of Morgan Crossroads had home mail delivery, but some opted instead to call for their mail in person. They figured there would be nothing in the box but the electric bill and a Publishers Clearing House sweepstakes entry anyway, so they would just pick their mail up whenever they wanted to. Traffic trickled in and out on normal days. However, on high traffic days, such as the week before Christmas, there might be three or four customers at the counter at one time.

Grumpy heard the distinct sound of metal crumpling when Dora Mae drove one wheel of her little red car up on the sidewalk and in the process, pinned one of Morgan Crossroad's two newspaper boxes between her bumper and the flagpole.

By the time he made it out the office door, Dora Mae was standing on the sidewalk.

"What happened?" Grumpy asked.

She smiled and barely above a whisper said, "I was distracted by Marcella's crepe myrtles. It's not like her to let them grow that large."

Dora Mae patted his arm. "Come in here. I have something I need to ask you." She marched through the front door and turned to face Grumpy only to find she had gone inside alone. She stepped back out and found him staring at the paper box, more in amusement than surprise.

"I have something to ask you, Grumpy," Dora Mae half whispered and half squeaked. She tugged at his shirt and dragged him through the door.

"What's that?" From the counter he picked up the coffee pot and held it toward her. "Coffee?"

"No, thank you. It makes me hyper." Considering his off and on relationship with Jack Daniels whiskey, she was glad to see Grumpy drinking coffee today. Just two years earlier she had written a notice in the Whipper County Gazette of the graveside service after his abusive alcoholic father died driving his car head-on into a tree.

"By the way, I think you should consider changing your name. You are far too nice a young man to have a name like Grumpy," Dora Mae said.

"Then I'd have to get used to people calling me something else. Besides, I kinda like Grumpy. Gives me an excuse on those days when people aggravate me."

Grumpy's real name was James, but Marcella had unofficially renamed him Grumpy on the first day she taught him in first grade. He tended to wear a scowl on his face, as if hoping to ward off anyone who might attempt to befriend him. The name had stuck with him so well that most people in town would have to think a while if someone asked them what his real name was.

THEN CAME EDGAR

"Well, you think about it," Dora Mae said.

She drew up next to Grumpy and half-whispered, "Have you seen anything suspicious going on across the street?"

"Nope. Nothing that I can think of. Why?"

"Nothing. It's just that I'm having a hard time finding out anything about this mysterious man who was seen walking down Main Street. Rumor has it that he was on his way to see Marcella, but that's all I know about him."

"Why don't you go ask Marcella?"

"Now, Grumpy, you know that would do me absolutely no good. Marcella Peabody's not going to give me any information like that. So, are you sure you haven't seen anybody about seven feet tall over there? I really can't see how you could miss him."

"Maybe this guy never really existed. Or maybe he's a ghost."

"Oh, stop it. You've just gone silly on me now."

Across the street Marcella pulled her front door to, and walked toward the street.

"I've got to go," Dora Mae said. "I wouldn't want her to know that I was asking about her. Keep this between you and me, okay?"

"Got it," Grumpy said.

Dora Mae waved at Marcella, got in her little red car, bounced off the sidewalk, and fled the scene.

Marcella stopped on the sidewalk and studied the wounded paper box. "Did she do this?"

"Afraid so."

"Why is she in such a hurry?"

"She gets that way when she's being nosy," Grumpy said.

Marcella raised an eyebrow. "About what?"

"She's chasing a seven-foot-tall man and can't seem to catch up with him."

"Oh."

Grumpy held the door open and motioned Marcella through it.

She found a chair and perched on its edge. "Grumpy, can you tell me how to drive to Mason's meadow? I know I go out toward Porterville, but I don't think I'd recognize the turnoff."

"What's at Mason's meadow?" he asked.

"Probably nothing. I just want to see if I can find it, to see if it looks like it did when I was a child," Marcella said.

"Why be so secretive about it? And why after all these years?" Grumpy asked.

"I'm not being secretive. I just don't want everyone in the neighborhood to know that I'm going. That's all."

"It's still there as far as I know. But I'm not so sure I'd try to drive that old car up to it."

"Grumpy, you know that I've been driving twice as long as you've been alive. It might take me a while, but I almost always find my way," Marcella said.

"Okay. Something tells me you're going no matter what I think about it." He gave Marcella his obligatory safe driving speech, then told her in the simplest way he could how to find Mason's meadow.

"Thank you. I'm going there right now. Say hello to your sweetie."

~

Marcella backed Papa's Chevy onto the street. She waved at Grumpy and set out toward Mason's meadow. *Let out real easy with the left foot while I press down with the right.* The old car lurched and jumped as Marcella aimed it down the street.

"Look at that grass," she said as she passed Morgan Chapel. "Why has no one mowed the church yard?"

Next door to the church, the Mooreheads kept their landscaping meticulously groomed. Compared to their yard, the church lawn looked as though it had been neglected.

Marcella waved at Stella, who was standing in the doorway at Lucy's Café. She made the turn just as Grumpy had instructed and headed out the Porterville highway.

Mack Johnson waved from his tractor when she drove by, but he'd as well have waved at a tree. Marcella didn't see him, nor did she notice that his cow was out again and grazing in the ditch, just feet from the pavement.

It was twelve miles from the light in Morgan Crossroads to the Mason property. The sound blasting from the angry horns of the six cars and three pickup trucks that passed her fell on deaf ears. "Speed up," one person yelled.

Marcella looked at her speedometer. "Twenty-five miles per hour. That's fast enough for anybody," she said.

Little was different about Whipper County's landscape now than it had been forty or fifty years earlier. There was no urban sprawl and so far, the county had stayed under Walmart's radar. Most of the houses that she crept by were older, with the occasional exception such as the fancy new brick and stone home that newcomer Fred Starnes had built just around the curve from the general store. Besides the house itself, he had gone far beyond the norm and installed a winding paved driveway and ornamental landscaping. Marcella had always thought that the property would look right at home in House Beautiful magazine, which she often dreamed her way through. She wondered what it would be like to live in a home that looked as if it had been meant for Beverly Hills, even though it had instead sprouted among the decades-old white farmhouses, rutted gravel driveways, and weathered tractor sheds of an Alabama county, which, if time had not forgotten, it had at least overlooked until the last decade.

On both sides of the road, red-roofed barns and yellow tulips popped against a background of deep green alfalfa and clover. Occasionally Stone Creek would run alongside the road, and soon it would go its own way across a pasture and on out of sight.

Two Johnson boys, muddy from their toes to their knees, prodded milk cows through a gate from one pasture to another.

Marcella caught a glimpse of a woman slowly driving her tractor beneath a faint rainbow left behind by a shower that had passed through. It started in her back pasture and ended beyond a hill on the opposite side of the road. After she passed the lady, Marcella waved out the driver's window. "Why, there's Jewell Crabtree."

Marcella had not been to the meadow since that day sixty years earlier when she and Papa had picnicked there. Will it still look the same? Of course not. It couldn't.

The Mason property rose from the pavement and disappeared over a hill to the left. Besides the rainbow, the early afternoon shower of rain had left behind it fresh clean air that somehow made the colors in the pastures and hillsides more vivid than normal.

Marcella might have missed the turnoff had she not remembered to look for a crumbling and blackened stone chimney standing alone in a field. Rumor had it that it had stood there for over a hundred years.

She made the turn and lined Papa's Chevy up as much as she could with the crumbling remnant of a road in front of her. "Ouch!" she said when she misjudged the depth of a hole in the road. The resulting bounce sent her freshly teased hair into the headliner. She dodged right and slowed to a stop, then lunged left again. Her head bobbed forward, to the right, forward again, then to the left. "Come on, car. You can make it." She wondered if perhaps the meadow no longer existed and was about to give up when young trees and brush yielded to a clearing on the left. Just as Grumpy had said, it was off the main road far enough to be out of sight to passersby on the highway.

The meadow seemed smaller to her now than she remembered. It smelled the same though. The sweet fragrance of honeysuckle hung in the air and dragonflies still called the place home. She took a long deep breath and savored that aroma. On the day she and Papa had come here, there had been a tree standing alone near the center. Now, over sixty years later, in the spot where Marcella remembered having the picnic, the split remnants of a large sycamore tree bowed toward the ground. Lightning had torn it, she judged from the charred wood on its trunk.

Marcella opened the trunk of her car and retrieved a large weathered picnic basket, the same one she and Papa had carried to the car. She draped a blanket over one arm and walked with slow steps toward the sycamore.

∼

The telephone in Eva Jo's kitchen rang and rang until whoever was on the other end gave up. Five minutes later it rang again, blasting through the open windows toward the barn. "Hang on. What could be so important that this can't wait until I get these eggs gathered?" Eva Jo asked. Just as she stepped on the porch, the ringing stopped again. "It figures. I bring myself back to the house just to talk to nobody."

She spread a towel on the kitchen counter and laid the

eggs out, ready to be washed. "They'll wait for me until I get Chelsea milked," she said, taking a stainless steel pail from a shelf near the door.

Eva Jo had been a rather robust tomboy as a child and grew up to be a busty, plump woman with plenty of size in her feet to hold her up and a head full of dark gray curly hair that made her appear more big-headed than she was. She'd as soon drive nails into barn doors as to darn socks. Whether it was to milk cows or bake biscuits, she found herself awfully handy to have around.

People had called Eva Jo by her full name ever since her elementary school days. That is, by everyone but Marcella and two other girls—they had pinky sworn in the third grade to always to leave off the Clomper when addressing her. Most of the time they remembered their oath. She always blamed her mother for giving her such an obnoxious three-word name and stayed agitated at her for using all three words every time she wanted Eva Jo for something. "Eva Jo Clomper, come in here this minute!" Or, "Eva Jo Clomper, you'd better hurry with that hair or you'll be late catching the school bus. You know the old man doesn't wait on slow children named Eva Jo Clomper."

Even now, she hated going into the post office to send off for a mail-order something or other, or into the beauty shop for her weekly shampoo and set and being attacked by a bevy of voices. "Well there's Eva Jo Clomper. Doesn't she look lovely today?" She sometimes wondered how they'd like her purse up side their heads.

Just as the milk pail met the floor under Chelsea, the phone rang out across the yard again. It seemed to be louder than before. "Hold on, Chelsea. Let me see who this clown is before they wear my phone out."

Panting, Eva Jo said, "Hello." Her other hand fell from the

hip where she had rested it and she sat down. "Jesse! How in the world are you? Where are you?"

"Chelsea, hang on!" Eva Jo yelled.

∼

Marcella spread the blanket out in the breeze and let it float to the ground. She placed the picnic basket and a few other necessities on it and made a slow descent from standing to sitting. "Oh, my knees," she said.

Overhead a red-tailed hawk scanned the fields for lunch. The creek still babbled along behind her, splashing against the larger rocks that dotted the creek bed just as it had the day she and Papa watched sycamore leaves floating past. Those leaves had no idea where they'd come from nor a clue where they were going. They were just happy being, Papa had told her.

In the limbs overhead, songbirds conversed with others in the trees across the meadow. Marcella ate a sandwich and a piece of fruit from the basket and after a few minutes of listening to nature's chorus, laid on her back as she and Papa had. Half a dozen decades earlier, had there been snow on the ground, she might have made a snow angel.

Above her, light wisps of clouds passed by in slow motion, interrupted for just a moment by the glimmer of an airplane slicing through the sky miles above her. She imagined what the passengers on the plane might think if they could see her, a fiery redhead well into her seventies lying on her back on a picnic blanket like a child still full of wonder.

A squirrel scurried across the corner of the blanket and snatched Marcella from her daydream. As quickly as she could, she sat up, barely in time to see the little intruder jump and run across the bowed and charred trunk of the tree. She looked at her watch. She had lain there, transported to a place of peace and quiet, for an hour.

Marcella had always favored large purses and never went anywhere without one, including picnics in the middle of nowhere. In fact, she had a collection of purses that was the same size as her collection of shoes. With the exception of gardening shoes, she never bought a pair without also buying a matching purse. She reached into the soft blue leather one she'd brought and found the photo of Papa, the man whom everyone else in Whipper County had known as John Robert Peabody. She sat the photo on top of the picnic basket. "Now, there you go, Papa."

~

"Jesse, where did you say you were?" Eva Jo asked.

"We're in Virginia, close to Bristol. Say, Eva Jo, I won't keep you long, but is Marcella alright?"

"Sure. As far as I know, she is. Why?"

Jesse said, "I don't know, really. I just want to be sure I didn't disrupt her life too much by stopping in like I did."

Eva Jo chuckled. "Oh, I don't think I'd call your visit a disruption. In fact, she seems to have a little extra pep in her step now."

"I'm glad to hear that. I didn't realize she's as old as she is until I got there," Jesse said.

"Oh, don't worry about that. There's a bunch of us around here that are a lot closer to sunset than we are to sunrise. You asked me a question, now here's one for you. Just between you and me, what's the real reason you came all the way to Whipper County, Alabama just to see an old lady you'd never met?" Eva Jo asked.

"Are you still there, Jesse?"

"Sorry, Eva Jo. Sorry." Jesse hesitated for what seemed like minutes. "Dad has always talked about this girl he knew in college named Marcella. Nothing makes him light up like memories of her. I just wanted to meet her myself."

"I've known Marcella since we were in grade school and we've talked about a million different things over the years," Eva Jo told him. "But this is the first I've ever heard about any boyfriends she had in college."

Jesse said, "I feel like I'm prying, but there's something else that I wonder about."

Eva Jo prodded him on.

"Why didn't Marcella ever mention her husband?" he asked.

"Who said she was ever married?" Eva Jo asked.

"Did he die?"

"Jesse, honey, there never was a he, unless she had one that I never heard about. If you came here thinking she had a husband stashed away somewhere, you probably just need to clear that up with her."

"I sure hope I didn't wreck anything by showing up like I did."

"Don't worry about that. You didn't mess anything up. In fact, something happened in her that day, something good. She'd been down in the dumps for quite a while. You came along at exactly the right time to help her snap out of it."

Jesse asked, "Do you think she'd mind if I stayed in touch with her?"

"I think she'll be very disappointed if you don't," Eva Jo said.

∼

"Papa, a visitor came by the house a few days ago," Marcella said, taking her skirt from the breeze. "He was a young man from Texas. You should have seen him, Papa. A most unusual person, he was. He was very tall like you and in a way, might have been mistaken for a Peabody, had there been any others after you. Oh, he didn't look like you at all. But once I saw through the rash of tattoos that covered almost every bit I could see of him, I found that there was an air of dignity hidden under all those flowers and birds and words. He carries himself proudly, but with a kind of meekness much like you."

"Jesse said his father was a man I knew in college. His name was Edgar. Edgar Garrison. He was the handsomest boy in all of Texas. Every letter I got from you ended with the line, 'Stay away from the boys.' So, I never told you about him. You needn't have worried about Edgar though. He was kind, like you. He was so gentle with me. He treated me like a dainty little flower, opening every door, always pulling out chairs for me. I suppose manners like that are a little out of date now, but I loved it when he made me feel special."

"Jesse said that Edgar calls me Rosie sometimes." Marcella poured iced tea from a Thermos bottle and brought the cup to her lips. "I like that name, Rosie. It seems like the name of a happy person, doesn't it? I remember him calling me that. He said my pink cheeks reminded him of roses."

Marcella squinted against the sunlight. "It was in this very spot that you and I had our picnic all those years ago. Because I had told you I had no one to play with, you played with me here after we ate. Do you remember that? You brought a kite; it was a beautiful yellow one that I could never get off the ground. You flew it so easily though. You ran and jumped and pretended to let it go. The sky was a deep blue like it is today. Against that sky your kite looked brilliant, like the sun with a sparkling tail. We played chase and you let me believe that you couldn't run as fast as I. You'd say, 'Slow down, Sweetie. I can't run that fast,' knowing full well you could catch me any time you wanted. Sometimes you'd catch me, just to make me think it was a fair game."

"Papa, I never forgot that day. From that time on, whenever I had no one to play with, I could see myself watching the clouds go by with you and I'd almost always feel better. You and I made a game of naming the clouds that passed, based on their shapes. 'There goes sailboat,' I'd say. And you'd point to one you had named apple or bird or fish. My, what an imagination you must have had."

Marcella laid back on the blanket, closed her eyes and watched spontaneous replays of dozens of memorable times that she and Papa had experienced together until the scenes faded into sleep. When she woke, the sun strained to peep through the trees on the hill behind her.

CHAPTER 8

Decades earlier, John Robert Peabody had been a towering presence at six and a half feet tall. People who knew him unanimously agreed that he was a gentleman in the strictest sense of the word, a gentle man apparently born without the ability to become riled about anything. He was born to Thomas and Anna Peabody, who lived in a cabin at the bottom of the ridge that formed the western boundary of the valley. By age four, he worked alongside his mother in the garden, learning to tell the difference between good plants and bad plants, between weeds and carrots. One at a time, he carried cantaloupes to the porch. At six, his assigned chore in the winter was to see that the wood box next to the fireplace never went empty.

John's education came from his talented father, not through formal schooling. His father taught him to add and subtract using practical examples. "If I pick three tomatoes, and you eat one of them, how many do I have left?" If his mother sent him to fetch six buckets of water from the well behind the house for his Saturday evening bath and he stopped at five, he would soon remember how to count to six.

His mother taught him to read the same way she had learned—by reading the King James version of the Bible and the Sears and Roebuck catalog. Rice boiler, 60¢. "The Lord is my sh, shep, shepherd." Men's cotton Union Suit, 80¢.

He discovered early on that he loved to read and devoured every book he could get his hands on. If a word presented itself that he could not manage on his own he would run to his mother or, if he thought the word had too many letters for her to read, he might run down the road to Miss Smithson.

The Adventures of Huckleberry Finn garnered the first position in his collection of literature. Miss Smithson was his Sunday school teacher and the local schoolmarm. Impressed that he had learned to read so well without a teacher, she gave it to him, a gift from her personal library. He would read it to his mother and sometimes he would take the book to Stone Creek and imagine that it was Huck's omnipotent Mississippi rather than the slow-running inches-deep tributary it was.

John Peabody also learned from his father the fine art of frugality. He learned to find money in places where no one else looked. His father had taught him that to walk past a penny without picking it up was to walk by a symbol of abundance without so much as showing it his respect. But he found money in other ways, too.

At the age of twenty, with money he had saved from doing chores for other people in the valley, he bought a languishing sawmill business. Every person he had talked to about the mill had told him it was hopeless. Eighteen hour days, a natural bent toward customer service, and patience worked together to build the business back to prosperity.

Without fanfare, John bought small pieces of property up and down the valley. He kept them a while and resold them at fair prices when he met the person who he thought needed the land.

In the same way he had a knack for finding buyers for his products and services, he had a quiet unassuming way of knowing who needed his help, but would never ask for it. There wasn't a person in the valley who would go hungry if John heard about their plight. They did not have to ask for his help; he just somehow would find them. There was no fanfare in his giving. He would just show up with a bushel basket of vegetables from his garden, or a pair of shoes from the general mercantile in Porterville. A widow might walk out one day to find that someone had replenished her firewood supply without her knowing about it.

Once, John gave a small house and an acre of land to a man who'd had to quit working so that he could care for his disabled wife. In most cases, though, the recipients never knew who their benefactor had been. Those who did, kept it to themselves.

"John Robert Peabody, do you take this woman, Clara Ruth Brown, to be your lawfully wedded wife?" the minister asked.

"Yes sir, I do. I most certainly do," said John, fulfilling a dream he'd had for half of his twenty-six years. The ceremony was short; neither the bride nor groom was fond of fanfare. On the day of the wedding people gathered from one end of the valley to the other to witness what they all surely believed was a marriage made in heaven.

Morgan Chapel had been organized in 1887 and still sat in its original location two doors down from the crossroads, convenient for worship on Sunday mornings and for potluck dinners, family reunions, and community meetings any other day of the week. Fan wielding spectators filled every pew inside. Well-wishers who could not fit inside stood three and four deep outside the building, watching and listening through open windows.

Prior to the wedding, John had set aside a piece of property near the church to build a house for his bride to be. Together, they would make it a home, and that they did. When he carried Clara Ruth across the threshold, she entered for the first time to find a fully furnished house, complete with furniture, dishes, and food. For the next two and a half years, they lived an idyllic life. He was frugal by nature, but generous in showering his bride with the answer to every need or desire that she had. Their love for each other was famous in the valley.

Clara Ruth became pregnant and glowed with anticipation of the day she and John would hold their newborn child. That day was not to be though. At twenty-three, in the bed where her only child had been conceived, Clara Ruth Peabody suffered complications that no doctor ever foresaw and died while giving birth.

John Robert Peabody fed Marcella her first meal and vowed to be, as much as he could, the father and mother that she needed.

CHAPTER 9

It was mid-morning between the breakfast and lunch crowds at Lucy's Cafe. Every table was empty except the large round one in the back corner where the Rosebud Circle met and where today, Henry Brown and Cecil Grey were drinking coffee, reading a three-day old Huntsville newspaper and waiting for their daily slices of pecan pie with vanilla ice cream.

At The Dairy Bar on the other end of town one could order chocolate-dipped soft-serve ice cream cones, cherry lime Cokes, and hamburgers served through a walk-up window, but Lucy's was the only dine-in eating establishment in that end of the valley. In an earlier life, the nineteenth century building that Lucy's occupied had housed a post office and general mercantile. Thousands of packages and love letters had exchanged hands across the massive old counter over the decades that the post office had been in operation. Now, huge home-made hamburgers, hand-battered chicken fried steaks, and an assortment of pies slid across it. Shelves nine feet tall still lined the walls, empty and sturdy.

Cecil was the unelected and unpaid overseer of Morgan Crossroads, Alabama. He had worn every public hat there was in Morgan Crossroads other than that of preacher. Even that exclusion was not because he had not been asked. "Why don't you give it a shot?" they'd said. "You can't do any worse than the last one."

"Who in the world is that sliding in here sideways?" Henry asked over the rattling and squawking and dirt and gravel peppering the outside wall.

"My guess is either Johnny Mack Durant or that boy of mine," Cecil said. Whichever it is, he'd better have a good excuse. Casey Grey, Cecil's youngest son, had snatched his rusty rattling pickup truck off the road and slid up to the building next to his father's much better kept blue Chevy truck. He slung the front screen door open, ran past Stella, whose hands were full of coffee and pecan pie, and came to a halt at his father's table.

"Slow down, man," Cecil said to Casey, then took his pie from Stella.

"Thanks, Stella."

Cecil asked, "What's got you all in a fizz?" He took in a mouthful of pie and chased it with coffee.

Casey said nothing, but shoved his cell phone in front of his father.

"What is that?" Cecil asked, trying to focus on the photo. "Is that Dora Mae's car?"

"Yep," Casey said. "Looks like she tried to turn in Eva Jo's driveway and missed."

"Is she alright?" Cecil asked.

"She's okay," Casey said. "But, she keeps saying something about a sign."

"Come on," Cecil said. He left his ice cream melting across his remaining pie, but took time to push in his chair and straighten the table.

"Should I come along?" Henry asked.

"Go ahead and eat your pie," Cecil said. "Mine, too, if you want it. Between Grumpy, Casey, and myself we'll get her straightened out."

Cecil stopped by the register and handed Stella some cash. "Sorry Stella, gotta run. I'll eat two pieces next time," he said with a wink.

Casey went ahead. Cecil stopped to enlist Grumpy and his tow truck.

When they arrived at the scene, an assortment of passersby stood in the road trying to figure out just how this woman had managed to plant her car nose first in the ditch. "How did she stand it on its bumper," one of them asked.

It took three people to get Dora Mae out of the car and one more to retrieve her gargantuan purse from the floorboard. Other than a tad of misplaced lipstick, a loose false eyelash, and a few rattled nerves, she had emerged from the spectacle unscathed. She stood on the side of the road with her purse, looking as though she hadn't given a thought to her disarranged hair.

Cecil convinced the onlookers that there were more interesting things that they could get excited about and watched them return to their cars and pickup trucks.

Grumpy studied the situation and within a few minutes had pulled Dora Mae's little red car out of the ditch. It would need work on its underside, but Grumpy assured her that he could handle the repairs.

Morgan Crossroads was too small to warrant its own police department and had always relied on the Whipper County Sheriff Department or the Alabama Highway Patrol to see that the law was respected. After a one-sided discussion with Dora Mae, the decision was made not to call either one out there to investigate what, in her mind, was nothing more than a little mishap. With that matter settled, Grumpy drove off with the car in tow.

Eva Jo had come out of her house to offer whatever help she could when the accident happened, and when the excitement settled she took the nerve-shattered Dora Mae into the house.

"Here," Eva Jo said, pointing to one of her reclining chairs. "Plop yourself down there for a while." She continued to the kitchen and yelled, "Coffee?"

Dora Mae said, "I'd better go for a glass of warm milk."

For the next hour the conversation rambled along, covering everything from why Eva Jo hadn't repainted her house to why the septic tank guy had changed his phone number after all these years.

"You'd think he'd let someone know," Eva Jo said. "And especially when he knows my field lines need work. On top of that, next time he comes by, he's gonna try to talk me out of a gallon of fresh milk. You wait and see. I've got a mind to tell him Chelsea ran dry."

Dora Mae found a smile.

Eva Jo said, "No, I guess I probably shouldn't do that. He might just disappear altogether next time." She chuckled. "And where would that leave me?"

"Who is your septic tank man?" Dora Mae asked.

"Jim what's his name. The only one in the valley," Eva Jo said. "You've got me to wondering something."

"What's that?"

"You were driving on a straight road out here in the country and you just suddenly decided to hook a left into the ditch."

"Uh huh," Dora Mae muttered.

"Why?" Eva Jo asked. "I just can't make sense out of that."

"Okay, here's the truth. You won't tell anyone, will you? I was on my way out here on a research mission. You know, trying to gather some facts about this giant man that came through town yesterday. I suppose I must have been concentrating too hard. From the corner of my eye I saw that sign on the side of the road."

"What sign?"

"That little sign out there." She pointed out the window in the wrong direction. "Somebody nailed it to the fence just before your driveway."

"What's that got to do with you deciding to just leave the road?"

"Well, it said, 'Turn or Burn.'" Dora Mae took a long swig of milk. "So I did."

Eva Jo heaved to the left and might have fallen out her chair laughing, had she not caught herself on the edge of the table. She tried to stop the entire top half of her body jiggling, but gave up.

"I shouldn't have told you. See there, you think it's funny."

"Honey, I don't know how you even managed to read that sign. It's been there for thirty years or more. The paint's so faded you can hardly read the words."

"Well, I read it, didn't I?" Dora Mae said.

"I reckon you did, Honey. I reckon you did. We could ask the old Pentecostal preacher that nailed it up there if he wasn't dead, but I really don't think that's what he had in mind."

CHAPTER 10

*P*olly's House of Beauty was quieter than usual. For the first time since early morning, Polly Brown had just two customers.

"Here's a question for you," Gertrude Gleaves said. "Why do people always latch on to rain when the weatherman says there's a thirty percent chance of rain?"

"Never gave it much thought," Jewell said from the shampoo station.

"Neither have I," Polly said, fingering the shampoo into Jewell's hair. "I can tell you this much. Henry's that way, but now let me tell you, he won't give that thirty percent that same respect if you were to say there was a thirty percent chance of sunshine today."

"That's my point exactly," Gertrude said. "I want my weatherman to tell me the good stuff. The way I look at it, if I turn on the Huntsville news and that weatherman says we have a twenty or thirty percent chance of storms, that means there's a seventy or eighty percent chance that it won't."

"Give me the good news," Jewell said. "I hate storms."

"Speaking of storms," Polly said. "Has anybody talked to Dora Mae since she drove her car into the ditch?"

"I reckon she's gone into hiding," Gertrude said.

"I don't know why. Everybody knows she can't keep her mind on the road," Polly said.

"I heard she drove up on the sidewalk at the Post Office the other day," Jewell said.

"According to Grumpy, and I guess he should know since he was just inside the door when it happened, she was busy snooping on whatever Marcella was doing. Then, bam, right up on the sidewalk she went," Gertrude said.

Polly finished rinsing Jewell's hair and sat her up. "I don't know what's gotten into Dora Mae. I've seen her go too far a bunch of times over the years."

"Yes, she has. Like that time she decided to go up to Mister Roper's for a story on honey bees. She wound up in the right place at the wrong time and came back with about a dozen bee stings," Gertrude said.

"I think she can't bear the idea that Marcella might have an acquaintance that she knows nothing about," Jewell said.

"What does she think is going on?" Polly asked.

"Who knows? The way that lady's mind works, she's probably decided that there's a new soap opera in the works and Marcella's in the starring role," Gertrude said.

"You don't think ...." Polly said. She shook her head. "No, that couldn't be. Not Marcella."

∼

Marcella wiped her hands on her apron and answered the door.

Eva Jo held two bags filled to overflowing with squash, zucchini, and red bell peppers.

"Here, Honey, let me help you," Marcella said as she pushed the screen door open.

"I sure hope you can use these. That garden is about to run me over," Eva Jo said.

"You know how I love squash. And zucchini. And bell peppers, too."

"Well I hope you still love tomatoes and cantaloupe. I swear, if that cantaloupe doesn't slow down, it's going to run straight up in my back door."

Marcella laughed. "Well, maybe it won't do that. Do you have time for a cup of coffee?"

"Why not," Eva Jo said.

"Good. We can sit here in the living room."

Marcella poured coffee and placed it on a tray along with two slices from a pecan pie that Eva Jo had dropped off a couple of days earlier.

"Eva Jo, I have an idea."

"What idea? I hope you haven't decided to order another one of those gizmos from that catalog."

"What gizmo? Do you mean that electric feather duster thing I ordered?"

"That one. The one that sent feathers flying all over the living room the first time you flipped the switch on it." Eva Jo bounced with laughter as she flung her arms toward one corner of the room, then another. "You should have seen the look on your face when you were trying to turn that thing off, Marcella! I couldn't tell if you were coming or going or already been."

Marcella straightened herself and her skirt. "Well no, Eva Jo. That is not my big idea."

Eva Jo mustered what small amount of seriousness that she had left. "Okay, then. Let's hear it."

Marcella shuffled to the edge of her seat. "I think we should climb into my car and drive to Texas. We could ...."

"Surely, you don't mean the same car that took you five minutes to get under the light that day," Eva Jo said. "Can we move to the kitchen? If I keep sitting in this easy chair I'm liable to fall out in the floor asleep."

"Sure. We'll both have to sit on one end. My sewing machine seems to have taken over the other end."

"Please tell me you're not serious about driving your daddy's car to Texas."

"Well, of course I am. Grumpy did a lot of work on it. It's like brand new, or at least as much as a fifty-year-old car can be. Lord knows we can't go in that rattly old truck of yours."

"Marcella, I don't mean to be ugly, but I just don't think I could manage riding with you all the way to Texas. It takes you ten minutes to get from your house to mine and it's only two miles," Eva Jo said. "Have you thought about how long it would take us to drive a thousand miles or however far it is?"

"No, I haven't. Not exactly. I just came up with the idea this morning," Marcella said.

"Do you know how far a thousand miles is? Well let me help you, Sweetie. You have a top speed somewhere south of thirty miles per hour. Whatever you'd be hoping to see when you got out there would've long ago dried up and blown away, I'm afraid."

Eve Jo reached across the table and patted Marcella's arm. "I've got an idea. You can make 250 round trips between your house and mine. That'd be how far a thousand miles is. Let's see, ten minutes times two for a roundtrip. That's twenty minutes. Do that 250 times and you could make the trip to Texas. Lord only knows how much we'd age before we got there."

Marcella pleaded. "I'm serious, Eva Jo. I'd like to take a

trip to Texas and I want you to go with me. If you don't want to drive, we can get Henry or Cecil to take us to the airport in Huntsville."

"What? And get on an airplane?" Eva Jo shrieked. "I'll go and sit there with them watching you take off, but you will not see my tail gracing a seat on anybody's airplane. I'm just not doing that."

"I flew one time, and it wasn't bad," Marcella said. "The pilot said all that bouncing and wiggling around that we did during the flight was normal for some days, and we'd be okay. And we were."

"Nope. I am absolutely not going to fly anywhere with anybody during this lifetime."

"Okay. How about the bus?" Marcella poured milk for herself and more coffee for Eva Jo. "I'm sure someone would be happy to drive us to the bus station in Huntsville. There has to be a bus from there to Texas."

Eva Jo narrowed her eyes and scrunched up her forehead. "You've already made up your mind, Marcella Peabody. Am I right? You have decided that the two of us are going to unleash ourselves on those poor Texans, haven't you?"

"Well, not entirely, I haven't. But I really do want to go. I haven't been outside this state since college and you know how long that's been."

Eva Jo took the last bite of her pie. "Let me guess. Jesse's visit stirred this up, didn't it?"

"Maybe."

"He called me the other day," Eva Jo said as she picked up her purse. "Did I tell you that? I've got to run to Haley's. Come ride with me."

Marcella asked, "What does Haley's have to do with Jesse?"

"Nothing. I just need to pick up some lard before I forget

it. Can't make decent biscuits without lard. Come on and I'll explain about Jesse on the way. Don't worry. I'll bring you back home."

Marcella climbed into the old truck with Eva Jo and together they roared to the corner and hooked a right down brick-lined Main Street. Marcella asked, "Are you sure we ...."

"Speak up. My muffler's got a hole in it," Eva Jo said.

Marcella turned up her volume. "Are you sure we aren't leaving little pieces of this thing behind us? Look down there, Eva Jo." She pointed to the floor board. "I can see the road passing by under us. The road, Eva Jo! What is keeping this thing from dropping both of us straight on to the pavement?"

Eva Jo said, "We'll be okay. That hole's been there for years. Just a little rust, that's all." She rolled her window up to stifle the noise.

"Jesse said he was somewhere up close to Bristol, Tennessee," she said.

"My, that's a long way from here. He must have gotten a ride from someone," Marcella said. "Was he okay?"

"He said that he and Spotlight were getting along just fine. He was worried about you. Said he was afraid he might have upset you, showing up out of nowhere like he did."

"I hope you told him that I'm fine," Marcella said.

"I told him that you didn't sleep for days."

"You didn't, Eva Jo," Marcella said, her face contorted with worry. "Tell me that you did not lie to that young man."

A laugh slipped through Eva Jo's grin. "No, I didn't. I told him you were doing just fine."

"He gave me a start when I first saw him," Marcella said. "But in the end, I enjoyed our time together."

Eva Jo braked hard against the curb in front of Haley's Grocery. "Better leave your window open. Remember this thing's got no air conditioning except what comes in through the windows."

"And the floor," Marcella added.

Eva Jo opened her door and sat with one foot hanging out. "You think you can find Jesse's dad, don't you?"

Marcella said, "His father is someone I knew when I was in college. If things were to work out right, I might be able to find him again. Several years ago I heard that he was an attorney or an accountant—something like that—in New Braunfels, Texas. That's not far from Austin if my memory serves me correctly."

"Honey, when I get you back home we need to talk. You're scaring me more than a little bit."

Marcella reached for the right words, but none would come.

CHAPTER 11

Ollie Smith, Grumpy, and Johnny Mack Durant had each finished off a Double Cola and a Moon Pie.

Johnny Mack had picked up a six-month-old magazine from the checker table in the back of Brown's General Store and brought it to the porch. He read a line or two, laid it down to argue the weather, read another line or three, and offered his prediction for the Auburn football season and whether California was going to slide off into the ocean with the torrential rains that channel thirty-one news said it was having. After ten minutes of sporadic reading, he laid the open magazine in his lap.

"You want to know what I think?" Johnny Mack asked, pecking on the magazine with his finger.

"I'm guessing you're going to tell us, whether we want to know or not," Ollie Smith said.

"Let's hear it," Grumpy said.

"Here's what I think about laxative advertisements," Johnny Mack said.

"Where in the world did you come up with something like laxatives to talk about?" Ollie asked.

Johnny Mack pecked the magazine again. "Right here." He raised the magazine from his lap. "It says here that this stuff keeps you regular twenty-four hours a day."

"What's wrong with that?" Grumpy asked.

"It's gotta be a lie, that's what," Johnny Mack said.

"You tried it yourself?" Ollie asked.

"No. Don't need to. I eat my oatmeal every morning. But that wife of mine does. She's been taking this stuff I reckon for twenty years and I tell you for dead certain that there's not a regular bone in her body."

"You'd better not tell her that," Ollie said.

"Oh, she knows it," Johnny Mack said. "If there was anything regular about her, I could figure out how to act when I walk in the door."

"What in the world are you talking about?" Ollie asked.

"If I thought this stuff would turn her into a regular old woman, I'd buy her four or five truckloads of it. It'd be worth it to come up with a few minutes of peace."

Grumpy and Ollie looked at each other, then at Johnny Mack.

"Maybe you need to go bale some hay or something. Work this out of your system," Ollie said. "Because I really don't think a laxative's going to do the job.

Marcella took the chicken breasts and tea bags that she'd bought on her unexpected trip to Haley's Grocery into the kitchen, then joined Eva Jo in the living room. She lowered herself into her favorite chair, a Queen Anne wing back chair that had been Papa's. She motioned Eva Jo toward a recliner near the front window.

"We may as well get this over with, since you're not going to let me rest until we do," Marcella said.

"This thing that you're trying to do, going to Texas and all, isn't like you, Marcella," Eva Jo said. "Not even close."

"Why wouldn't it be?" Marcella asked.

"Because it's not. That's why. You are the world's most cautious woman on most days."

"I'm still ...."

"For Pete's sake, you drive like you think if you go slow enough nothing can happen to you. When you go somewhere you check the lock on the front door about forty eleven dozen times. But not today, or yesterday or any other day since Jesse came into your life."

"Well, why ...."

"And I'm afraid you're going to drop straight into a bucket of scalding hot water if you don't watch yourself," Eva Jo said. She paused. "Your turn."

Marcella fingered the piping around the front edges of the chair arms. "I haven't gone anywhere or done anything that's even the slightest bit dangerous, so I don't understand your concern."

"No, not yet you haven't. But what would you call a trip to Texas, just you and another old lady who's never been anywhere to speak of? Do you know anything about Edgar—what's his last name, Garrison? Do you know where he's been or what he's done? What about other women? How do you know there's not someone else hanging out in the shadows? Don't you wish you knew that much about him?"

"Jesse said that Edgar talks about me all the time," Marcella said.

"Remember Thomas, that first husband of mine? Good riddance, I said. He talked about me all the time, like I was his prize watermelon, yet he had enough women scattered out between here and Georgia to keep him doing dishes for the rest of his life."

"Well that certainly doesn't mean that Edgar is like that," Marcella said.

"No, it doesn't. And if he's anything like Jesse claims he is, he'd be a good catch. But you don't know that yet, do you?"

"That's why I want to go to Texas. I want to see if I can meet him and see how similar he is to the Edgar I knew in college."

"You mean how different he is?"

"No, ma'am, I don't mean different. I intend to see how similar he is. And I'd be willing to bet you that other than a few years of age, he's the same person he was then."

"Don't you think you should at least call the man before you go zipping out there like I don't know what?"

"What would I say to him if I were to call him?"

"What would you say to him if you went diddly-bopping on out there and showed up unannounced?"

Marcella clasped her hands in her lap and fell silent. She laid her head against the chair back and stared at the light on the ceiling.

"Look, Honey," Eva Jo said, leaning forward. "I'm not trying to trample on your petunias or spoil anything for you. But it worries me that you are going into this like you were sixteen again and going to the dance at Porterville school, just hoping and praying that Leroy Jones was going to pick you, God rest his soul."

"Perhaps I am hoping that Edgar picks me. Maybe I do hope that he's my Prince Charming. And you know what? It would be a marvelous thing if he were to pick me up from the loneliness I've felt for all these years," Marcella said.

"Why haven't you ever told me about this? About Edgar and college. I'm telling you, Honey, I don't know if I'm mad or hurt. Why'd I have to wait until Jesse came along to find out something so important about you? We've been practically glued at the hip for more than sixty years and I just days ago learned that there was a man somewhere in this world that you had loved so much that you would drive a thousand miles to get him back."

Marcella pushed herself up from her chair as quickly as her knees would allow. She scooted an ottoman beside Eva Jo's chair. "I've certainly never meant to upset you. And maybe that's what's wrong with me. Maybe I can't figure out whether to be angry with Edgar for not calling me occasionally or hurt that he left me at U.T. in the first place. Had Jesse not found me, would I ever have heard from Edgar again?"

"That's something I hope you'll give some serious thought to before you drag me halfway across the country living on hope that he'll be there with open arms."

For a long moment silence filled the room. Marcella sat with her eyes closed, a tear escaping.

"I just couldn't do that myself," Eva Jo said, barely above a whisper. "I just could not do it."

Eve Jo said, "I've got to go. I've got milking to do.

Marcella walked her to the door.

Eva Jo opened the screen and stepped out onto the porch. She held the screen door for Marcella.

"Why didn't Edgar come looking for you?"

"I can't …."

"If you loved him that much, why didn't you go looking for him?"

"There was …."

"Honey, I've been married three times and not one of them was anywhere near the man that Edgar probably is. I just wish I'd had a man worth going after."

Marcella wiped a tear first from one cheek, then the other.

Eva Jo touched Marcella on the shoulder then went to her truck.

Marcella watched as the truck's single tail light crept away and turned at the corner.

CHAPTER 12

Three days after Eva Jo's visit, Marcella sat in her Queen Ann chair, late in the evening, holding Papa's photo in her lap.

"Papa, my life is changing so fast. I can hardly believe all that's happened. My mind has been in a haze ever since Eva Jo was here. Oh, I know. She said exactly what a true friend should have said, but I'm not so sure I thought that at the ..."

Marcella bolted upright. "Who could be calling at this hour?"

On the fourth ring she picked up the receiver. "Hello. Peabody residence."

There was silence for two or three seconds. "Hello. Who is this?"

"Is this Rosie?" a smooth baritone voice asked.

Marcella's hands momentarily dropped to her lap, still holding the phone receiver. Tears formed in her eyes as her trembling hand returned it to her ear.

"Yes, Edgar. This is Rosie," Marcella said.

"I hope you'll forgive me for calling at this hour. Jesse

called this morning to say that he had met you. He gave me your phone number."

"It's fine, Edgar. I'm so very happy to hear your voice. I wasn't in bed yet."

"I was, but all I could do was toss and turn, thinking of you."

By the end of the thirty-minute conversation, Marcella was satisfied that he was not married. She was surprised to hear that Edgar had lived most of his life believing that she had gone on with her life and left any memories of him behind. He would explain later, when they had more time. She would explain her distance, too. If she could come up with the right words, that is.

"This is short notice, I know," he said. "But I'd love it if you could fly out and spend a few days getting reacquainted."

"My friend, Eva Jo, and I have already discussed taking a trip to Texas," Marcella said. She would love to fly, but other, stronger forces dictated that they take a Greyhound bus instead.

Edgar tried to convince her that flying would be safe and the most comfortable way for her and Eva Jo to travel, but gave up after hearing the full story of Eva Jo's refusal to fly.

An hour after she'd heard him call her Rosie for the first time in more than five decades, Marcella said goodnight to Edgar and made her way to bed. She lay in bed listening to the whump whump whump of the ceiling fan as it sliced through the air above her. There was a clear full moon and the security light in the yard next door joined with it so that light burst between the slats in the blinds, causing the bedroom to take on a dusk-like aura. Shards of dim light danced on the walls.

Just after midnight she woke, a train of thoughts chugging by with Edgar's call in the background and the conversation she'd had with Eva Jo loud, front and center, in her ears.

~

Almost two weeks had passed since that phone call. A conversation or two with the agents at Greyhound had convinced the women that their trip to Texas would get off to a better start if they boarded the bus in Birmingham, rather than Huntsville.

The clock on the bedside table said three a.m. and there Marcella was, wide awake, wondering one minute if she was doing the right thing, and convinced the next that of course, she was. Jesse hadn't just shown up on her front porch to pass time. Of course not, he had come because it was time for her and Edgar to see each other again. Serendipity had to count for something.

Eva Jo had spoken to her in a tone that she had rarely heard since their school days. But privately, she'd had to admit that Eva Jo was right. She'd just spent an hour reminiscing over fifty lost years. Still, she didn't really know anything about the inner parts of Edgar. During the evening that Jesse had spent with them, the conversation had never veered into the personal side of Edgar's life. And even now, after her time on the phone with him, she still didn't know much more. How much can one really learn about five decades of a person's life in such a short conversation? What were the chances that she was making the worst mistake of her life?

She had waited for Edgar. For more than fifty years she had, but had he waited for her? He said he had. Was it possible that he had actually lived a celibate life or that he had saved his entire heart and soul for her? No one but

Edgar knew the answer to that question and somehow, she just couldn't accept that such a question could be given the time it deserved over a telephone line.

Today, in just a few hours, she and her best friend would board a bus full of strangers and ride straight into a world of unknowns.

∽

"You can get that idea out of your head," Henry Brown said into the phone receiver. "You ladies are not driving yourselves to the bus station. Especially not one in Birmingham."

"You don't think we can find it?" Marcella asked.

"Oh, I'm pretty sure you'd find it if you asked enough people along the way. But I'm not so sure you'd make it in time to catch your bus. No ma'am, I'll drive you two down there. What day are you leaving?"

"Today. This afternoon."

Henry dropped his bacon and egg sandwich. "Today? Did I hear you right? This ain't Eva Jo's idea, is it?"

"It's my idea, Henry. And yes, you heard me right. Our bus leaves Birmingham this afternoon. If you don't mind, pick up Eva Jo first."

Henry enlisted Cecil to help with the luggage and driving and Cecil's son, Casey to watch the store while they were gone. Henry gave Casey a key to the front door in case he wanted something for lunch that he couldn't find on the store shelves and made certain that he knew about the coffee can under the counter.

When the men arrived at Eva Jo's house, she was standing on the porch ready and waiting. She wore tan slacks and a blue speckled cotton button up blouse. "Look at you," Cecil said. "You're all dressed up."

Eva Jo said, "I thought I should probably change out of my milking clothes."

"The other passengers would appreciate that," Cecil said, smiling. "Where is your luggage?"

"Right here," Eva Jo said, pointing to the suitcase next to her leg. "You mean to tell me that I'm about to trust you to drive me all the way to Birmingham and you can't even see this big old suitcase. I tell you what, Cecil Grey."

"I saw the suitcase, but I figured you'd have a truck full of luggage for a trip this long."

"I've never been to Texas, but I'm sure it doesn't take a truckload of luggage if you only pack a handful of clothes. They do have laundromats in Texas, don't they?"

"I'm sure they do. But I'd bet you a nickel to a hole in a donut that Marcella Peabody's not planning on using a laundry while she's gone," Henry Brown said. "Have you ever seen her iron a handkerchief? It's a piece of art when she gets finished."

Eva Jo turned to her sixteen-year-old grandson, Justin. "You're sure you won't go off with your buddies and forget?"

"I won't forget, Granny."

"You know where her bucket is, in that ...."

"Granny, I know where everything is. I've been milking and feeding since I was little. Remember?" he said.

Eva Jo dug two twenty dollar bills from her purse. "Here's a down payment. I'll pay you the rest when we get back."

The moment Cecil, Henry, and Eva Jo turned into Marcella's driveway, they began imagining which of them would be walking to Birmingham.

"Would you look at that?" Henry asked.

"Where did she come up with a herd of luggage like that?" Cecil wondered aloud.

"I thought we were only going to be gone for a week," Eva Jo said.

The three of them climbed out of the SUV and stared at Marcella sitting on her porch swing with two overgrown vehicular suitcases and three smaller pieces of luggage laid out in an arc before her.

"Look at her," Eva Jo said. "She looks like the Queen of Sheba sitting there waiting for her subjects to load her carriage."

"And what is that she's wearing?" Henry asked, his face wrinkled with confusion.

CHAPTER 13

Marcella was quite the dresser and owned what most Whipper Countians considered the most extravagant wardrobe they'd ever seen. Most of her collection of finery came to her doorstep via a UPS delivery person.

"Neiman Marcus this time, Miss Peabody," the deliveryman would say. Or it might be Macy's or Bergdorf Goodman. He always smiled and when Marcella signed for the package he'd wink and add, "Happy birthday."

Marcella had an uncanny ability to do almost anything without getting her clothes dirty. She was just as likely to mow her lawn wearing silk as she was to fill her car's gas tank while wearing cashmere. She was not given to dullness, which accounted for the fact that her closets were full of skirts in vivid colors and crisp white pants. They hung alongside tops with huge florals and abstract patterns in every possible shade of yellow, red, and blue.

She had asked Casey Grey to build what she called her glamor wall, a special closet area just for her stash of shoes. In a community where suits and ties for Sunday church would have been extravagant, her habit of choosing bold or exotic color combinations had garnered more than one sideways glance from certain residents of Morgan Crossroads. She had chosen to keep her penchant for expensive clothes behind closed doors and as a result, most of her finer fabrics and shoe collection had never been seen outside her home.

For the trip, Marcella chose a sharply creased ocean blue two piece suit, a subtle but lavish white silk blouse, and a pair of faux jewel encrusted mid-heel shoes with sharply pointed toes that reflected whatever light hit them. She carried a larger purse than normal, one that might have qualified as carry-on luggage, had she been flying to Texas.

Neither Eva Jo nor the men could form the words to ask why or how she had decided that such an outfit was a good idea for bus travel. This was Marcella's trip, though, so let her wear whatever she wanted.

Eva Jo walked toward the porch and when she made the step onto the first landing, she saw that Marcella's makeup was meticulously perfect in a way that seemed to make her face glow. Coincidently, or not, her lips matched the belt and purse she had chosen.

Eva Jo looked at Marcella but said nothing.

"What?" Marcella asked. "Did I miss something?"

"You look like a china doll. That suit might be a little more than I could handle myself, but your face ...." Eva Jo leaned forward a few inches. "You look like you could break, like you're so...so fragile."

"Well, thank you, Honey. I think I'm supposed to take that as a compliment. Let's hope we get to Texas without cracking up."

"I'm pretty sure we can do that, but I might have to watch you a little bit closer than I had planned," Eva Jo said.

"Why?" Marcella asked. "A girl has to do herself up as well

as she can when she wanders out into the world. A properly made up face is the first thing a man notices, isn't it?"

Eva Jo had only recently found out to which man Marcella might have been referring. "I don't think my face was ever much of a consideration. My husbands only wanted to know if I could make biscuits from scratch or if I could milk cows." She wagged her finger in Marcella's direction. "I could out-milk every one of them, too."

Marcella had heard from the time she was four or five years old how beautiful and long her eyelashes were. Just a touch of mascara, artfully applied was all they needed. And she had done a spectacular job with her rouge. Her prominent cheekbones were perfect for her to paint a subtle pinkish mauve.

Eva Jo suggested they go inside. "Honey, you do know that we're taking a Greyhound bus to Texas, don't you?"

"Of course, I know that. What kind of question is that?"

"Well ... you've got all that Volkswagen-sized luggage laid out on the porch like we're going to spend a month on The Love Boat or the Queen Mary," Eva Jo said.

"I only packed for a week. You never know when you might need something."

Eva Jo asked, "If Henry and Cecil manage to cram all that luggage into that one vehicle, how are you and I getting to Birmingham?"

"You don't think it will fit?" Marcella asked, her eyebrows following the freshly formed furrow on her forehead.

"Sweetie, I'm not sure it'd all fit on that bus. The thing might not even be able to take off. Then we'd be just sitting there, watching that poor driver trying to figure out why his bus won't go."

"Surely not," Marcella said. "I thought everybody carried luggage with them."

"Well, I suppose they do. But I doubt many of them carry everything they own on the trip. I suspect things have changed in the past fifty years or however long it's been since you took a trip of any length."

"Well, the two largest suitcases are empty. We can leave them if you think we should."

"Honey, please tell me that you weren't really going to drag two big old empty suitcases all the way to Texas and back."

"No, I wasn't. Not exactly. I thought we'd probably have a chance to go shopping and we'd need some way to get our new goodies back home," Marcella said.

"Let's cross that bridge if we have to," Eva Jo said. "If nothing else, we can drag the new stuff home in shopping bags."

Back on the porch, Marcella pulled the two empties aside and pointed to the remaining luggage. "Henry, Cecil, can you fit these into your car?"

The men each took a bag and waddled lopsided toward the rear of the SUV. Under his breath, Cecil asked Henry, "What in the world do you suppose Marcella has in these bags? You reckon she's trying to catch up for all those other trips she used to talk about taking, but never did?"

When Marcella was younger, she would sometimes tell Henry and Eva Jo and her other friends her private daydreams that she was going to Hollywood to become the next Betty Grable. She even said she might just become the next Marilyn Monroe, but then she decided against that because Marilyn's dresses probably wouldn't fit her properly. Once, for a day or two, Marcella had considered moving to an idyllic island in the Caribbean where she would become a famous author. She might even surpass Hemingway in the fame department. In the end, though, except for her years away attending the University of Texas, she remained firmly planted in Morgan Crossroads, Alabama.

Eva Jo said, "Just one more question."

Marcella, standing now and pointing toward the SUV, said, "Look. I believe it is going to fit."

"Where are we going to sleep, assuming we make it all the way to Texas with this truck load of stuff?" Eva Jo asked.

"Why, in the hotel room. There will be plenty of space. Don't you worry about that. The travel agent promised that the room would be plenty large enough for us and our luggage. You'll see. It'll be fine."

"Do you remember that time Jewell and Polly went to New York City?" Eva Jo asked. "They both said their closets at home were bigger than the room they had up there."

"Well, it's good we're not going to New York. We're going to Texas and I'm certain the room will be plenty large enough for the two of us and our luggage," Marcella said.

The SUV seemed to groan a bit as mile by mile, Birmingham came closer. Every window in the rear was blocked as was the seat space between Marcella and Eva Jo. By leaving the two empties at home, Cecil and Henry had been able to fit all of the luggage and the four of them in somewhat comfortably.

Whether in pity or joy, she wasn't certain, but Eva Jo thought the trees along both sides of the road must be bowing as the four of them drove past. She caught herself wondering if they might even be laughing among themselves at the site they beheld. *We look like ten pounds of junk stuffed into a five-pound sack*, she almost said aloud.

After three hours and two potty breaks, Henry made the final turn onto 19th and stopped in front of the Birmingham bus terminal. He and Cecil went inside to inquire where they might find a porter to help with the bags and returned pushing a troublesome wobbling luggage cart. Apparently, bus station porters all take their lunch breaks at the same time, or maybe they don't exist anymore.

The cart was small and they found themselves in serious need of sideboards to keep everything corralled. Henry pulled. Cecil pushed and steered. Marcella and Eva Jo walked alongside and grabbed whatever tried to fall off. The waiting room was sparsely populated, with only a person or two scattered here and there.

On the wooden church pew that sat nearest the aisle where the luggage was being wrangled into submission a toothless man of obvious advanced age chewed on nothing, his head following very slowly from right to left as the spectacle passed in front of him. Marcella saw him just in time to dodge his feet which jutted out like two planks. She could not help but notice the profile that a Jimmy Durante nose and a Sammy Davis chin presented. It seemed that his chewing was done in a rhythmic fashion. Three quarter time, she thought. Chomp, chomp, chomp. Chomp, chomp, chomp. With every beat his chin rose to meet his nose, missing it barely.

Neither Marcella nor Eva Jo had considered the possibility that there might actually be a limit on the amount of luggage that they could check onto the bus. By the time the ticket agent had figured the costs for over-sized and over-weight luggage, Marcella's trip to Texas had suffered a substantial cost increase. "Are you sure you want to pay for all that?" Henry asked. "We can haul one of them back if you want us to."

Marcella said, "No sir. I'm going to Texas and my luggage is going with me. We will make do just fine. The man at the counter said that senior citizens can request help with their bags. I told him I was glad because Eva Jo was a lot older than she looked and she would probably need a little assistance."

Henry and Cecil watched through the window as Marcella and Eva Jo ventured out to the loading area. "I sure hope those two make it," Henry said.

"They will," Cecil said. "They won't do it quite like anybody else would, but they'll make it just fine."

The women turned to wave goodbye one last time then set about in search of the right bus.

"This one must be ours," Eva Jo said. "The guy said dock four, and this is it, plus the sign on the front of the bus says Dallas. That would at least be headed in the right direction."

"I hope we're boarding the right one. The driver wouldn't let us get on the wrong bus, would he?" Marcella asked.

Eva Jo said, "I'd hope not. Wait a minute." She pointed frantically at the Dallas sign on the bus. "A minute ago, that sign said Dallas. Now it says Atlanta. We can't get to Texas on a bus going to Atlanta."

The driver stepped off the bus onto the platform and called for passengers going to Atlanta and several other cities that interested neither Marcella nor Eva Jo.

Eva Jo stepped around the four people in front of her. "Driver, a few minutes ago you were going to Dallas. Now you're going to Atlanta. Who's going to Dallas in your place?"

Unfazed and almost as uninterested, the driver said, "The bus that comes in after this one. Just stand right over there and wait for twenty minutes or so. He'll be here."

"Will it say Dallas on the front of it?" Eve Jo asked.

"No, ma'am. It should say Los Angeles or Phoenix on it."

Eva Jo motioned Marcella out of line and told her that the Dallas bus was going to Atlanta, but in a few minutes they would get on the bus to Phoenix or somewhere in California and she guessed they could just get off in Dallas. "That is if he stops long enough," she added.

Half an hour later a bus labeled San Diego pulled into the dock where the Dallas bus that went to Atlanta had been. Eva Jo took herself straight to the driver and asked if that might be the bus that would let them off in Dallas.

"Oh, they'll do more than that. They'll make you get off there. That's the end of the line for this bus. It goes in for maintenance there," the lady who drove the bus told her.

"So this really is the right one?" Eva Jo asked, holding her ticket for the driver to see.

"I promise. This is the one. We'll be out of here in about fifteen minutes," said the driver, a jovial black woman who Marcella guessed to be in her late forties, a lady with plenty of heft to manage the job.

Marcella and Eva Jo herded their carry-on luggage to the boarding area and fell in line behind a young couple that Marcella had trouble figuring out. There was a younger, shorter version of Jesse, but pierced in some of the most inconvenient places and considerably less kept. A great cloud of flaming pink hair sat atop a chunky girl with ripped jeans that, according to what Eva Jo had whispered to Marcella, must have been painted on. Between them, on the floor, sat a thin but apparently healthy child, perhaps five years old with a head of long mussed up, half dread-locked hair. Marcella couldn't quite make out whether it was a boy or girl.

The pink-haired girl turned around for no apparent reason. "Hi," she said.

"Are you folks going far?" Eva Jo asked.

"Santa Fe, eventually," the girl said. "We'll probably have to stop a couple of times and like, make a little money to feed ourselves."

Eva Jo said, "Santa Fe. That's in Arizona, right?"

"New Mexico," the young man answered through pierced lips. "It's real nice there—laid back and comfortable."

"So I've heard," said Marcella, wondering what kept the rings that graced the corners of his mouth from somehow hooking themselves together. What if they locked his mouth shut, or worse, open? she wondered. Young people!

Marcella turned to find the source of a shuffling sound. Scoot, sush, scoot, sush. The bent over man with the rhythmic face made his way past in slow motion, leaning on the arm of a bus company employee who deposited him at the bus labeled Memphis.

"This bus will get you to Corinth, Mississippi," the animated employee said in a loud exaggerated drawn out way. The man lifted his hand a few inches in a wave of thanks. Chomp, chomp, chomp.

Marcella, Eva Jo, and the Santa Fe bound couple watched as the driver struggled to help the man onto the bus. The chains that hung from the young man's belt clanged and rattled as he broke from their line and hustled over to help.

"He loves old people," the pink haired girl said, smiling. "He's such a kind, gentle spirit."

"I see," said Marcella, thinking back a few weeks to another gentle spirit that had appeared in her life. "Does he scare any of them?"

"She means, with all the tattoos and hardware and ...." Eva Jo said.

"Sometimes, I suppose his does," the girl said. "But they get over it after they hang out with him for about five minutes. Did you know he can quote Shakespeare?"

"No, I don't suppose I did," Marcella said. "That's great. My father could quote him as well."

When the young man returned, the girl told him with a brightened face, "This lady's father could quote Shakespeare."

He smiled, exposing clean but misaligned teeth between the stainless steel loops that framed his mouth. "Which line was his favorite?"

Marcella adjusted her shoulders and stood straighter. "Papa would often quote this one. 'In time we hate that which we often fear.'"

"Cool! That was from *Anthony and Cleopatra*," the boy said.

"That's exactly right," she said. "Which quote is your favorite? Sorry, what did you say your name is?"

"I'm David. This is Sonia." He pointed to the child on the floor. "This is Moon."

"Okay, David, which Shakespeare line do you like most?" Marcella asked.

The driver stepped from the bus and motioned the passengers to move forward. "Have your tickets out where I can see them," she said. "If you're going to ...." A bus from somewhere pulled in on the next dock and drowned her orders in a sudden hiss of air brakes. From the overhead speakers, a robotic voice announced the departure of the Memphis bus and requested passengers going to points west to make their way to dock four.

David stepped onto the bus and shouted back through the door, "I have been in such a pickle since I saw you last."

Marcella laughed, oblivious to the heads that had turned her way. "That was from *The Tempest*. He knows Shakespeare," she said, looking at Eva Jo, but pointing excitedly at the young man.

How is she doing this? Marcella has stood right here on this sidewalk and found herself yet another Jesse, Eva Jo thought.

CHAPTER 14

The decision where to sit on the bus proved more difficult than either Marcella or Eva Jo had anticipated. There were more than forty seats on board and at least half of them were filled with people who were already on the bus when it arrived. They first sat in the front row seats nearest the door, but found that they could not settle in. It was not a question of comfort. They supposed that no bus seat would feel quite like Eva Jo's Lazy Boy or Marcella's Queen Anne chair, but the front ones probably sat as comfortably as the rear ones. Neither of them felt any joy in the notion of lugging their carry-on bags all that way.

The real question that begged for an answer was, what would they do if nature called their names between stops? Eva Jo looked at the narrow aisle and let her eyes trace the path from her seat to the phone booth sized restroom in the rear. She saw herself springing down the aisle, bracing against each seat as the bus pitched back and forth, then planting her double-wide backside straight down in some old man's lap. *I might never make it to the restroom.* And what if after all that, it turned out to be a false alarm? *I'm far too old for that.*

For a moment she tried to consider what it might be like for the other passengers if Marcella were the one who had to make the trip. *As dignified as she is, I can just see that saddle bag of a purse slapping those poor people in the head.*

In the end, they decided that they would manage the risk of hiking to the rear if the necessity arose. Besides, they figured that at least they would be able to catch a breath of fresh air every time the bus door opened.

The driver, whose name tag identified her as Betty, stopped next to Eva Jo's seat and spoke toward the rear of the bus. "Hey, tall skinny dude. No, not you. The other guy," she said, aiming her pointing finger and voice over the heads of all but the most distant passengers. "You need to hang out right there, young fellow. You're not going to be moving all around the bus."

She and her abundant chest leaned into Marcella and Eva Jo and barely above a whisper said, "They say it takes all kinds to make a world. But I swear, I can't for the life of me figure out why they all have to ride my bus at one time."

An occasional wave of excited chatter found its way from the rear.

"You'll be in Tuscaloosa in a little while. Relax," she said to tall skinny dude.

A few turns and stoplights, then they were on the Interstate, finally pointed in the general direction of Austin, Texas.

"You ladies going to visit anyone in particular?" the driver asked over her shoulder.

"We're going to try to," Marcella said.

"Sounds like this trip may be a hunting expedition," the driver said with a grin. "You must be trying to surprise somebody." Her hands suddenly jerked to a death grip on the steering wheel. Both the pitch and decibel level of her voice shot to the top. "Did you see that?" She pointed toward a car that had nearly clipped her bumper during a lane change.

The driver went silent. Eva Jo watched her look toward the left mirror then the right mirror, to the left again, to the right again, then straight ahead.

Marcella leaned toward Eva Jo and whispered, "Maybe we shouldn't talk to her while she's trying to drive."

Eva Jo said, almost whispering, "Not if we want to make it to Texas. If she stands this thing on its nose in a ditch like somebody else I know, we'll never get it back down on its wheels."

"Don't make fun of Dora Mae. Occasionally she just has a day that doesn't work out for her," Marcella said, thinking back to the day Dora Mae Crawford had driven her little red car nose-first into a ditch.

After a few minutes on the highway, the bus seemed to settle into a steady rhythm of rocking and humming that had an anesthetic effect on some of the passengers. Tall dude did in fact get off in Tuscaloosa, along with several others.

Minutes morphed into hours as one sleepy little town after another yawned past. Daylight morphed into night. In Jackson, Mississippi, Betty got off and a different driver took over. A tall quiet man with wisps of silver in his hair, he was gentle in his manner with people and his handling of the bus. It was almost as if he considered his job to be that of delicately rocking his passengers to sleep.

Eva Jo sat with her seat reclined and her head cranked over onto her shoulder.

Next to the window, Marcella laid back against the head rest and watched the world go by through raindrops that streaked across the glass. A street light here, a billboard there, everything was the same yet different. The smallest light took on a star-like appearance. She strained to see the time on her watch. "Ten until two," she said under her breath. A semi-truck lumbered past, leaving behind a swirling misty cloud.

Marcella thought back to the letter she'd found in the attic. It had been a long time. At least fifty years had passed since that rainy evening when she had sat with Edgar in the corner booth at Josie's Diner for the last time. The two of them huddled, hardly taking their eyes off each other. From the jukebox, Chubby Checker tried his best to talk them into doing the twist, and they might have, had they been aware the song was playing. Words came few and far between. For the first time since that breezy Wednesday when Marcella had caught Edgar's eye in the library, neither she nor he knew what to say.

Theirs had been a whirlwind romance in a way. It had been one that swept them both into a vortex of irresistible attraction and held them there for nearly three years.

Across the street from the diner, a train trumpeted its presence then rumbled on into silence. Marcella took his hand in hers and asked, "Are you going to be like that train?"

His somber face made an attempt at smiling. "Probably not, whatever you meant by that."

"Are you just going to belt out your goodbyes, then disappear into the darkness, never to be heard from again?" Marcella asked. "I'm watching you board the train into your future, wherever and whatever that means. I'm staying here and you're moving on to graduate school somewhere. But you won't even tell me which school you are going to. Is it Yale? Harvard? Or maybe Stanford? Who knows what will happen to you or where you'll be."

He drew Marcella closer and gently cupped her tear-soaked face in his hands. "You have to know that I love you more than I could ever express. I promise you that there will never be another woman."

"If that's true, why won't you at least tell me where you're going?" Marcella asked, dabbing streaks of watery black from beneath her eyes.

Edgar stared into his tea glass. "Because I don't think I can stand it."

"Stand what?"

His eyes met hers and he let out a sigh. "Harvard accepted my application."

"That's great," Marcella said. "Isn't it?"

"For my career, it's wonderful. I've dreamed of going to Harvard for a long time. But I'm not sure it will be great for us. They've offered me a fellowship that requires me to teach undergraduate history classes while I complete my graduate work. I will be so busy that I won't be able to give you or our relationship the time that I should. It would be easier if I just went my way and you went yours."

"No, no. It just couldn't be better that way. Why would the pain of being apart be easier than the work of being together? I'll go with you. We can get married. No fancy wedding or anything like that. I'll find a job and help you while you finish your education."

"It still wouldn't work, Marcella. I'd still have no time for anything but my studies. That wouldn't be fair to you or to our marriage. After a few months, you'd feel neglected and left out. What kind of marriage would that be?"

"The kind that teaches us to work out the hard times. And what about last night? We've known each other for three years and we've never even come close to going beyond a kiss. Then last night happened." Marcella gripped his hand. "What about last night?"

"Last night will be a bright spot in my memory from now on, but it doesn't change what I have to do."

Marcella straightened and knit her fingers into a two-handed fist. "Okay, Edgar. If you think a few years of hard work and education are more important than our relationship, then go on. Go on and become a high-powered lawyer. Do well. I hope you do. But don't bother keeping my phone number. It won't work in Alabama."

⁓

When the sun rose it found Marcella and Eva Jo in the Dallas bus station, huddled around a vending machine, trying to decide which microwavable breakfast biscuit sandwich they wanted. Should they choose the one with the rubber looking sausage and egg or the more expensive one with the plastic-like bacon and egg white? The one with the plain white label or the one with the fancier, "I'm the most exquisite example of a biscuit you will ever experience" label?

Eva Jo said, "Five dollars for that? I'll tell you one thing, Marcella. If you ever in my life find me making biscuits that look as pathetic as those, I hope to the good Lord above that you wap me over the head with a rolling pin."

Marcella said, "If you think the biscuits are sad, you're really going to get a kick out of the coffee."

Eva Jo wandered over to the drink area and returned with a bottled water.

"Not brave enough to try the coffee?" Marcella asked.

"Couldn't quite muster enough nerve to try whatever that was squirting out of that machine. I've had dishwater that looked more like coffee than that stuff did," Eva Jo said, shaking her head. "And did you see the price? You could buy a coffee pot for that."

Marcella asked, "Do you have any idea where our bus should be?"

Eva Jo looked over the departure sign, searching for any hint that one might be going toward Austin. After a question and answer session with a ticket agent, she took Marcella by the hand and went in search of the bus labeled McAllen.

If this is the right one, we should be heading for Austin in about thirty minutes, Eva Jo said.

Marcella stopped a passing station employee and asked, "Is this the bus going to Austin?"

"Yes ma'am, but you probably wouldn't want to wait that long."

Eva Jo propped an out-turned fist on each hip and asked, "Why not?"

"Because you're going to be standing here for about five more hours." He pointed in a bent kind of way to a bus that they could not see. "That San Antonio bus will get you there a lot faster. It leaves in about fifteen minutes."

Marcella said, "Thank you, sir."

She and Eva Jo hoisted their bags and scooted in the general direction of the San Antonio bus. "That was close. You were going to have us standing out here looking like two lost hillbillies for five hours."

Eva Jo punched Marcella with her elbow. "At least, we'd have been the two best looking ones they'd ever seen."

"Listen," Marcella said.

"Now loading in lane three. Waxahachie, Waco, Austin, New Braunfels, San Antonio." The robotic announcement rambled on with several other arrivals and departures.

"Did he say New Braunfels?" Eva Jo asked.

"I believe he did," Marcella said.

"Why don't we go there instead of Austin?"

"Why would you want to go to New Braunfels?"

Eva Jo held up a brochure she'd taken from the counter inside. "See this? We could go floating down the river in an inner tube. I haven't done that in forty or fifty years."

"Well you can go if you want to, but I won't be doing that. At least, not in this lifetime," Marcella said.

"Where's your sense of adventure? Just because we're as old as dirt, that don't mean we can't go blow it out a little bit."

Marcella said, "Well, I think it might be too late to change our hotel reservations. And, have you forgotten how easily I sunburn?"

Eva Jo cocked her eyes toward Marcella and asked, "I thought you said your long-lost friend lived in New Braunfels."

Marcella adjusted her skirt and pressed the front of her blouse with her hands. "Look. I've lost a button. When did that happen? All of these people around, and you've not said a word about it."

CHAPTER 15

"I don't think I want that dog hanging around here, mister," said Judy, who managed the Four Trees Campground outside Middletown, Virginia.

"He won't be any trouble. I promise you that I'll keep him on a leash," Jesse said.

"Every time I've let someone keep a dog on a leash, it's wound up waking up everybody at two or three o'clock in the morning." Judy took a drag from her cigarillo then stamped it out. "Some raccoon scoots itself from one tree to the next, and the dog goes crazy barking and lunging at it, and then whines because it got away."

Jesse scratched Spotlight on the head. "His barker's broken. You won't hear a peep from him."

"Do what? How can his barker be broken?" Judy asked, staring down at Spotlight as one of his eyes stared at her.

"He can't bark," Jesse said. "Before you ask, I'm not sure why, but he can't. And he couldn't care less about raccoons."

Judy peered at Jesse from the corners of her eyes and handed over a key. She wagged a finger in the air without saying anything.

The cabin was small and sparsely furnished with a strong slant toward the sixties. It was clean, though, and had all of the basics covered. And, in any case, it was a step up from sleeping outdoors as he and Spotlight had done every night since they left Morgan Crossroads. In just a few days, they would arrive at the writer's retreat in New England. The cabin would give him a chance to make some calls and catch up on current events.

Judy had given him a tiny bar of soap with some fancy Baltimore hotel's name printed on it, a washcloth and a half-size bath towel. There was a closet turned toilet in the corner and a freestanding shower in the opposite corner hidden only by a plastic green paisley print curtain. Jesse settled into a large olive green padded chair with tired springs that barely kept the seat cushion off the floor. He clicked through one snowy television channel after another then hit the off button.

"Spotlight, what shall we have for dinner?" The dog lay stretched out on the floor, his jowls draped flat across one foot. His wagging tail betrayed the busted down expression on his face. "Will you be having a granola bar?" Jesse held the bar with one hand and with the other, a can. "Or will it be Super Meaty Dog Chow with faux gravy?"

Spotlight looked up with his right eye and sniffed toward the granola bar.

Jesse said, "That might not be such a great idea. How about this canned stuff?" Spotlight had his nose in the food bowl before it touched the floor and had finished his only course before Jesse could make it back to his chair.

Spotlight's wagging tail seemed to propel him across the room when he heard Jesse mention that he was going to call his sister. Jesse knew nothing of the life that his four-legged sidekick had led prior to them discovering each other. But for some reason he always became excited when he heard the word sister.

The phone rang once, twice, three times. Jesse held his finger to his mouth as if Spotlight's delighted attitude might be heard on the other end. On the sixth ring, an out of breath female voice answered.

"This is Jesse. What's got you so excited?"

"Oh, nothing out of the ordinary," his sister, Gloria said. "Brian just fell out of a tree—again."

"Again? How many times ...."

"Twice this week. Fortunately, he hasn't broken anything yet," she said. "I happened to glance out the kitchen window just in time to see him hit the ground butt first. He kinda got the wind knocked out of him for a second or two, but would you believe the kid didn't even whimper?"

Brian, at nine years old, was the oldest of three boys. The others, eight and six years old, were quiet and reserved. Brian, on the other hand, was precocious and afraid of nothing.

"Guess who I met a few days ago," Jesse said.

After three failed guesses, Gloria said, "I give up. Who?"

"Marcella."

Gloria gasped. "You met who?"

"Marcella Peabody, the lady Dad always talks about," Jesse said.

"I know who Marcella is. How did you find her?"

Jesse recounted the story of his trip to Morgan Crossroads and his time with Marcella and Eva Jo.

"Send me a picture of her, just as soon as we hang up."

"Sorry, Gloria. I never thought to take any pictures. I don't know if she would have liked that."

Gloria said, "Jesse! You should have taken at least one. Is she pretty, like Dad remembers her?"

"Even more so," Jesse said. "She's probably a little older than we had imagined, but she's still a very pretty lady. Kinda classy, actually."

"Wow. Have you told Dad?"

"I told him a couple of days ago. I never had told him that I was going to try to find her," Jesse said. "You know how he always says it wouldn't be right to just show up after all these years."

Gloria said, "Have you noticed how he pretends that he has no clue how to find her?"

"He's always been that way, like the town had disappeared from the map or something."

"Was she hard to find?"

"Not at all. Morgan Crossroads is one of those tiny places that isn't on the way to anywhere else. But I found it, and the first place I stopped to ask about her, the guy knew her. He just happened to be her cousin."

"Has Dad called her?" Gloria asked.

"I don't know. I hope he has."

Jesse heard his sister blow her nose, and when she returned, her voice cracked.

"Jesse, I can't believe you found her. She ...."

"I'll probably call her in a few days. Do you want me to tell her anything?" Jesse asked.

"Just that I'm so glad you found her." The simultaneous sounds of a door slamming and boys yelling roared through the phone.

"Mom, Christopher won't let me ...."

"Jesse, I've got to go. Call me." The phone sang its hang up tone.

CHAPTER 16

Outside the bus station in Austin, Marcella stood beside a small suitcase and spoke through the passenger side window of the sub-compact-sized taxi. "Sir, do you think you could give us a hand with our luggage?"

The driver, a man of oriental descent with sprigs of gray that sprouted randomly around his head, jumped out and eagerly latched on to the bag. He lifted it into the trunk of the car, then opened a door and politely bowed and motioned her into the car.

"Oh, sir, we have more luggage just inside the door," Marcella said. "My friend is there with them."

He scampered across the sidewalk and met Eva Jo babysitting a small groaning two-wheeled luggage cart that seemed to have a pathetic, "Would you come and take me out of my misery?" look about it.

"That small one outside was mine," Eva Jo said, pointing toward the taxi. "These belong to the other lady."

The driver was a short man, approximately five feet tall, a little taller when he tip-toed. He stared at the pile of luggage which was stacked about eye-level to him. The longer he looked, the more his shoulders drooped. For two or three minutes, he pondered the situation that had presented itself to him. The quiver in his lips seemed to hold back the question, "Why me?"

Eva Jo patted him on the back. "I feel that way sometimes, too ... right after Chelsea kicks over her bucket for the third or fourth time." She hung her purse on her elbow and braced herself behind the cart. "I'll help you. You get the door."

Outside, Eva Jo took one look at the tiny taxi and asked the driver, "Where's the rest of it?"

"Is there more?" the driver asked, looking despondent.

"No. I mean the car. Where's the rest of it?"

The driver shrugged. "I'm sorry."

"Never mind," Eva Jo said and began to hand the luggage to the driver.

A few minutes later, the taxi stopped four blocks away in front of Hotel Austin. Marcella stepped out of the front seat and Eva Jo stepped out of the right rear. One piece of luggage tumbled out when the left door was opened.

~

Inside the hotel room Marcella watched as Eva Jo dragged and hoisted herself over a bag and then a chair, partly along the wallpaper and part of the way across the dresser top, until she had reached the other end of the luggage and carry-ons, which, together constituted a pile. She propped the knuckles of each hand on a hip and stared first at the floor, then at Marcella. She said, "You know, I used to absolutely hate it when Mama'd toss one of her told-ya-so's at me. But I have to tell you, this would be a real good time for one of them. Do you suppose you could tell me how you define a 'plenty large enough room?'"

Marcella straightened the collar of her blouse then crossed her arms delicately across her belt. "I'm sure there is a way to arrange things so that there will be plenty of room," she said. "The desk clerk promised that we would be in a regular-size room tomorrow night."

"Are you sure they didn't stick us in the broom closet?" Eva Jo asked.

"I'm sure they didn't. This room is just a tad petite, that's all. Tonight we get to share a bed. Tomorrow night we'll each have our own."

"Do you remember the time Ben—I think he must have been eleven or maybe twelve—lost a back tire off of that old Oliver tractor? When that wheel fell off, he couldn't figure out what to do with the tractor and started cutting donuts right there in the middle of Dough Springs Road." She laughed and motioned circles in the air. "They said he looked like a kid on an overgrown two wheeled tricycle. And might you know it, just as Ben started riding in circles, here came Johnny Mack Durant's daddy pulling a hay wagon and dumped the whole thing right there in the ditch trying to miss Ben. It was after dark before that brother of mine found his way home. He was covered from head to toe with that stuff. The boy looked like a scarecrow standing there."

Marcella, arms still crossed, said, "I suppose you're going to say that he was carrying a suitcase with him when he got there."

Eva Jo waved at nothing. "No, he wasn't. But by the time he got over that told-ya-so that Mama threw at him, I'd had a six-week vacation from milking, and mopping, and ironing. Just about forgot how. I figured out what brothers are for. I can tell you that for sure."

"Well, if we don't get this luggage situated and hang our

clothes up, we'll never be able to iron the wrinkles out of them," Marcella said.

For half an hour, Eva Jo and Marcella shuffled luggage around the room. The reading chairs and table went from one side of the room to another and back. The dresser might have found a new temporary home, had it not weighed as much as the two ladies combined. No matter what went where, it seemed there was no way that the little room was going to work.

In the end, most of the floor in front of the window had been relegated to luggage duty. Eva Jo thought it better never to veer off into the subject of where Marcella might keep her little bags full of make-up and other primping necessities and volunteered to just keep her own lone lipstick in her purse.

CHAPTER 17

"It's ringing," Marcella said with a little girl squeak in her voice. She motioned for Eva Jo to hurry over and held the phone so that both could hear.

"Hello," a sleep drugged voice said.

"Is this Jesse?"

The rustling of bed linens and squeaking mattress springs muffled the voice. "Hello? Yes, this is Jesse. Who is calling at this hour?"

Eva Jo twisted to see the alarm clock. "It's 7:53 a.m.," she whispered.

Without reading it, Marcella held the watch on her arm out for comparison. 5:06.

Eva Jo squinched her face. "He's going to kill you Marcella, door knob dead."

"I'm sorry, Jesse. This is Marcella. I thought it was quite a bit later. How are you doing?"

Jesse cleared his throat and stammered that he was fine.

"I'm glad to hear that. And I suppose Spotlight is still with you." Marcella smiled at Eva Jo and pointed into the phone.

"He's a good dog. A bit unusual, but in a good way, I suppose."

"What is the weather like in Alabama?" Jesse asked.

"I don't know. We're in Austin, Texas, Eva Jo and I. If the sun ever comes up, I think it will prove to be a beautiful day."

"May I ask why the two of you are in Austin?"

"Well, we thought, or rather, I thought we could come out and visit your sister."

Eva Jo whispered just south of a yell, "We what?"

Marcella waved at Eva Jo, then continued, "This morning it occurred to me that I don't have an address or phone number for her."

Jesse said, "She has an unlisted number, so I'm afraid you wouldn't find her in the phone book."

Marcella said, "No, you're right. She's not in there. I looked last night and didn't find a listing for her."

Eva Jo squinted through the corner of her eye and wagged her finger as if to say, "I knew you were up to something."

Marcella squeezed the phone closer. "Oh, she doesn't? Where does she live?"

"She lives in New Braunfels," Marcella whispered across the bed.

"How far is that from here?" Eva Jo asked Marcella.

"So we could rent a car and drive down there in just a little while, then," Marcella said. "I'm sorry, what was that last sentence?"

Jesse said, "Gloria has a thing about keeping her address and phone number private, so if she wonders how you found her, you might have to deal with that little issue."

After a second or two of hesitation, he gave Marcella the address but chose to keep the phone number to himself.

After listening to her read it back to him, he said, "She has three boys, and one of them is especially rambunctious so don't be too surprised if you find things in an uproar when you get there."

~

After ten minutes of going back and forth between Marcella and Eva Jo, the car rental agent handed Eva Jo the keys. Eva Jo convinced Marcella that trying to get the old Chevy under the light in Morgan Crossroads was a minor inconvenience compared to the traffic that she would face during the drive to New Braunfels.

"They don't tend to favor people who drive twenty or thirty miles an hour on the freeway," Eva Jo said. "At least on TV they don't."

Marcella said, "These people have probably never heard that they'd live longer if they just slowed down a tad or two."

The two of them looked the little car over, and after a short introductory session that the agent had offered, they climbed in.

Eva Jo said, "What's this thing hanging on the key ring?"

Marcella craned her neck over to investigate. "Well, I don't know. Whatever it is, my car doesn't need one. Didn't he tell you?"

"No, he just pointed it at the door, opened the door and handed me the keys," Eva Jo said.

Marcella pointed at a button on the remote. "What does this one do?"

Eva Jo shrugged and pressed the button that indicated a horn. Both women jumped back in their seats, held there by the blaring repeat of the horn.

"It's stuck," Eva Jo shouted. She punched every button on the remote, inconveniently leaving the horn button until last.

Silence.

When they settled down and found their breath, they heard a tap on the driver's side window.

Eva Jo opened the door. "Why on God's green earth did they put the horn button on this thing and not the steering wheel?"

The clerk looked away, choking back a snicker. "Ma'am, that's the alarm button. The horn button is here," he said, pointing to the steering wheel.

Marcella said, "Well, I certainly hope we don't need to use that little button. That is the most annoying little horn sound that I've ever heard."

The agent straightened himself. "Is there anything else we missed going over?"

Eva Jo said, "Just one more thing. What did they do with the clutch pedal?"

"What did they do with what?" the agent asked.

"The clutch pedal. You know, the one that's supposed to be over here." Eva Jo pointed to the left side of the floorboard. "Like in my old pickup truck."

The agent struggled to constrain his facial expression to a smile. "Have you really not driven a car with an automatic transmission, or are you just joking with me?" he asked.

Marcella steeled herself for whatever might be about to happen. *Young man, I sure hope you're ready for this.*

Eva Jo straightened herself in the seat, cleared her throat, and said, "Son, I've got biscuit pans older than you, so I don't know if you'll quite be able to grasp what I'm about to tell you."

The agent lost his smile and stood as still as a stone.

"I reckon you've probably never heard of Whipper County, Alabama. Have you heard of it?"

"No ma'am," he said with a cracked voice.

"Well, that's a place where you can live your whole life and never need a car without a clutch pedal. I've lived there for more than seventy years and this is the first time I've ever tried to drive without one. Some of my kids and grandkids have cars like this, I suppose. Never really paid any attention to that. But, I don't need one, and I don't want one. Now, how do you work this thing?"

The agent relaxed and felt his face warm. He explained that they didn't need a clutch in this car. All they needed was the D, the N, and the R on the shifter.

Once convinced that the car wasn't defective or missing any necessary parts, Eva Jo and Marcella ventured onto the street and headed toward Austin.

Eva Jo sat silently. Marcella wasn't sure if Eva Jo was peeved or pouting.

"What's wrong?" Marcella asked.

"Nothing's wrong. I just want to know what the problem was with the way they used to build cars."

Marcella said, "I guess they're like anything else. We used to have party-line phones that weighed five pounds. Now we can stand on a street corner somewhere and talk on a phone that weighs nothing and has no wires."

"Well, cars are different," Eva Jo said. "I've been driving since I was nine years old. Daddy sat me on his lap on that old tractor and away we went. I've driven all kinds of stuff, from tractors to dump trucks, and today is the first time I've ever noticed that there were cars with the clutch pedal missing."

Marcella patted Eva Jo on the forearm. "Honey, you've

never driven anything outside of Whipper County. Maybe you should get around a little more."

Eva Jo said, "It's been about a jillion years, but you ventured all the way out here, and look at you. You still drive a car with all its parts. Well, you did drive that Cadillac for a long time. But now you're driving Papa's old car. Granted, sometimes you have a hard time keeping it straight which one to use next, but you usually get it done."

When the fourth car horn sounded, Eva Jo looked at the approaching speed limit sign, then at the speedometer. "I swear, these people must think that sign means the minimum speed is seventy," she said.

Marcella had a death grip on the arm rest with one hand and on the shoulder belt with the other.

Eva Jo said, "I'm driving fifty miles per hour, and look out there, Marcella." She pointed through the windshield. "These people are passing us like we're parked."

"Maybe we should park somewhere until it slows down some," Marcella said.

"What if it never slows down? Then how are we going to get to New Braunfels?" Eva Jo asked.

"Did you happen to pick up a map at the car rental office?" Marcella asked.

"No, I thought I saw you pick one up."

Marcella said, "I did, but it wasn't for Texas. It was just for Dallas."

They crept down the ramp and into the parking lot of a convenience store at the first New Braunfels exit. Lottery and Deli, the neon sign in the window flashed. Inside, they waded through the smell of tired fried chicken grease, found a restroom, then two bottles of water. After paying for the water, Eva Jo showed the clerk the address Marcella had written down.

THEN CAME EDGAR

"Do you have any idea where this might be?" Eva Jo asked.

The clerk stretched his neck and wadded up his forehead before saying, "Don't think I do." He turned to a young woman dipping chicken pieces into a fryer. He said a few words to her in Spanish. She shook her head.

He said, "She's never heard of it either. It's not on this side of town, I'm sure." He directed their eyes to the police officer who had just walked in. "She can probably help you."

After a round or two of questions and a couple minutes of drawing directions in the air, Eva Jo and Marcella rolled back into traffic and headed farther south to the fourth exit.

Marcella held the note she had written from the officer's directions. "Off the ramp, then right to the third light, then left two blocks, and right to this address. Does that sound right?"

Eva Jo said, "Well, it can't sound wrong when you're going somewhere that you've never been to in your life. Let's try it."

A few minutes later, they stopped along the curb in front of a small bungalow. Run-away dandelions carpeted the lawn with yellow. Unkempt shrubbery below the windows hid a calico cat. Next to the sidewalk, a bicycle lay on its side. Water twinkled in a large blue above ground swimming pool that was partially visible behind the house.

Marcella emerged from the car first, then Eva Jo.

"Do I look alright?" Marcella asked Eva Jo in a hushed tone.

"Of course, you do. What are you so nervous about? Remember this lady has never met you. She has no idea what you look like. As long as we don't look like missionaries, we should be fine."

"Be serious, Eva Jo."

"I am serious," Eva Jo said. "Listen, we can go in and

spend a few minutes with her, try to explain how we met Jesse and how we just wanted to meet her, then we'll be on our way."

Marcella turned toward the house. A curtain in the picture window fell into place.

CHAPTER 18

The gossip mill settled in at full steam at Polly's House of Beauty. An almost empty coffee pot and a cake plate sprinkled with brownie crumbs hinted at the prevailing mood.

"You should've seen her," Gertrude Gleaves said over the hum of the hairdryers. "She was beautiful."

"And do you know she had said absolutely nothing about taking a trip?" Stella said from her gossip chair along the wall.

Polly's House of Beauty was the only beauty shop in the valley and was home to the grandest gossip circle in the entire county. Polly Brown, Henry's wife, had owned the shop for decades. It was located in a converted garage behind their home. There were no signs by the street and no advertisements in the county paper. Word of mouth and the routine of regular appointments provided all the business Polly could handle. She rarely had to write appointments down since most of the women had been coming in at the same time on the same day for twenty years or more.

Speculation was the real fuel that kept the front door

open at Polly's House of Beauty. Most of the women who dropped in every week could do without their monthly colors or another hair teasing, but without speculation and gossip, there was a distinct possibility that two or three of them might suffer physical withdrawal symptoms. On some days, the conversation consisted of little more than rehashed gossip about why Haley's had raised their prices on eggs. The next day the conversation might be about how egg prices hadn't gone up after all. It was milk that had gone up, instead. Today, the subject was juicier than normal.

"I heard someone in Texas had sent her flowers, a huge arrangement of roses," Dora Mae Crawford said from the manicure table. "Mary Beth at the flower shop could probably tell us who they were from, don't you think?"

Stella said, "No, Mary Beth would never give out such information. At least I don't think she would."

"Who saw Marcella getting any flowers?" Gertrude asked. "Did anybody actually see a bunch of roses being delivered?"

"Well, no, not exactly," Dora Mae said. "But why else would a lady get herself as gussied up as Marcella did, then take off on a long bus ride to somewhere she hadn't been in half a century? There had to be some flowers involved, if you ask me."

Stella said, "All I know is that neither she nor Eva Jo said a word about taking off on a trip Tuesday at the Rosebud Circle. They just chit-chatted about this and that, gathered the dishes and left."

Polly finished the color she had been working on and moved to Bernie, who had been toasting under the hair dryer. "Okay, gal, your turn."

"Who was that young man that Grumpy saw leaving Marcella's house in the back of Eva Jo's truck?" Bernie asked.

"What young man," Dora Mae asked.

"He was quite large, and didn't appear to be Marcella's type at all," said Bernie, who occasionally wondered in from Porterville with no apparent reason other than to stir the gossip pot a bit.

"If it was the guy I heard about, he was too young for her," Dora Mae said. "And besides, he obviously wasn't from around here."

"What would classify a person as not from around here?" Stella asked.

"Tattoos. The fellow had more of them on his arms than the rest of Whipper County's population combined."

Polly stopped pulling curlers out of Bernie's hair and stared at Dora Mae for a suspended second. Then, waving one curler in the air said, "Henry said he first thought Marcella was going to take just about everything she owned on that trip. Poor old Eva Jo was barely going to have room to sit on the ride to Birmingham."

"I saw them going out of town," said Gertrude. "Eva Jo was scrunched up against the door like she had just gone along as an afterthought."

"Does anybody know when they're coming home?" Gertrude asked.

"We should throw a welcome home party for them," Stella said. "I'd be glad to open up the cafe for it."

"Or maybe it'd be easier to use the church hall," said a lady in the corner buffing her nails. "Does anyone know when they're coming home?"

"Henry will know," said Polly. "He and Cecil are supposed to pick them up in Birmingham when they come back."

"Good," Gertrude said, a broad smile shining across her face. "I know just what we can do to surprise them."

CHAPTER 19

A curly haired boy with dirty bare feet, deep-set eyes, and a Dallas Cowboys jersey that was too large for him studied Marcella and Eva Jo from behind the storm door. He fixed his eyes first on Eva Jo, then on Marcella. After a few seconds, he tightened his eyebrows and said in his deepest nine-year-old voice, "I don't think my mom knows you."

"Do you think you could ask her to come to the door?" Marcella said as she adjusted her bright blue blazer and skirt. Her bracelets rattled as she brushed her skirt with her fingers.

"Brian, who is it?" a voice shouted from somewhere else in the house.

"Somebody you don't know," he said without taking his eyes off them.

A tired looking, but pretty woman appeared and tried to greet Marcella and Eva Jo. "Brian, would you kindly move?"

"I don't think you know them," he said, robotically removing himself from the doorway.

"Sorry, he goes into his protector mode every once in a

while. He's not like that all the time." She smiled sheepishly. "I promise."

Marcella said, "We're looking for Gloria. I'm Marcella Peabody and this is my friend, Eva Jo Clomper."

An excited smile grew across her face as she fumbled with the latch on the storm door. She opened the door and invited them in, hugging and pulling at the same time. "Jesse told me he found you," she said with watering eyes. "But he didn't tell me you were coming. Ohhh, and my house, it's such a mess."

The scent of apples and cinnamon cooking filled the air. Marcella gave Gloria a quick hug. "Don't worry about your house, Honey. It smells wonderful in here."

"You should've seen my house when the kids were little," Eva Jo said through a chuckle. "Looked like a war zone most of the time. Is that apple pie I smell?"

Gloria picked up a couple of action figures and a video game console from the sofa. "Actually, I'm baking some apple dumplings. Please, have a seat. Would you like something to drink?" she asked, still excited. "There's tea and water, and let's see, I think there is some Coke in there. I can make some coffee, if you'd rather have that."

Eva Jo said, "I think I'd just like some ice water."

"That will do for me, too," Marcella said.

Gloria scurried out of the room and returned with the glasses of water then settled into a chair across from Marcella and Eva Jo.

Brian the protector and his brothers, both younger, stood in the doorway like stair steps. They stared into the room, taking in the strangers.

"Go on, guys," Gloria said. "Go outside and play. Christopher, isn't that your bicycle I see out in the front yard?"

In turn, each of them went slump-shouldered and slowly out the front door. Once outside, they stopped and plastered their noses against the storm door in one final effort at not missing anything. Gloria's eyes and forehead expanded into one of those "I'm going to get you" looks. She pointed with a finger that seemed to reach through the door's glass. The boys cowered away and disappeared.

"Sorry. I don't know what gets into those kids. You'd think they'd never seen a living soul outside this family. How did you find me?" Gloria asked.

"Jesse gave me your address," Marcella said.

"Well, I'm glad he did. He told me that he had met you, but I had no idea you were in Texas. Are you staying here in New Braunfels?"

Eva Jo said, "No, no. We're staying in Austin."

"That makes sense," Gloria said. "Austin has the nearest decent airport. San Antonio has one, too."

Marcella explained that Eva Jo hadn't been up to driving all the way out, so they had taken the bus from Alabama to Dallas, then to Austin.

"I knew that Jesse was planning to hitchhike across the country to that writing retreat in Connecticut, but he never said one word about trying to find you," Gloria said. She hugged her arms as if she were freezing. "Look at this. Goosebumps."

Eva Jo said, "He was only there for one afternoon, really, but we had a ball. Didn't we, Marcella?"

"I'm so glad he came by. I was taken aback by his, his ...."

"She didn't know what to do with a guy that big. And Lord, does he have some tattoos," Eva Jo said.

"Jesse's always been tall. He was six feet tall in the seventh grade," Gloria said. "I'm not sure who he gets that from."

Marcella said, "Well, what about you, Honey. How are you doing?"

"Good. In fact, most days I'm great," she said, not so convincingly.

Four framed photos sat on a simple table across the room. There were individual school photos of each boy and a family portrait that included Gloria and her sons.

"Do you work?" Eva Jo asked Gloria.

"As much as I can without having to pay for child care," Gloria said. "I wait tables at the truck stop over on Interstate Thirty-five. I was going to culinary school to become a baker, but I've had to drop that for now."

Marcella said, "I'm so sorry that things are tight for you. I hope I'm not prying, but is your husband not around?"

"No, he hasn't been here since I was three months pregnant with Joshua. He's my youngest. The boys' father just decided that he needed to go find himself. As far as I know, he's still looking."

Eva Jo said, "Well, you just try to stay strong. It may not be easy every day, but just know that you got the long end of the stick. He's the one who's missing out, if you ask me."

"We're doing okay. We never go hungry. We always have clothes to wear and gas in the car. Dad lets us live in this house rent-free."

Marcella flushed with a familiar feeling that she had last felt more than fifty years earlier. *That sounds just like him.*

"Does your Dad live in New Braunfels?" Eva Jo asked.

"No, no. He lives in Austin, out near Lake Travis."

"Sounds like a pretty place," Marcella said.

"It's beautiful out there," Gloria said. "His home sits on one of the highest places around so he can see almost the entire lake from any room across the back of the house."

"I bet his wife loves the view," Marcella said.

A door slammed against something in another room. "Mom, Christopher is chasing Joshua into the street again."

"Go tell him I said to stop it and get back in the yard."

"I already tried that. Joshua is standing in the road. I told him he was going to get mashed if he didn't come back," Brian said.

"Excuse me," Gloria said, already half-way to the back door. In a minute, she returned, followed by two boys with puffed out cheeks and pouting lips. "Go to your room and don't come out until I tell you to."

She turned to Marcella and Eva Jo. "I'm sorry. There are some days when I think they're just trying to get on my very last nerve. Say, I'm ready for more tea. Would you like more water, or maybe something else?"

Gloria walked to the kitchen. Eva Jo and Marcella followed.

"Maybe tea this time. Can I give you a hand?" Eva Jo asked.

"If you'd like some ice, you may have to crack some. The ice maker is taking a vacation right now, so I have to use ice trays."

"That's perfectly fine," Marcella said, smiling. "We can crack ice with the best of them."

"How about we just sit around the table," Eva Jo said.

"Sure," Gloria said. "The chairs aren't too comfortable." She caught Marcella half-way through her sitting motion. "Sorry, Marcella, you might like that one over there better."

Marcella smiled and moved to the suggested chair.

Gloria dished up desserts and served them around the table.

"Look at this," Eva Jo said, holding hers in front of Marcella. "Apple dumplings. Take a whiff of that. I know people who would pay serious money for one of these."

"They're my favorite dessert to bake," Gloria said through

a smile. "I took some of what I learned in school and added my own little secret to it."

"Well, you hang on to that secret," Eva Jo said. "As far as I'm concerned, you could make a good living with this kind of baking."

Marcella sipped her tea, and then with both hands, lowered the glass. "Gloria, what is your dad's wife like?"

"I guess Jesse told you that Dad adopted us when our mom died."

"Yes, he did. And we're so sorry for your loss," Marcella said. She laid her perfectly manicured hand on Gloria's.

"Dad had never been married, yet he took us in like we were his own. He's still single, even though he probably could've had his choice of women."

Marcella cleared her throat and tried to keep her heart rate and voice under control. "He never married? Not in all this time?"

Eva Jo watched Marcella for signs that she was okay. She saw moisture glistening in the corner of Marcella's eye.

"No, he didn't. Jesse and I tried to talk to him about it a few times, you know, to talk him into meeting someone for companionship."

"Did he ever say why he wouldn't marry?" Eva Jo asked.

"He won't tell us. Once he said something about he had made a pact with someone to never marry. We never figured out what or who he was talking about."

Marcella's lip trembled. She looked around for a tissue.

Eva Jo retrieved a napkin from the counter and slipped it to Marcella.

Marcella straightened in her chair and dabbed at the tears that laid on her cheeks like beads of joy. "I'm sorry, ladies."

Eva Jo said, "Honey, there's nothing to be sorry about.

You just let it go if that's what you need to do." She squeezed Marcella's free hand.

Gloria scooted her chair closer to Marcella and in the process, saw two boys' noses, one above the other, sneaking in from behind the door frame. She waved them back into the other room and wrapped her arms around Marcella.

"It was me. I was the one who he promised that there would never be another woman," Marcella said, her bottom lip quivering. "But I never truly expected that he would live his life alone for the sake of a youthful promise."

Gloria said, "I want to hear how you two met."

Eva Jo said, "I do, too. But first, I need a little more tea." She went to the refrigerator and helped herself to the pitcher, then held it toward Gloria and Marcella. "More tea, anyone?"

Marcella regained control and sat with her typically proper posture. "Oh my, where do I begin?"

"I had decided that I wanted to go off somewhere to college," Marcella said. "No one in my family had ever gone beyond high school. My father was extremely successful in business, but he never went to college. I wanted to be the exception. I'd never been outside of Alabama except for the few times that we went across the line to Huntland or Winchester in Tennessee to visit a cousin or something. I had always loved hearing Minnie Pearl say "Howdy" on the radio, so one time Papa drove me all the way to Nashville to see her in person at the Ryman Auditorium on the Grand Ole Opry. I'll never forget the infectious smile on her face when she walked out on the stage. Other than that trip, I'd never ventured far from Morgan Crossroads."

"Texas was far enough away that coming here would've been like going to a foreign country to me. So, I applied to the University of Texas in Austin. I did well there. Being the shy person that I was, I had never been part of any social groups. I held no sorority aspirations or anything like that. I was halfway through my second year and sadly, I think my closest friends were my textbooks. They were the only thing I gave my time to."

Marcella paused, as if wafting away into a dream. "Then came Edgar."

"Good-bye books," Eva Jo said, laughing. "Hello, Edgar."

The telephone rang in another room. Gloria said, "Excuse me a second."

Gloria yelled through the door, "Brian, see who that is. Tell them I'll call them back."

"I remember the morning vividly." Marcella looked upward into the past. Her finger traced the rim of her tea glass.

Brian appeared in the doorway. "It was Grandpa. He said to call him."

"Look at this," Eva Jo said, trying to rub away the goose bumps on her arms.

"Was that your dad?" Marcella asked.

Gloria said, "Yes, isn't this exciting? I don't know what he'd do if he knew you were sitting here talking about him."

Marcella, her voice weak, said, "I don't know if I can tell this without becoming emotional again."

"You don't need to worry about that," Gloria said.

Eva Jo said, "Maybe we'll join you. Go on."

Marcella said, "I'll try."

Eva Jo grabbed a handful of paper napkins from the counter next to the refrigerator and laid them in the center of the table, "Here, just in case our eyes start to leak."

Marcella said, "It was a windy Wednesday morning. I remember that because I normally went to the library on Wednesdays and that day it was so windy that I could hardly walk, try to keep my skirt under control, and still carry my papers and all that I needed. I'm sure that I probably was quite a sight. The harder I tried to keep my slip from showing, the harder the wind tried to blow my skirt over my head."

Eva Jo said, "I bet you were a sight to behold." She cackled, her body bouncing while she halfway acted out what she saw in her imagination. She stood and hobbled across the kitchen with one hand squeezed between her knees and another on her shoulder. "I can just see Marcella trying to keep her petticoat under control."

Gloria laughed, amused at the friendship between Marcella and Eva Jo.

Marcella wagged her finger toward Eva Jo. "You can laugh if you want to, but I was struggling that day. I barely weighed ninety pounds soaking wet. My books were so heavy that it was all I could do to carry them. When I finally made it to the library, I slipped into the ladies' room. And my hair. I wanted to cry when I saw myself in the mirror. I had ironed my dress that morning and I had worked on my hair for half an hour, and there I was, a total wreck. My dress was just a wrinkled mess and my hair looked like it belonged to someone else."

"How did you meet Dad?" Gloria asked.

"Once I had gotten myself straightened out, I found a seat at a table," Marcella said. "I had probably been reading and studying for an hour or so when a young man caught my eye from far down at the other end of the aisle."

"Did you go meet him?" Gloria asked.

"No, I didn't. I was afraid to. But I just sat there staring at him as though I'd never seen a boy, or a man, before."

Eva Jo asked, "Was he better looking than Benny Goldman?"

"Benny who?"

"Benny Goldman. You know who I'm talking about, Marcella. He was that boy that always wore a red shirt to school. You were kinda sweet on him, if I remember right."

"Eva Jo, that was more than sixty years ago. We were in the third grade. Every girl in the class thought he was cute, but you were the one with the crush on him. That was you," Marcella said, poking Eva Jo's arm.

"Oops," Eva Jo said, holding her hand over her mouth.

"You guys have known each other for sixty years?" Gloria said.

"More than that," Marcella said.

"Neither of us can remember not knowing the other." Eva Jo said.

"Wow, that must be some kind of a record," Gloria said. "We should call those Guinness people and tell them we have the world's longest friendship right here at this table."

Eva Jo winked. "That might not work. Marcella stopped going up in age when she hit sixty-five. And that was how many years ago?"

"Anyway, for a while, every time I looked up, this man would be looking in my direction," Marcella said. "And just as I'd raise my head, I'd catch him jerking his head back down. That went on for thirty minutes at least, and then he disappeared."

Marcella said, "I tried to study, I really did. But the harder I tried to keep my mind on my research, the less I was able to do it."

Eva Jo asked, "Did you ever figure out where he went?"

"No, but just as I stood to return my books to the shelves, this rich baritone voice behind me asked, 'Do you like Josie's Diner?'"

"Where did he come up with a question like that?" Gloria asked.

"Oh, Honey, that question let me know in no uncertain terms that whoever that was standing behind me had excellent taste in food, that he was part of the in crowd, and that he was not new around there," Marcella said. "Josie's was a popular place for students to hang out. It was a loud, happy sort of place. I'd always been somewhat shy and not at all comfortable being in social settings and the one time I'd been there, I'd found myself sitting alone. I'll have to say, though, they made the best hamburgers in the world and every student at U.T. knew that."

"I turned around expecting to see the young man that had been at the other end of the shelves," Marcella said. "But what I saw instead made my knees weak. There was this handsome and meticulously dressed man. He had beautiful dark brown hair. Oh, girls, you should've seen it. It was wavy and not a strand of it was out of place. He wore sharply creased pants with a button up shirt that looked like it had just come from the cleaner."

Marcella stacked her hands across her chest and raised her eyes toward the ceiling. "He was so tall that I had to look straight up to see his eyes. And when I did, it was like the blue in them melted and covered me with something that I had never felt before."

"Well, did you speak to him?" Eva Jo asked.

"I couldn't. Not at first," Marcella said. "For the life of me, I could not form audible words. We just stood there, peering deep into each other's eyes until finally he said, 'I'm Edgar.' He stammered and seemed so shy when he told me he'd been watching me from over there since I walked in.'"

Marcella pointed toward the wall. "He nodded toward a table far across the room, one that I hadn't seen. I was so embarrassed to learn that he had seen me in such a state as I was when I'd walked in. I hadn't even known anyone was sitting there."

"So, that wasn't Dad that you'd been watching at the other end of the library?" Gloria asked.

"No, it wasn't. Whoever that young man was, I never saw him again," Marcella said.

"Did Edgar take you to Josie's?" Eva Jo asked.

"That day and many other times," Marcella said.

CHAPTER 20

*E*xcept for the conversation that Eva Jo had with the police officer after she had turned the wrong way up a one-way street, the trip back to Austin had been uneventful.

After dinner in the hotel restaurant, the women sat on the terrace of their sixth floor room taking in the view and sounds of a Friday evening in downtown Austin. On the streets below, horns squawked and honked and people laughed. Broken bits of music floated by from somewhere in the distance.

Marcella and Eva Jo looked at each other. Eva Jo said in a loud voice, "Listen to all that noise. Constant! Back home it'd take a year to make that much racket."

Directly across the street, a cleaning crew vacuumed floors and washed windows in an office.

"Do you think those people know the world is watching them work?" Marcella asked.

"Maybe," Eva Jo said. "But I doubt they give it a second thought."

"I wonder if Edgar's office was in one of these buildings,"

Marcella said. "It could have been, you know. That one over there is somebody's office, maybe even a lawyer. See how big that desk is?"

"Marcella," Eva Jo said, looking out into the city. "Why had you never told me about Edgar? We've known each other forever, but you never told me about him."

Seconds passed. Marcella said, "I never told a soul about Edgar. Not even Papa. I didn't tell him until a couple of weeks ago."

"You what?"

"I told Papa about him."

Eva Jo turned her chair toward Marcella. "How did you do that?" she asked, her brow scrunched over her eyes.

"Oh, it's really not a big deal, Eva Jo. I just have conversations with Papa every now and then. It's how I say the things that are on my mind that I don't want anyone else to hear."

Eva Jo let that answer simmer for a minute. "I told you about all of my husbands and boyfriends. You were the first one I told when I got pregnant with Jimmy. We were just starting the tenth grade. Do you remember that, Marcella?"

"Sure, I do, Honey." Marcella rubbed her knuckles. "Did you bring Bengay?"

"There's some in my suitcase, I think. What about the Rosebud girls?" Eva Jo asked. "You never told any of them?"

"No, none of them."

"Surely, you couldn't have thought ...." Eva Jo's voice trailed off.

The sounds of the city seemed to fade away. Across the street the lights in the office went out and from overhead, a nearly full moon lit the ladies as if on stage before the world.

Marcella smiled. "Edgar made his promise to me in Josie's Diner on the last night that we saw each other. That evening I insinuated that I didn't want him to ever call me again. I certainly didn't mean it, though. And even though I would've understood if he had broken it, I've held on to that promise for more than fifty years. I never told anyone about the two of us because I didn't want to somehow jinx us."

"For the first time in my life, I'm just out of words," Eva Jo said.

"You don't have to say anything. You've been a sister to me for longer than most people have been alive and I would've told you ... if I hadn't been afraid that I might cause my dream to fall apart. Oh, I know that sounds superstitious, but honestly, that's the only reason."

"Every time we have an old folks dance at the school, or a sweetheart banquet at the church, you're always pouring punch or cutting cakes," Eva Jo said. "You never, ever have a date or even dance with anyone—and I know you love to dance. Now be honest. Is that why? Because you promised him you'd wait on him?"

Marcella studied the floor for a minute. "No, I never said anything like that. I sure never told him that I would wait on him. Not out loud, anyway. But I told myself over and over that someday he'd come back into my life and when he did, I was going to be ready."

"And you are," Eva Jo said.

"Oh, Honey, I hope so." Marcella studied her hands folded in her lap. "I surely do hope so."

Inside the room, the phone rang.

"Who could this be?" Eva Jo asked as she reached for the receiver. "Hello."

"It's for you," Eva Jo said, handing the phone to Marcella. She whispered, "You might want to sit down."

"This is Marcella."

Eva Jo took her purse and indicated that she was going downstairs.

"Edgar. Of course I recognize your voice."

～

Thirty minutes later, Eva Jo returned with a newspaper and a cup of coffee. Marcella was back on the terrace. "Was that who I think it was?"

"Yes, it was. Edgar Garrison actually called me," Marcella said with her face suspended somewhere between a smile and tears.

"How did he know where to find you?" Eva Jo asked.

"I suppose Gloria told him."

"Well, what did he say?" Eva Jo asked as she moved her chair closer. "Don't keep it all to yourself."

Marcella smiled. "He asked me out on a date."

"You're kidding. When?"

"Tomorrow evening. He's picking me up at five o'clock."

"What are you going to wear? Out of all that luggage, you did bring something for a night out on the town, didn't you?" Eva Jo asked.

"We'll need to go shopping tomorrow. It seems I forgot to bring the right shoes."

CHAPTER 21

The next morning Eva Jo woke to find Marcella sitting straight up in bed, staring across the room at her reflection in the television screen.

"What are you doing?" Eva Jo asked.

"Do you think I look old?"

"Isn't it a little early in the morning for a question like that? Of course, you ...."

"How old do you think I look? Be honest," Marcella said.

"We both know you don't look sixteen anymore. But neither do I," Eva Jo said as she leaned over to join Marcella in the reflection. "I'd say you look a little younger than me."

"Eva Jo, you're half-way through your seventies, so how old does that make me look?"

"Early seventies," Eva Jo said. "You look like you could be no more than seventy-one or maybe seventy-two."

"I was afraid of that." Marcella pointed into the television. "Look at me. Edgar is going to be shocked at how old I look."

Eva Jo laughed. "Is that what this is all about? You're worried that Edgar is going to think you look too old. I swannee, Marcella. You need to stop that right this minute."

Marcella said, "But Edgar is so handsome. He has all that beautiful wavy hair and all those muscles. And I've got …."

"I'd be willing to bet you a dollar to a hole in a donut that you look better than he does. Have you forgotten that he's not twenty something anymore, either? Why, I bet he has more wrinkles than you. He's probably still got a handsome streak in him, but I'd bet you anything that he ain't hung on to his beauty like you have."

"I'm just afraid he might be disappointed when he sees me," Marcella said.

"Not going to happen. You are going to sweep that man straight off his feet … again." Eva Jo swung her feet off the side of the bed. "Now, it's almost six o'clock. Don't you think it's about time for breakfast?"

"Let's have breakfast in bed today," Marcella said. "There's a menu on the table."

Eva Jo retrieved the menu and found the breakfast items. "French toast points, sprinkled with powdered sugar and served with wedge of fresh melon. Eggs Benedict. Omelet of fluffy egg whites, filled with creamed spinach and topped with smoked gouda and roasted mushroom caps. Fifteen dollars. Your choice of fresh coffee, skim milk, or fresh orange juice, seven dollars." She dropped the menu to her side and stared at Marcella.

"What?" Marcella asked.

"Stella'd have a fit if she saw this," Eva Jo said. "What are you supposed to eat if you want a real breakfast?"

Marcella said, "I suppose that is a real breakfast for some people."

"After whatever that was in that machine in the bus station, I thought for sure we could find some good homemade cat head biscuits and gravy and maybe a couple of sunny side up eggs."

"Maybe we can find something like that tomorrow. For now, let's be adventuresome and try something here. I'll have the spinach omelet and orange juice on ice," Marcella said.

Thirty minutes later, a young lady with sharply pleated black pants and a crisp white shirt pushed a linen covered cart into the room and set the table as elegantly as was possible, given the cluttered circumstances. Marcella tipped the girl and joined Eva Jo at the table.

Marcella had the meticulously prepared spinach egg white omelet. Eva Jo had French toast and, for the first time in her life, Eggs Benedict. They shared a carafe of coffee.

Marcella dabbed her lips with her napkin. "Now, you will never be able to say that you don't know what Eggs Benedict is, will you."

Eva Jo said, "I need to go down to that kitchen and show them what Eggs Eva Jo is. I don't know who these are named after but whoever he was, I bet he's rolling over in his grave long about now."

∽

Eva Jo and Marcella walked three blocks in search of a ladies' wear shop that the hotel concierge had recommended. He had offered to call a car for them, but they said they'd rather walk.

Marcella had decided that the shoes she'd brought from home just would not do for dinner with Edgar.

"Do you have a particular style or brand in mind that you'd like?" the clerk asked. "By the way, those are beautiful shoes you have on now."

Marcella sat in the fitting chair and held one foot a few inches off the floor. "Thank you. These are very comfortable," she said. "I need something similar but less flashy."

"Do you have a particular color in mind?"

Marcella picked up her purse from the floor beside her and pulled a scarf out in a delicate kind of way. "I brought this." She pointed out the stream of blue silk that wound through the scarf. "I'd like something that matches that thread."

Eva Jo looked at Marcella and wondered what else she just happened to have brought along with her. *This is why I like plain ole dresses. Takes longer to zip them up than it does to pick them out.*

The clerk measured Marcella's foot then dashed off and disappeared behind a curtain. When she reappeared, she carried a stack of five or six boxes. "These are size five and all have a similar construction."

It took more than an hour of trying on and walking around the store in each pair, but Marcella finally settled on two pairs of closed toe pumps. A peacock blue pair perfectly matched the thread in the scarf. A taupe pair would work as a backup.

"That will be $1,127.00," the clerk said.

Eva Jo caught her breath and fought to keep her eyes in their sockets.

Marcella produced a credit card from the depths of her purse. "Here you go," she said without batting an eye.

Eva Jo and Marcella started toward the hotel. After a few steps, Eva Jo stopped. "All the clothes and shoes that I own cost less than that," she said.

"It's a special evening. I just splurged a little."

"I'd hate to see what you'd call a big splurge," Eva Jo said.

They took in the wonders of what they considered the big city. Any city would dwarf Morgan Crossroads, but to Marcella and Eva Jo, they'd just as well be wandering the sidewalks of New York City or London.

Eva Jo screeched to a halt. "Look over there."

"Over where?"

"Across the street. Read that sign, Marcella."

Marcella followed Eva Jo's pointing finger to a small diner across the street. A sign in the window said, "Fresh sourdough biscuits and homemade sausage daily. Come early. When they're gone, they're gone."

"I know where I'm going for breakfast tomorrow," Eva Jo said. "That place will be right down my alley."

Marcella patted Eva Jo on the arm. "We'll do it." She strained to read the opening time on the door. "They open at six."

Eva Jo walked a little taller the remainder of the way to the hotel.

∼

"Thank you. You've been a life saver," Marcella told the concierge. Outside, the doorman helped her into a taxi and gave the driver the address of Daniel, a reputable hairdresser who could take her on short notice.

Marcella showed Daniel a photo of her that had been taken during the years she had dated Edgar. "Can you fix my hair like it is in this photo?"

Daniel stood off center between Marcella and the mirror. He leaned to the side and looked first at her, then the photo, then her, and back to the photo. "I will make you look like you are twenty-one," he said. "You've kept your natural hair color and that's good."

Wow. I wish Polly could see this, Marcella thought. *Look at those mirrors, and those paintings.* Daniel showed her to the shampoo station and when she was finished, the shampoo tech escorted her back to Daniel's chair.

Marcella had never had her hair done by a man, but she began to hope that this wouldn't be the last time. Looking at the photographs of his clients on the wall, she could tell that Daniel was more than a hairdresser. He was an artist and the way he handled and pampered her hair was an unexpected treat. Every word he said made her feel special. For the first time in her life, she felt a tinge of disappointment when her hair appointment was over. She smiled at herself in his mirror, deeply satisfied.

Marcella had asked the taxi driver to return in an hour and right on time, he stopped in front of the salon. At the hotel, she tipped the driver, thanked the doorman for helping her out of the car, and went upstairs.

When she walked through the door of their room, she found Eva Jo setting the table in front of the patio door with hand-patted burgers and fresh-sliced french fries from the sourdough biscuit diner down the street.

"I thought you'd be hungry by now," Eva Jo said.

"I'm starving."

"Your hair looks really nice. It's been years since I've seen you wear it like that."

Marcella asked, "Do you think Edgar will like it?"

"He'll love it. You watch what I'm telling you. When that man sees you, he's going to fall over in surprise."

"Oh, I don't really want him falling over, but I sure hope he likes it."

"Don't you worry one more second about that, Honey." Eva Jo stood up and with crossed arms and an appraising stance, said, "The man will never be the same after this evening."

CHAPTER 22

At precisely five o'clock, the phone in the room rang. "Ms. Peabody, this is the front desk. You have a guest—a Mister Edgar Garrison."

Marcella's lip quivered. "Thank you. Thank you. Yes ... please tell him I'll be right down."

She held the phone and said nothing for several seconds.

"You'd better go on, Honey. You don't want to keep your date waiting," Eva Jo said.

They hugged and Eva Jo walked Marcella to the elevator. "You will do fine," Eva Jo said.

"How about my makeup? My lipstick, is it okay?"

"You did good," Eva Jo said, brushing Marcella's shoulders for good measure. "Now go have some fun."

Marcella stepped off the elevator and walked past the desk into the center of the lobby. Two Queen Anne sofas and four high-backed chairs bordered a large oriental rug just off the center walkway made of pink marble. Behind two of the chairs, a grand carved fireplace dominated a wall.

Is that him? Scattered around the lobby were several

couples chatting and three groups of men in business suits, obviously involved in serious conversation. *I'm sure none of these men is Edgar.* She walked to the front door and looked out, but thought, *No, he wouldn't be outside. He has to be in this room.*

She made another pass through the lobby and this time noticed a tall, slender, distinguished man standing next to the hearth. Under the lights that accented the fireplace, his wavy silver hair seemed to have a gentle glow about it—a perfect top for the dark blue of his tailored suit. She stopped and looked him over. *Could that be him?*

The man's eyes met hers. *That's him.* Her heart raced and her knees felt weak.

He walked slowly toward her, his eyes never venturing from hers. "Marcella, is that you?" he said in a quieter, older version of the same voice she'd remembered.

"Edgar," she said softly.

"My Rosie, I can hardly believe you're here."

She wrapped her arms around him and stayed there for several seconds.

Edgar hugged her and paused a second to take in the floral notes of her perfume, as delicate as the lady who wore it.

Marcella stepped back and looked him over. "It is so good to see you, Edgar."

"You look stunning," he said. "I'm absolutely breathless."

"So am I," Marcella said. "You are just as handsome this evening as you were the first time I saw you."

Edgar said, "Say, I've picked out a nice little place where we can have dinner, if that's okay with you."

"Wherever you take me, I will love it."

At the door, Edgar handed his parking ticket to the valet

who quickly disappeared around the corner of the building. In a minute, he returned with a long ivory-colored BMW sedan.

The valet reached for Marcella's door. Edgar gave him a healthy tip and gently said, "Thanks. I'll get it." He opened the door and helped Marcella in.

Edgar drove for fifteen minutes before he stopped in front of The Burger Palace.

"Is this ....? This is Josie's Diner! Is that right, Edgar? It's been more than fifty years and it looks much like it did the last time I saw it."

"It's the same building. There have been several owners since we were here, but the new owners have taken it back as it was in the early sixties. The furnishings are newer, but the menu and recipes are the same as when we were in school."

Edgar helped Marcella out of the car and held the door for her to enter the diner.

"I held your table for you, Mr. Garrison," the girl at the checkout counter said.

He thanked her and escorted Marcella to a booth in the same spot where he and Marcella had last eaten together.

"She called you by name. You must come here often," Marcella said.

"I stop by on a fairly regular basis. Do you still like the same foods?" Edgar asked.

"Sure. My tastes have hardly changed at all."

"Then, may I order for you?" he asked.

"I'd love it. We'll see how good your memory is."

The server placed glasses of water on the table and when she was ready, Edgar ordered. "Miss Peabody would like a cheese burger with lettuce, tomato, and pickles, no onion and a side of onion rings. I'll have the same."

The waitress jotted down the order. "Drinks?"

Edgar started to reply, but yielded to Marcella who was halfway into a word.

"We'll both have Coke with half a glass of ice."

"Make mine Diet Coke, please," Edgar said.

The server disappeared and for a few seconds neither Edgar nor Marcella voiced a word. With their eyes, they each told stories of longing and anticipation.

"Do you know that there has not been a single day gone by that I haven't dreamed of this day?" Marcella asked. "For fifty years I've wondered if I'd ever see you again. I've thought of your health, what you did for a living, if you had found another woman who loved you as much as I did."

Edgar stared into his glass, then at Marcella. "It's been the same for me. In my mind, I've sat right here in this spot a thousand times and asked myself if I did the right thing by going away so secretly."

"And what was the answer?"

"I'm not sure if I did the right thing or not. But, I can tell you this much. When I promised you that there'd never be another woman, I meant it. I have not been out with anyone else, not once."

In their solitary cocoon, the silence drowned out the flurry of laughing families and the jukebox and dishes rattling. Their food appeared without their noticing it.

"Neither have I," said Marcella. "My best friend has been married several times. But, I've not been on a single date since the day you went away except when I'd sit on my porch swing at night and relive our evenings together over and over again."

Edgar straightened and stared across the table, neither smiling or frowning. "You never ...."

"I never what?" Marcella asked.

"You never married?"

"Of course not. Edgar, you seem surprised."

"So you never married, not when you were young and living with your father?"

"No, Edgar. What is this about?"

"About a year after I went to Harvard, I called information and found your father's phone number. You had told me not to bother calling, but I had to see how you were doing."

"You called Papa? He never said a word to me about that. What did he say?"

Edgar sipped his Coke. "He said that you were out on a date."

"Surely he didn't say that. I got lonely and thought about dating–I'll tell you that. But I never did. Not one time."

"Well, I remember the conversation very clearly. He said that you were on a date with your boyfriend ...."

"Boyfriend? There was no boyfriend for me to date." Her brow furrowed. "Are you just teasing me? You are, aren't you?"

"I promise. I'm not joking."

"What else did he say?" Marcella asked.

"Just one thing. He told me that you were getting married in a few months. I thanked him and hung up."

Marcella's face took on a red hue. "Papa was fiercely protective of me, but I can't believe he said that. Who would I have married? I just can't believe my ears."

"I'm sorry, Marcella, but that is what he told me and that is the reason I never tried again to find you."

Marcella's hand trembled as she reached for a napkin. "I'm so embarrassed. I can hardly stand it."

"Why?" Edgar asked. "You had asked me not to call you again. I was sure you would go on and someone else would come along to love you and take care of you. So, to me, your father's conversation just confirmed what I thought."

"I only said that about not calling me because I was hurt and more than a little bit angry. But deep inside I didn't mean a word of it. Not a single word," Marcella said.

"I'm so sorry that I hurt you. In hind-sight I can see that I did what I did out of the fear that I might somehow fail if I didn't concentrate all my energy on my education. In truth, I'm sure the whole experience was more difficult than it would've been had you gone with me."

"Gloria said that you never dated," Marcella said.

"That's true. From the night we parted until this evening, I have not been on a date with anyone."

"Not even to business functions?"

"Not even to business functions. If anyone ever questioned me about my love life, I just ignored them or let them know that it was none of their business," Edgar said.

"I wanted to believe that you had kept your promise, although, to be honest, I wasn't sure you would be able to. I mean, you were handsome and intelligent. And you're human. You surely had girls lining up for a chance to date you."

Edgar smiled. "If the line was there, I never noticed it."

"I heard that you've occasionally talked about me," Marcella said.

"All the time. Sometimes the kids would be there to hear me. Let me guess. Jesse told you where I was."

"When he came to see me, I was almost knocked off my feet. Of all the things in the world that I might have expected, that certainly was not one of them."

"Excuse me," Edgar said as he lifted his glass to signal the server for more.

THEN CAME EDGAR

"Be honest, Edgar." Marcella pointed playfully at Edgar. "Did you ask Jesse to find me?"

"No. In fact, I knew nothing about it until we spoke last night. He took that challenge upon himself."

"Well, he's a fine young man and I'm glad he found me. Has he told you about that dog of his?"

Edgar chuckled. "You mean the one with the unruly eyes?"

"That one. Jesse named him Spotlight."

After they had finished their burgers, the server brought a double fudge brownie sundae with whipped cream and two cherries. She set it in front of Marcella.

"I don't remember ordering ...." Marcella looked at the girl who brought dessert, then at Edgar. "Did he ....?"

She looked at Marcella and nodded toward Edgar, then walked away.

"Edgar Garrison, you had this all planned, didn't you? You ordered this before we got here. How in the world did you remember this?"

"It wasn't hard. It was the only dessert you ever ordered," he said.

"How about your dessert? What was it, pecan pie with one small dip of vanilla ice cream and one of strawberry?"

"That was it, but I've had to slow down on the desserts. I'm diabetic now, so pecan pie is off the menu."

Marcella stopped eating. "I'm sorry to hear that, Edgar. How long have you been diabetic?"

"More than thirty years now. I'm fine. It's well managed and doesn't slow me down in the least. Did you go on to teach?"

Marcella told Edgar about the one room school on the edge of Morgan Crossroads. "The county eventually closed that school and I moved to the new middle school out on the

Porterville highway. I taught for nearly forty years before I retired."

"Forty years. That's a long time to teach in one school."

Marcella smiled. "A lot of my students have grandchildren going to that same school now. Sometimes I think about the people I see walking around Morgan Crossroads and I can hardly believe how much history they're carrying around. One went on to become a doctor working in impoverished areas. Another one lost an arm in Afghanistan. A girl that I had taught took her family to Florida on vacation. While she was there, she bought a lottery ticket and won some huge amount of money."

"Morgan Crossroads sounds like a place I'd like to visit," Edgar said.

"How about you?" Marcella asked. "Where did life take you?"

"Right back here," he said. "I went to Harvard and earned my law degree. I stayed up north for a couple of years, but came back to Austin. I've been here ever since."

Marcella said, "Gloria mentioned that you were retired."

"Last year I sold my interest in the firm and a couple other business ventures. I still tinker with a few real estate investments, but that's about all I do now."

"Good. You probably need a break. I know I would if I had worked that long in the business world," Marcella said.

"I've been blessed so that I can do just about whatever I want to now. Life has been good for me." He laid his hand on Marcella's. "But right now, it's absolutely grand."

His eyes went to the brooch she wore pinned through her scarf. "Marcella, is that the brooch that I gave you when we were dating?"

Marcella looked down at it. "Yes, it is. You said it had been your grandmother's."

"I hadn't even considered that you might have kept it. It looks lovely on you. Accents your eyes, I think."

"Thank you. This is the first time I've worn it since I graduated. It's been hidden away all these years."

"It is perfect on you. My Rosie."

CHAPTER 23

A massive chandelier and hundreds of small white lights that lined the edges lit the portico in front of Hotel Austin. When Edgar stopped his car, a white-gloved doorman opened Marcella's door and held it while Edgar walked around to help her out.

"Good evening Madam," the doorman said.

Marcella smiled. "Good evening. Thank you."

"I'll only be a minute or two," Edgar told the valet as he handed him the ignition key. "If you need to, just pull it over out of the way."

Edgar placed his hand gently on Marcella's lower back. They walked toward the lobby.

"Marcella!"

Edgar and Marcella both turned to see who was shouting.

"That's Eva Jo," Marcella said, watching her pay a taxi driver. "I want you to meet her."

Marcella introduced Edgar to Eva Jo. "We've grown up together."

"I'm glad to finally meet you," Edgar said. "Marcella told me a few things about you."

"Where have you been?" Marcella asked.

"I've had more fun tonight than I've ever had in one night. The girl at the biscuit place told me about a little comedy club across town."

"You went to a club?" Marcella asked.

"Oh, it wasn't a honky-tonk or anything like that. It was called The Laugh Mill, I think. I've never laughed so hard. Lord, I know I had more fun than I was entitled to."

"I'm familiar with that place," Edgar said. "Did you sing?"

Marcella looked at Edgar, then at Eva Jo, smiling. "Did you?"

"That depends on who you ask, I'd say. There were a couple of people in the back that told me to quit trying to call the hogs. But those nice ladies in the front row just clapped and smiled. I'd say I sang as good as I do in the choir at church. Marcella, you should try it some time."

"No thank you. I can't imagine myself even thinking of singing to strangers, especially without someone to play piano."

Edgar said, "You sing to recorded sound tracks."

"They called it carry something. I never did get the whole name for it," Eva Jo said. She laughed and said good night to Edgar. "I'm going on up to the room. See you when you get there, Marcella."

Edgar waved and turned to Marcella. "I'd like to pick you up tomorrow and take you to another special place."

"I'd love that," Marcella said.

"Casual dress," Edgar said. "Ten o'clock?"

"Got it."

In the room, Eva Jo demanded to hear every detail about Marcella's evening. She listened as Marcella recounted the parts she wanted to share.

"Are you going out again tomorrow?" Eva Jo asked.

"Edgar's picking me up at ten. He's going to take me somewhere special, he said."

"Honey, I'm so glad that you are getting to know him again. I still don't know how you managed to keep him a secret for all those years, though." Eva Jo leaned in to have a closer look at Marcella's brooch. "Were you wearing this when you left?"

"Yes, I was. You just overlooked it."

"Well, how could I have done that? When did you get it?"

"Edgar gave it me when we were in college. It had been his grandmother's."

"So you've had this beautiful piece of jewelry stashed away for fifty years? Let me look at it," Eva Jo said. She scrunched her eyes and started counting stones.

Marcella said, "Forty-six. There are fourteen diamonds and thirty two rubies."

Eva Jo asked, "Marcella Peabody, do you have a clue how much ...?"

"I don't want to know how much it's worth in dollars. It's priceless to me," Marcella said.

"I wonder what else you've had stashed away that I wish I'd known about."

Eva Jo sat down and removed her shoes. "Well, I've got a surprise of my own."

"Great," Marcella said. "Let's see it."

"It's not something you can see. Guess," Eva Jo said, waiting just long enough for Marcella to open her mouth. "Michael's coming home."

"When? When will he be home?" Marcella asked.

"Justin called and said that Michael's coming home toward the end of next week."

Michael was Eva Jo's oldest grandson, Justin's brother,

who had spent several months in Afghanistan, and later, another year at an Army base in Stuttgart, Germany.

"That is great news. Is he coming home for good this time?"

"Yep, this is it. He's moving back to Morgan Crossroads."

"I'm really happy for you, Eva Jo. I know you've been worried about him."

"You know, I never wanted the little stinker to enlist in the first place. I was hoping he 'd stay around and help his mama out a little, maybe find himself a girlfriend. You know, settle down. But I reckon it was his life to live. I lived mine and who am I to stop him living his?"

"You've got a point," Marcella said.

"Oh, and before I forget, I called Polly before I went out."

"Good. How is everyone?"

"They just want to know when we're coming home. Apparently we've been giving the gossip line plenty to feed on. Jewell Crabtree has been trying to convince everybody that the only reason you really wanted to come out here was to see if you could meet Willie Nelson. Polly said Jewell's been going around singing *On the Road Again*. One of Stella's grandkids came down with the measles. I think it was that littlest one, the one with a freckle on the end of his nose. Fred Starnes has something going on with his mother or somebody, so he's selling that big old house he built and he's moving back to California. Oh, and the traffic light went out and backed up traffic for more than a block in every direction. Polly said Grumpy got tired of watching everybody trying to take off at once and took it on himself to direct traffic until the sheriff patrol happened along and took over."

"Did you tell her when we'd be back?" Marcella asked.

"Who?" Eva Jo asked.

"Polly."

"I just told her we'd probably head for home in a couple of days. She said Henry's getting all antsy about it. He got worried about your yard and talked Johnny Mack Durant's boy into mowing it for you. I sure hope he does a better job on your yard than he does on his hair. Have you seen that kid's hair, Marcella?"

"I don't guess I have. What's wrong with it?"

"Looks like he ran it through a blender. That's exactly what it looks like. Somebody said he paid good money at some hair styling place in Huntsville. They must have used a weed trimmer instead of scissors."

Eva Jo poured a glass of water and took her arthritis pills. "I guess you know that Henry's afraid he's going to have to rent a U-Haul trailer to get our stuff back home if we stay too long."

Marcella laughed. "That's Henry for you. Always fretting about something. Maybe we should leave pretty soon."

Eva Jo said, "We'd better. We've only got this room for tonight and tomorrow night. After that, it's either Greyhound or the street."

CHAPTER 24

The sky could not have been bluer when Edgar rolled back the sunroof in his BMW and whisked Marcella away from the hotel. Just as he had the night before, he had called for her at precisely the time they had planned. They drove across Austin and northwest until Marcella began to see glimpses of water.

Edgar pointed to his left. "That's Lake Travis."

Marcella pushed herself up in the seat for a better view.

"There has been so much development around that it hardly looks like the same place you probably remember."

"No, I don't see anything familiar."

Edgar drove on, occasionally pointing to a different sliver of the lake that shone between large houses and small ones. At an intersection past the Shell gas station, he turned left and followed a smooth ribbon of asphalt that took them through gentle hills and curves until they arrived at an ornate gate attended by a security guard in a small brick and stone building.

"Good morning, Mr. Garrison."

"Good morning, Emily. Nice to see you. How's that baby?"

"She's fine. She can be quite a handful at times."

Edgar handed the guard some folded money and said, "Go do something nice for yourself and the baby."

"Thank you, Mr. Garrison."

"She seems like a sweet girl," Marcella said.

"That young lady has had a rough time of it. She's a fighter, though."

The gates opened slowly and allowed them through.

"She recognized you," Marcella said. "You must come out here often."

"Every day."

She tried to see every house that they passed, peering between stone pillars down winding driveways and through fences. On one side, a gated compound of Mediterranean design. On the other, a cobblestone driveway wound past cacti and a Spanish fountain and stopped at a six-car garage. A man who had just pulled onto the roadway driving a Bentley waved at Edgar. Who in the world could live in one of these?

At the end of the road, Edgar pulled onto a brick entrance and stopped at a metal privacy gate framed in thick mahogany. He punched a code into the box beside the driveway and the gate swung inward. They drove in on a curved hand-laid stone driveway that was lined on both sides with gloriously tall decorative grasses rocking lazily in the breeze. The largest home Marcella had ever seen outside a magazine came into view. Terracotta roof tiles topped beautiful stucco arches. A curved pathway, also hand-laid, wound its way across a lush lawn. Recessed into an entryway, heavy doors with large hinges stood guard as though they might have secured a castle in some previous life.

THEN CAME EDGAR

Edgar stopped the car outside one of five garage doors. He clicked the remote garage door opener on the car's dash, and then pulled the car into its resting place next to three other vehicles whose names Marcella could not begin to guess.

Marcella sat quiet and still, her breath faint and unsettled. "Is this your house?"

"This has been home for more than ten years."

"You live by yourself?"

"Almost, but not quite. I have a grounds keeper who lives here and doubles as a security guard. And I have a lady who cleans and occasionally cooks for me if I'm having guests. They live in a couple of small apartments upstairs above this garage."

"I'm absolutely stunned. I had no idea in this world that you might have such a beautiful home."

"When I was senior partner in the law firm, I wanted some place where I could have complete privacy, yet entertain guests when I needed to. This house came on the market and after some research and a little back and forth with the trust that owned it, I was able to buy it."

"Oh, Edgar, I'm so happy that you've had so much success. I always felt that whatever you involved yourself in, you would come out on top."

"I've been blessed, Marcella. There is no doubt about that. This house is much too large for me, but it's paid for and I haven't been able to come up with a good reason to sell it."

"Can we go in?" Marcella asked.

"Sure, but I'd like to show you something first."

Edgar helped Marcella out of the car and escorted her across the spotless garage to a door that opened to a courtyard. Streaks of sun and shade alternated across the grass.

They walked past the sparkling water in the pool and through a short wrought iron gate onto the lawn.

"This is beautiful," Marcella said.

"Do you have any idea where we're standing?" Edgar asked.

"Well, I know that this is your gorgeous yard." She waved her hand toward the water. "And I know that is Lake Travis. Is there something else I should remember?"

"Right now, you and I are standing in the same spot where I gave you the brooch you wore yesterday."

Marcella braced her hand across her chest. "Are you kidding me? Right here?" She looked around for anything that might be familiar. "How can you tell?"

"That was one reason I bought the house." Edgar turned and formed a border of sorts in the air with his arms. "In my research, I studied the process that development had followed in this area and realized this point is what was then just a green field, the one we came to that day."

"Is that the real reason you bought it?" Marcella asked.

"I had already decided that I would buy the house, but when I realized exactly where it was built, the deal was sealed. We closed on the property a few weeks later."

A refreshing lake breeze blew over them. Sailboats leaned with the wind on their way past. A grinning young lady on a jet ski bounced by in the other direction.

Oak and cypress trees gently swayed in a rhythmic dance as the breeze swelled and faded.

"I thought you might enjoy a picnic lunch out here," Edgar said. "Would you like that?"

"I'd absolutely love to do that. And I'd love to help prepare it, whatever you had in mind."

"Done! Let's go to the kitchen and see what we can scare up."

Edgar wrapped his arm lightly around Marcella's shoulders and escorted her back to the house. They passed through the garage into a spotless mudroom.

At the next door, Marcella stopped, stunned at the sight of a culinary wonderland. *My word,* she thought. *This kitchen is bigger than my entire house.*

Overhead, oak beams crisscrossed a high ceiling. One held a massive hammered iron chandelier. Commercial grade appliances blended into beautiful cabinetry on three walls. Mediterranean tiles covered the floor.

"Are you okay?" Edgar asked.

"Sure. I'm sorry. It's just that I've ...."

"Don't worry. I still get lost in here sometimes. After all these years, there are times that I can't even remember where I put the coffee. Now, if it's something cold that I'm after, it's a pretty good guess that I'll find it in the fridge. Otherwise, it can be like going on a safari."

Marcella smiled and walked to the center island. She ran her hand across the tile surface. Next to the vegetable sink sat a picnic basket that had been stocked with festive plates, silver, and napkins. "You've already been busy, I see."

"Take a look in here to see if anything stirs your taste buds." Edgar said, holding the refrigerator door open.

Marcella stared at the shelves, trying her best not to look surprised by the variety. "This looks like tuna salad. Did you make it?"

Edgar grinned sheepishly. "No, I'm afraid not. I get that from a deli in town. It's good though. I promise."

She set the tuna out, and at Edgar's request, handed him the shaved ham and roast beef.

"We'll need some cheese," Edgar said.

Marcella explored the dairy drawer and brought out a

block of Gouda, a marbled cheddar, and a mozzarella ball. "How do you want yours sliced?"

Edgar told her he preferred thin slices and found a cheese knife for her. He brought out three Roma tomatoes and a container of butter lettuce. "Onions? On second thought, maybe not."

Marcella caught a glimpse of him out the corner of her eye and smiled.

"I've got pumpernickel, multi-grain, and sourdough. There are probably several types of crackers over there in that cabinet if you prefer. Which would you like?" Edgar asked.

"Sourdough," she said.

With their basket full, they walked toward the door.

"Would you grab that blanket, please?" Edgar asked.

Marcella took a blanket that Edgar had laid on a table near the door then held the door for Edgar. Together, they walked to the spot he'd shown her.

Edgar spread the blanket under the oak tree and anchored it in the center with the picnic basket. While he looked for ways to secure the corners, Marcella unpacked the food and dishes. They both were slightly slow in the process, but they managed to find a comfortable sitting position across from each other. Edgar watched how the dappled sunlight set off the blue in her eyes, aided he thought, by the color of her outfit. She had taken to covering her arms as she aged and to do that, today she had chosen a blue V-neck cardigan with raglan shoulders. She wore a pair of silk slacks that the catalog had described as Ottoman blue.

Marcella asked, "What's the matter?"

Edgar sat as still as a stone. "Nothing. Nothing at all. I don't mean to stare, but I just can't believe how beautiful you are. Still to this day, you are every bit as beautiful as you were in college. Your red hair, your skin, the color of your eyes and your delicate but confident way of walking. I'm just amazed."

"I, uh ...."

"And your hair, it's so shiny today," he said. "Did you know that, Marcella? In the sun it just seems to light up somehow."

A blush of embarrassment overtook the pink of her cheeks. "No one else has ever spoken to me that way, Edgar. The last time I heard such words, we were dating."

"Well, someone should have," he said.

"Last night when I first saw you in the lobby of the hotel, I found it hard to speak," Marcella said. "I expected that you'd still be a good looking man. But somehow what I saw in you went beyond that. You were, and are, so distinguished looking. You seemed so tall, so debonair, like a movie star. You look so healthy and athletic, like time has been good to you."

Edgar said, "Thank you. For years I ran when I could and I tried to work out some. I had a gym installed in the house, and there's a lap pool inside off the den, but it didn't stop me having a heart attack a few years back."

Marcella's eyes sprang open. "You had a heart attack? But you are in such good shape."

"There's no need to worry about me, Marcella. It was a minor attack, just sidelined me for a couple of weeks. And it forced a new way of eating, but I'm okay. The only thing I have to concern myself with daily is my diabetes. That's under control, too. How's your health?"

"Thank heavens, I've never really been sick other than a cold or stomach virus. My doctor says my heart is in good shape and I should just go on living. So that is what I intend to do."

"I'm glad to hear that," he said. "That's exactly what I intend to do, too."

They finished their lunch and spent time walking along the water's edge. They stopped occasionally to watch a houseboat floating by full of sunbathers or a ski boat zipping toward more open waters in the wider part of the lake.

Edgar pointed out unusual homes across the lake and told Marcella interesting stories about some of the residents, including one whom he had defended in a court case. As he talked, she gingerly placed her hand in his. She felt the gentle grip of a soft, but masculine hand, one that was there to nurture her and to keep her safe.

Inside the house, they settled into dark leather chairs in the library. Beneath a pair of antique gas chandeliers, Marcella and Edgar sipped iced tea. She tried to absorb the ambience of a room with an eighteen-foot ceiling and lined on two walls by shelves filled with thousands of books old and new. On one end was a floor to ceiling fireplace built of stone with a mahogany mantle and a black Italian marble hearth. The other end was a wall-to-wall, floor to ceiling view of the lake, framed by cypress trees on the sides and lush green grass below.

"I'm not used to being in rooms like this, but I love it," Marcella said. "Your home seems so warm and inviting."

"Maybe that's because you've been here the whole time, that is, in my thoughts and dreams."

She patted his hand. "I told you that I never dreamed you had a home like this, but I have dreamed at least a thousand times of living with you."

For a moment, Edgar lost his attorney-bred skill of asking questions without hesitation. He looked toward the lake and hesitated, then faced Marcella. "When are you leaving to go back home?"

"Tomorrow morning. Our reservation will be up and Eva Jo needs to get on back."

"That is so soon," he said.

"I wish I could stay longer, but the only reason she came on the trip was to keep me company. I couldn't let her make the trip home by herself."

"She's a great friend, isn't she?" Edgar said.

"We've been friends since we started to school. That's a very long time."

Edgar said, "We should invite her to dinner with us. Do you think she'd like that?"

"She'd love it so long as we went to a casual restaurant. She'd be more comfortable there."

"What if we invite her to Josie's Diner so she can see where we used to hang out?"

"That would be perfect," Marcella said. "I've told her about it. I know she'd love to join us. I should call her to give her a little warning, though."

"There's a phone right over there," Edgar said, pointing to a desk near the fireplace. "If you don't have the hotel's number, it's written on a pad by the phone."

Marcella telephoned Eva Jo. Edgar smiled when he heard Eva Jo's laughter escaping the phone.

"As I expected, she said she'd love to join us," Marcella said. She walked back to take a seat, but this time she sat next to Edgar.

"I hope I don't sound too forward, but there's another question that I need to ask," Edgar said.

Marcella turned on the sofa to face him.

"I'd hate to think that we had this time together and that it could be our last."

"Oh, no, Edgar. We won't even entertain that idea. You hear me?"

"There is only one way that I can imagine would guarantee we spend the rest of our lives together and that would be ...." He looked deep into her eyes.

"What?" Marcella asked.

"That would be if you married me."

Marcella jumped to her feet and facing Edgar, clasped her hands together across her chest. "There is nothing in this world that I'd love more than to marry you, Edgar Garrison."

Edgar stood and wrapped his arms around Marcella. Together they danced, swaying to the sound of inaudible music. Edgar pulled back enough to see Marcella's face, and for the first time since that final night at Josie's Diner more than fifty years earlier, they kissed. They embraced with Marcella's face pressed tight again Edgar's chest. With tingling arms, she held on to him and the sound of his rapidly beating heart, the one that had waited for her. Then their lips met again, this time lingering until they were finished.

"Marcella Garrison. I like the sound of that, Edgar. Mrs. Edgar Garrison."

"Then you might want this," Edgar said. From the drawer of the lamp table beside him, he brought out a velvet-covered box.

Marcella gasped and covered her mouth with the fingers of both hands. She fought unsuccessfully to hold back the tears.

"Open it."

Her hands trembled until Edgar helped her steady them. She lifted the lid and lost her breath. For a moment she said nothing, staring at the piece of jewelry that glistened as it reflected the light of the chandelier.

Edgar removed a four carat diamond and platinum ring. "May I?"

Marcella watched as he slid the perfectly sized ring on her still trembling finger.

"Perfect," he said. "I knew it would be."

"How could you know that?" Marcella asked.

"Instinct, I suppose."

"When have you had time to buy this ring? You couldn't have shopped for it last night, could you?"

"No, no. I didn't shop for it. It came from the same collection as the brooch. You probably remember that the brooch had been my grandmother's. My mother died about twenty years ago and in her will, she left me the remaining jewelry that my grandmother had left to her."

"I took it out of the safe last night," Edgar said. "It's yours now. It has your name written all over it."

"It's absolutely beautiful, Edgar. I just don't know what to say. If you pull any more tricks like this out of your hat, I won't be able to walk," Marcella said, laughing as she dried her cheek.

By the time they had talked and laughed for a few more hours, it had grown dark outside. Marcella walked to the window. "Can you dim the lights?"

Edgar turned the lights down and rejoined Marcella. They turned to face the lake and for the next several minutes, Edgar held Marcella snugly against himself as they watched shards of light bending and flickering across the water.

"There is something that I think you should know," Marcella said. "After I graduated from college, I went straight back to Morgan Crossroads, back to the same house where I was born. I still live there."

"That's wonderful," Edgar said. "I like stability in life."

"My point is, I've lived a very simple life ever since we last saw each other. Morgan Crossroads has barely changed in all this time. Most of the new people in the community are there because they're born there. You have all ...." She swept her hands toward the garden and the lake and around them. "You have all of this. Your life seems so much more complex ... it's so different from mine."

Marcella looked up at Edgar. "Don't get me wrong. I love nice clothes and pretty shoes. I have closets full of clothes that I've ordered from Bergdorf Goodman and Saks and Neiman Marcus. I have all of the money that I'll ever need. Papa saw to that in his will. But, I've lived such an ordinary small town kind of life, and you live so opulently. How can we make those two work together?"

"I love ...."

Marcella continued. "Edgar, you drive that beautiful car and I love it. But, would you believe that, until this trip, Eva Jo had never driven a car without a clutch pedal? She has now, but I drive a 1953 Chevrolet that Papa left me. I started driving it after my other car was hit by a tractor driving through the middle of town. My car's not at all fancy and it has a few dings in it where it sometimes takes a mind of its own and goes places I never intended it to go. Still, it gets me to Haley's to buy milk and down to Lucy's Cafe for our weekly Rosebud Circle meetings. I walk just down the block to church. And my entire house would fit in this room. Do you know that? All of it, right here in this room."

Edgar laughed. "I love it. Simplicity, that is. This house and the trappings that go with it are just things. They have nothing to do with happiness. I told you the story of why I bought it. Now, I have it and until now have had no good reason to sell it. Let me show you something." He led Marcella by the hand to a doorway across the room. "Look down that hallway. There are six bedrooms and five bathrooms scattered through that part of the house. I use the same bathroom all the time and I sleep in one bedroom.

Actually, I only sleep there part-time. The rest of the time, I wake up in my recliner with either the television on or a book in my lap."

Marcella chuckled. "I thought I was the only person who did that."

"Oh, no. I'm sure I have you beat in that department. The only time those other rooms are ever used is when the grandkids spend the night with me. I just let them pick whichever room they want and it's theirs for the night. Sometimes Gloria will come with them and when that happens, the house is all theirs. I just hang around in case they can't find the Fruit Loops."

He continued. "I think I live a pretty simple life. I use my house as a place to sleep and for protection from the heat and cold. I drive my car because my knees just won't let me walk everywhere. I could live just as happily in a smaller house as I can here. So please don't let that bother you."

Edgar said, "Over the years I've built an estate of mostly commercial property and investment funds that are much more than I can spend in my remaining years. As far as I'm concerned, it is just there as an inheritance for Jesse, Gloria, and the grandkids. In fact, much of my estate is in trusts for them."

"See, you really haven't changed, have you?" Marcella said. "You are the most giving person I've ever known. Papa was like that, you know."

Edgar jerked his arm up so that he could see his watch. "Sorry, I didn't mean to startle you. I just about forgot about Eva Jo and dinner at the diner. Don't you think we'd better get going?"

CHAPTER 25

*E*very head in Josie's Diner turned when Eva Jo squealed, "You're getting married! Marcella and Edgar ...." When applause broke out across the diner, Eva Jo turned the volume down a notch or two. "I'm so happy for you two." She wiped a tear from one eye, then two from the other.

"Honey, are you okay?" Marcella asked as she patted Eva Jo on the arm.

"Sure, I am. Just this morning I was sitting on the patio outside our room and I saw couples zipping up and down the sidewalk and I said to God, you know something, God? Marcella really needs Edgar. I hope you can work that out for her."

Edgar said, "You said that to God, this morning?"

"Sure did. Most of the time, I'm pretty sure my prayers don't make it any higher than the ceiling, but ...."

Marcella said, "It looks like you shot that one all the way up there this time." She looked at Edgar and laughed.

Edgar and the ladies chatted about their days, how the

picnic had gone so well, and how Eva Jo had enjoyed walking around downtown Austin.

They had each ordered a cheeseburger and onion rings in honor of the occasion. Marcella and Eva Jo ordered sundaes and Edgar asked for a scoop of sugar free ice cream.

"Have you told your kids about their new mother to be?" Eva Jo asked.

"Not yet. I will, though, and I'm sure they will be thrilled," Edgar said.

"I like Jesse," Eva Jo said. "And Gloria. She's a sweetie."

Edgar said, "They're both good kids. Well, they aren't exactly kids anymore, but compared to me, they are."

"Compared to all three of us, they are," Marcella said. "Almost anybody is younger than us."

"Speak for yourself," Eva Jo said, chuckling as she turned her spoon upside down and licked the last bits of ice cream from it.

"Are you coming to the bus station to see us off tomorrow?" Marcella asked Edgar.

"I've been meaning to talk to you about that. What do you suppose would happen if I were to escort you two back to Morgan Crossroads?"

Marcella jerked up straight in her seat. "You want to go back with us?" Her eyes widened and a smile stretched from ear to ear.

"See there, Marcella, Henry was right," Eva Jo said.

"What do you mean? Right about what?"

"He was afraid you were gonna come back with more than you left with." Eva Jo gestured toward Edgar. "But I'd bet he never had a clue just how much more."

"Eva Jo!"

"Edgar, just don't let her try to stuff you in a suitcase.

Henry Brown would probably keel over trying to get you out of the car."

Edgar said, "I won't. I promise. Who is Henry?"

"He's my cousin, the one who drove us to Birmingham to catch the bus. How long has it been since you road on a Greyhound bus?" Marcella asked.

"A very long time. When I was in high school, probably."

"I'm sure it's a lot different now than you remember," Eva Jo said.

"I was thinking that we might get there a little faster if we flew," Edgar said.

Eva Jo's face lost all of its color. "Fly? All the way to Birmingham? From Texas?"

Marcella said, "Eva Jo is a little shy about flying."

"You two can fly. Lord, my knees are knocking just thinking about it. I'll ride the bus and see that the luggage finds its way home," Eva Jo said. "You might beat me by a couple of hours, but I'd catch up with you."

"Honey, we'd beat you home by a day or so."

Edgar said, "Once the plane took off, you'd be in Birmingham in a couple of hours. Then it would all be over and you'd wonder what all the fuss was about."

"Can they knock you out, like a dentist?" Eva Jo asked.

"That's usually not necessary," Edgar said, laughing.

"It might be this time." Eva Jo sipped her Coke. "I just don't know. What if I get up there and ...."

"They have little bags for that," Marcella said, hoping to head Eva Jo off before she said something that emptied the diner.

"How about this," Edgar said. "I'll show you the least stressful way to deal with flying, and you just follow my lead. You, too, Marcella."

"Sounds like great fun," Marcella said. "What do you say, Eva Jo? Are you willing to give it a shot?"

Eva Jo let out half a chuckle and muttered under her breath, "Somebody better bring along a shot of something for me."

"You'll be fine," Edgar said.

They drove back to the hotel and agreed that he would pick them up at ten the next morning. He said he knew what time the flight left and he had a way to get tickets even if the flight was filling up.

Marcella and Edgar kissed. The ladies waved as Edgar drove away.

"You know that I'm a nervous wreck, don't you?" Eva Jo asked.

"I know." Marcella held her hand on Eva Jo's back as they walked toward the elevator. "You'll be fine, though. I promise. You'll have something new to talk about for years to come."

CHAPTER 26

The driver steered the black van with Eva Jo, Marcella, Edgar, and a mountain of luggage and shopping bags toward the airport.

"Did you get the flight you wanted?" Marcella asked Edgar.

"No problem. We got the best seats on the plane."

Eva Jo said, "We need to tell Henry what time to be in Birmingham. He'll need some warning, you know."

"I must have forgotten to tell you that Henry's not picking us up. We're renting a van and driving ourselves to Morgan Crossroads," Marcella said.

"Who's gonna drive?" Eva Jo asked. "I hope you're not planning to do it, Marcella."

Edgar laughed. "None of us is. The van comes with a driver."

The van stopped in front of a terminal building.

"This sure looks like a small airport," Eva Jo said.

"It is. But, we won't need a large one. It's easier this way," Edgar said.

"Where are the planes?" Eva asked.

"Edgar, are you sure we're at the right airport?" Marcella asked. "I don't see any Delta airplanes or United. They go to Alabama, I think."

The driver loaded the luggage onto a cart and delivered it to the correct place inside.

"Thank you," Edgar said as he handed the driver a tip.

Edgar pointed through a window to a cream-colored private jet, the largest one there. "See that plane? It's ours for the next two or three hours."

Eva Jo and Marcella stared through the window, trying to hide their astonishment and saying nothing.

Marcella saw the fear in Eva Jo and took her hand.

A tall gray haired man in a flight crew member's uniform approached Edgar and asked the three of them to follow him to the plane. They fell in line behind him as he walked across the tarmac and up the steps into the plane. After a few minutes of pointing out the emergency exits and instructing them on how to adjust their seats and their seat belts, he said, "Go ahead and fasten your belts. We'll be rolling toward the runway in just a few minutes. You won't be able to swivel your seats until I turn off the seat belt light. Enjoy your flight." He joined the pilot in the cockpit and closed the door that separated the cockpit from the passenger cabin.

"Is this ...?" Marcella said.

"No, it belongs to a friend of mine. He owed me a small favor," Edgar said.

"Look at this," Eva Jo said as she ran her hands across the soft leather upholstery. Along a wall across from them was a highly polished teakwood bar that the co-pilot had told them contained snacks and an assortment of beverages. On the wall next to their seats were magazine racks stocked neatly with *The Wall Street Journal*, *The Atlantic Monthly*, and other publications, mostly business or sports related.

The door closed and within a few minutes the plane began to move. Through the overhead speakers a gentle male voice reminded them to keep their seats upright and to be sure their seat belts were fastened. Eva Jo gripped the arms of her seat like a vise. Her jaws grew tense and her eyes closed.

"Are you alright, Eva Jo," Edgar asked.

No answer.

The plane roared down the runway and lifted off. When the whine of the engines pushing them skyward replaced the vibration and rumble of the runway, Eva Jo slightly relaxed her grip, giving the chair arms a break.

"You did it, Sweetie," Marcella said. "Look out the window. It's beautiful."

Eva Jo slowly opened her eyes and when she saw nothing but blue in front of her and above her, she smiled. Below, she saw the patchwork of fields and pastures and towns and asked, "Is this what I've been afraid of?"

A chime sounded and the seat belt lights went out.

"We've leveled off and plans are to stay right here for a little while. Please feel free to have whatever you want from the bar. The restroom is in the rear of the cabin," a voice said through the speakers overhead.

Edgar swiveled his chair toward the bar and scanned its contents. "Would either of you like something to drink?"

"Do you see any moonshine in there?" Eva Jo asked through a laugh.

"I don't see anything quite that strong. How about a soft drink or milk?"

Marcella accepted a Coke and one of the chicken salad sandwiches that the pilot had told them were freshly made just prior to their boarding the plane.

Edgar passed Eva Jo a milk and sandwich and took one for himself.

They soon passed over the corner of Louisiana, then Arkansas and Mississippi and started their descent.

The seat belt sign came back on and the voice spoke again from the overhead speakers. "We're starting our approach into Huntsville. Please return your seats to their forward-facing and upright positions. We'll be on the ground in just a few minutes."

"He said Huntsville, Edgar. I thought we were flying to Birmingham," Eva Jo said.

"That's one of the perks of flying in a friend's private plane. We can land almost anywhere that there's an airport. Isn't Huntsville closer to Morgan Crossroads?"

"It's a lot closer."

"Look out your window, Eva Jo," Marcella said. "You've never seen Huntsville from this angle, have you? See, there's the Space and Rocket Center. And look. There's the mall."

Eva Jo saw Huntsville, but she also saw the ground coming closer a lot faster than it had gone away when they had taken off.

Edgar noticed her gripping the chair arms again. "You're going to feel a little bump when we touch down, and once we're on the ground, you're going slow down real fast. But it'll be over before you know it."

The plane touched down and while it slowed, Marcella smiled at Eva Jo who was giggling like a girl on her first roller coaster ride.

Inside the terminal, the women made a pit stop so that Marcella could double check her makeup and hair.

Eva Jo talked to Marcella in the mirror. "Do you see this face? It may not be all that pretty, but it's low maintenance. I like it that way." She studied Marcella touching up her lipstick. "Did you ever wish you'd been born with your makeup already there?"

"What kind of question is that?"

"Well, then you'd be like a shirt. Permapress. No wrinkle, no iron. No paint required."

They looked at each other briefly. Eva Jo hugged Marcella and said, "I love you and I'm so happy for you."

Marcella dabbed her cheeks with a tissue, first one, then both.

"What's this?" Eva Jo asked. "I hope these are tears of joy."

"They are," Marcella said, trying to avoid sniffling. "This whole thing may make no sense at all to you, or to anyone else in Morgan Crossroads. Here I come with a man that even my dearest friend had not heard of until a stranger and his dog hiked into Morgan Crossroads. I can't imagine what must be about to pass through their minds when the Rosebud girls find out about him."

"If I were you, I just wouldn't worry myself about that. I got over it real quick and I think everybody else will, too. Now, don't ask me how you are going to make them understand how you fell so deeply in love in such a short time. You'll have to work that one out yourself."

"But I didn't fall in love with Edgar on this trip, Eva Jo. I've been in love with that man for more than fifty years. Not one day has my love for him ever been weak."

Eva Jo swallowed Marcella in a two-armed hug. She whispered, "Edgar loves you, too, Honey. He's loved you like you've loved him. I can tell that from the look in his eyes when he talks to you. Now you take your future husband home and show him off." She patted Marcella on the back and coached her in removing the traces of tears from her cheeks. "And when you two decide on a date for your wedding shindig, I'd better get front row tickets."

Laughter returned and when they reappeared in the lobby, Edgar escorted them to the van which had already been loaded.

"Poor thing looks like it's trying to squat a little," Eva Jo said just before she climbed on board.

CHAPTER 27

No one in Morgan Crossroads knew the exact day or time that Marcella and Eva Jo would be home. That is, until Polly Brown stepped out of Haley's Grocery just in time to hear the large black van rumbling by on the old brick pavement. The strange driver in a black suit and dark glasses was a mystery, the way he looked like a Secret Service agent, but there was no mistaking that head of red hair glowing through the window from the back seat.

Across the street from Haley's, Dora Mae Crawford had been resting on a bench in the shade of a tall sycamore tree. She shot up from the bench as if she'd hit the eject button and headed toward Marcella's house, her hands fumbling between her cell phone and a note pad.

Before the driver had opened his door, half of the Rosebud Circle was walking up Marcella's driveway. And right behind them came Henry Brown.

Giddy chatter filled the air when Marcella and Eva Jo stepped out of the van. Then awestruck silence took over as the dignified looking silver-haired man unfolded himself from the van and stood beside Marcella.

Eva Jo elbowed Marcella. Out of the corner of her mouth, she said, "Introduce him so they'll start breathing again."

Marcella jerked back to reality. "Everybody, this is Edgar Garrison, an old friend from my college days in Texas."

Ladies nodded. Most tried to keep their curiosity at bay, but some, like Dora Mae, couldn't keep words from tumbling out of their mouths. "Marcella Peabody, you've been keeping secrets from us all these years. And good looking secrets, too."

Some reached out to shake his hand, as did Henry.

"Henry, you remember Jesse, don't you?" Marcella asked. "Edgar is Jesse's father."

"Well, I'll be," Henry said. "I'm glad to meet you, and to see that you are real."

Edgar said, "To see that I'm ...."

"I'll explain later," Marcella said. "Now what did I do with my house key?"

Henry helped the driver carry the luggage to the front porch, and answered his question about the shortest route back to Huntsville. He drew a map in the air to help the driver along.

Edgar tipped the driver and waved as he backed out of the driveway.

Eva Jo phoned Justin, her grandson, but got no answer. There was little need for a phone call since he had already heard that she was back in Morgan Crossroads and was sitting in Marcella's driveway before she could hang up. He tossed her luggage in the back of the pickup truck and climbed into the driver's seat. Eva Jo waved through the back glass until she could no longer see Marcella's house.

When Henry was satisfied that Marcella would be perfectly safe with Edgar, he shook Edgar's hand then coaxed the Rosebud women off the front porch and out to the sidewalk. A couple of them, the Pearle twins needed an extra tug to get them moving. "Come on ladies, I'm pretty sure Marcella will still be around in a few days. Give her a chance to rest up."

Henry returned to his duties at the General Store.

Most of the ladies walked to Polly's House of Beauty where there was a certain palpable energy, a sense that exciting changes were in the air.

Dora Mae Crawford burst through the unlocked door just ahead of Polly Brown.

"Did you see that man?" Dora Mae asked Polly.

"If I weren't already married I'd ...." Polly said.

"Polly, I said did you see that man? Did you seeeee him?"

"Of course, I did. Everybody did." Polly motioned toward the manicure table. "Come on, Dora Mae, let's get those nails done."

Jewell Crabtree walked in. "Where in the world did Marcella find a man like that?"

"Looks like he dropped in from a soap opera," Polly said.

"I was born right down the road from here," Dora Mae said as she waved her hand toward the south. "And in all of my sixty something years, I have never seen such a specimen as that man in this town."

"Keep still," Polly said. "You're going to have red polish all over you if you don't."

"Here's what I want to know," Dora Mae said. "Where has she been keeping him and why hasn't she told us about him before now?"

"That's what I want to know, too. Around my house, about the soupiest secret you'll ever miss is what color of slippers I bought Henry for his birthday. But I'm telling you, Marcella takes the cake with this one," Polly said.

"You don't suppose ... you don't ... she's not about to get married, is she?" Dora Mae asked.

"Marcella Peabody. Marcella, what was his last name?" Jewell Crabtree asked. "Garrison. That's it. Marcella Garrison."

"That could take some getting used to," Dora Mae said.

Polly said, "Well, I hope she really is getting married. Marcella's no spring chicken, but she could be a spring bride."

"And good for her," Jewell said as she clutched her hands against her chest. "If she's been waiting on this guy for all these years, she deserves a wedding."

"You know, I wore a plain little white dress when I married Eugene," Dora Mae said. "We didn't have much money, so Mama was going to make mine out of cotton flour sacks. I cried and pleaded with her until she finally let Daddy take me to Porterville so he could buy me a proper dress. I think he paid six dollars or something like that for it."

Gertrude Gleaves hollered from under the hair dryer in the corner, "Does it matter what color your wedding gown is if you're seventy-something years old?"

Polly dropped her hands to the table, nearly spilling the bottle of polish. "Well, I doubt anybody's given that much thought."

"I'll tell you one thing," Jewell said. "If I had waited as long as Marcella has for Mr. Perfect to come along, I'd wear red or purple or whatever color I wanted. That's what I'd do."

"I'll tell you something else. Marcella Peabody just came sliding back into town and completely messed up any idea of a surprise party," Dora Mae said.

"Sure did. It was us that got the surprise," Jewell said with a laugh.

"I need to do some investigating," Dora Mae said. "I bet there's a soap opera somewhere missing its leading man."

Jewell Crabtree clasped her hands and closed her eyes. "And he's right here in Morgan Crossroads, Alabama."

∽

Edgar wrangled Marcella's luggage from the porch to her bedroom and when he had finished he settled into a recliner near the window.

Marcella eased herself slowly onto the sofa and rubbed the backs of her hands.

"Your luggage is still on the porch," Marcella said. "When you feel like it, I suppose we should find a place for you to sleep."

"This is not going to start something is it?" Edgar asked. "Your friends won't think ...."

Marcella laughed. "No, no. That's already happened. I guarantee you that the rumor mill is running so hot over at Polly's that you could hardly breathe in there."

"Polly's?"

"The beauty salon," Marcella said.

"Well, I didn't think to discuss sleeping arrangements before I invited myself to come along with you because I thought there'd be a motel or hotel in town."

"There was a little motel out on the highway toward Porterville, but it closed down several years ago. I have an idea, though. Would you be willing to sleep in Papa's old room upstairs? There's a real comfortable feather bed and plenty of room for your luggage. I offered it to Jesse when he was here."

"That would be perfect," Edgar said. "What are your friends going to think about it?"

"They've already come up with some story in their minds. It wouldn't matter if you slept here or at the church. Their imaginations would tell them the same thing, whatever that is."

"Then it's settled. I'll get my things from the porch."

After they'd finished unpacking, both Edgar and Marcella opted for a nap. Edgar took his upstairs in Papa's feather bed.

Marcella lay down on her bed. As tired as she was, and as hard as she tried to summon it, sleep just would not come. She lay on her back, eyes wide open, staring at the ceiling fan. Thoughts—new and exciting ones—ran a steady stream through her mind. The last time she'd stared at the ceiling like this, she was on the brink of a journey into her past and her future at the same time. She'd wondered if she was doing the right thing, if he would still be the man she'd last seen more than fifty years earlier. *He's here, sleeping in my home. He really is here.*

After half an hour had passed without a wink of sleep, Marcella went to the living room and sat in her Queen Anne chair next to Papa's photo.

Though she had always tried to hide it publicly, life in this house had mostly been a lonesome existence. Sure, there was always Eva Jo, just a short drive or a phone call away, to talk to if she wanted. But Eva Jo was not Edgar. Marcella had always kept a space open in her heart and mind for Edgar to occupy this house with her.

Opposite her chair sat a large heavily cushioned chair that she had bought soon after Papa died. It was designed for a tall man, with a long seat cushion and large comfortable arms. Eva Jo didn't know it and neither did anyone else, but Marcella had bought it as a placeholder of sorts for the day that Edgar might come back into her life. She would sit in her chair and talk to Papa, then look across the room for

THEN CAME EDGAR

long periods of time conjuring up visions of Edgar sitting in his chair with a book or newspaper.

Marcella took Papa's photo from the table next to her. "He's home, Papa," she whispered. She laid her head back, closed her eyes, and held Papa against her chest.

The sound of strong footsteps coming down the stairs shook her back to the present. She set Papa back on the table and turned just enough to see Edgar standing behind her.

"Do you mind if I join you?" he asked.

"I'd love for you to. Just make yourself comfortable. Would you like some iced tea? I can brew some if you'd like."

"No, I'm fine."

Edgar looked around at the options and sat in the chair across the room, the one she'd bought for him. "Who is that man in the picture next to you?"

"That's Papa. It's the only photo I have of him."

"He looks like a strong man."

"He was. And he was so kind-hearted. He was a great Papa."

Edgar looked out the window just in time to see a dog chase a boy on a bicycle past the post office. He turned toward Marcella and paused for a second or two. "Are you okay?"

Marcella twisted a handkerchief in her hands. "You're home, Edgar. You're finally here."

He walked over and stood beside her chair. He gently laid his hands on her shoulders, his long fingers draped over them. "I like it here. It seems so peaceful and ...."

"Right," she said.

"Exactly. It feels exactly right." He stood still for several minutes with his hands covering her shoulders.

Marcella said, "I bought that chair for you years ago. I ordered it from a store in Huntsville and had it delivered."

"You bought it for me?" He looked at the chair, then stepped around so that he could see her face as she spoke.

"I sure did. I bought it thinking that some day you'd come and sit in it."

"Is that what was wrong?"

"You're home, Edgar. That's all."

CHAPTER 28

The sun hung low over the hills behind Brown's General Store. A gentle breeze wafted across the porch, temporarily keeping the heat at bay. A truck driver threw up his hand on the way by. Grumpy stopped at the light, then crossed the intersection and parked in front of the store.

Henry Brown and Ollie Smith were in their rocking chairs on the porch, busy discussing whether the fish were biting at the lake and other similarly important matters.

"A fellow I was talking to at the hardware store in Porterville said he caught a string full of bluegill, said they were all as big as his hand," Ollie said as he held his ham-sized hand out flat.

"I hear crappie are biting pretty good down at Guntersville," Grumpy said. Before he sat down, he went inside and picked up an RC Cola and a bag of salted peanuts. The screen door squeaked and slammed shut when he came back out. He gave Henry a wrinkled dollar bill and two quarters, which Henry promptly stashed in the bib pocket of his overalls.

Grumpy found himself a rocker and poured his peanuts into the RC Cola. "Looked like quite an uproar over at Marcella's this afternoon."

Henry said, "I'm thinking those gals tried to sneak back into town."

Ollie laughed. "Didn't work too good, from what I hear."

"Looked like half of Morgan Crossroads was standing in her front yard," Henry said. "And that was before she even got out of the van."

"Who was that gray headed fellow?" Grumpy asked.

"My wife said he looked like a doctor or somebody like that," Ollie said.

"Ollie, do you remember when that tall young fellow showed up here?" Henry asked. "Had all that hair on his head and tattoos everywhere."

"I remember him. He had a dog following him around that was about the strangest dog I'd ever seen," Ollie said. "Name was Jesse, if I remember right."

"That's him. Well, Jesse is that gray headed fellow's boy," Henry said.

"You didn't trust him much when he was here," Ollie said.

"Nope, sure didn't. Didn't trust him any further than I could throw him, but Marcella did."

"Looks like she might have been right," Grumpy said. "I was watching out the post office window and it looked to me like she was a little bit more than comfortable with him."

"Yep, and that bothers me," Henry said. "If Marcella knew that man way back then, and knew him well enough to be that comfortable with him now, you'd think she'd have said something about him. She's my cousin, you know."

Ollie said, "I guess she wanted to keep him a secret."

"Well, I knew something was in the air about him that day his boy showed up. When she heard his name, Marcella got so weak in the knees she had to sit down. I could tell." Henry took a drink from his water glass. "It was like a ghost had come roaring up into Morgan Crossroads from somewhere way back in the past."

"You reckon she's secretly had a boyfriend all these years?" Grumpy said.

"No, no. I don't think that," Henry said. "I think she and this guy, what was his name?"

"Jesse," Ollie said.

"No, that was the boy. Edgar. That's his name. I think Marcella and Edgar must have been sweet on each other when she was out in Texas going to college."

Grumpy said, "If she still has something going on with him now, it must have been way more than being sweet on each other. You don't think they ...."

"Watch your mouth," Henry said with his eyes lit up. "I can see that stuff you're thinking written all over your face. Marcella would never have done anything like that before she got married, and even if she did, we wouldn't be the ones discussing it. Ain't none of our business."

Grumpy threw a hand up in surrender and downed a swallow of peanuts and RC Cola.

"Well, whatever it is," Ollie said. "I hope this fellow is everything she thinks he is. Ain't neither one of them reached their expiration date yet, but they will some day. And if they're gonna have any kind of life together, they'd better get on with it."

~

Marcella closed the refrigerator door. "Edgar, I don't have a thing in this house for supper." She looked at the clock on the wall. A quarter after six. "Haley's is closed for the day,

I think."

"Don't worry about it. Is there a cafe where we can eat?"

"Lucy's Cafe is open. She has the best hamburger you've ever eaten."

"Really?" Edgar asked with one eyebrow raised.

"Well, Josie's Diner might have her beat, but not by much," Marcella said with a smile. "She cooks the best Coca Cola baked ham you'll ever eat, though. I guarantee it."

"Then Lucy's it is," Edgar said. "Do we walk or drive?"

"We'd better drive. The mosquitoes might get us this time of the day."

"Okay. Who's driving?" Edgar asked.

"I'll drive." With a playful tap on the arm, she said, "You might get lost."

Edgar opened the car door for Marcella and closed it after she had gotten settled. He got in on his side of the car.

"Where are the seat belts?" he asked, looking around for them.

"There aren't any," Marcella said. "Cars didn't come with seat belts when this one was made."

"Oh," he said, looking for a place to steady himself, should the need arise.

Marcella ground the gearshift into reverse and let the clutch out, a little too suddenly. The car lurched backward. With her hands firmly clamped on the steering wheel at ten and two, she eased the car toward the street. Because she'd never been able to organize which way to steer when looking backwards, Marcella never used her rear view mirror. She had told herself years earlier that if she drove the car straight up the driveway when she came home, she should be able to back straight out the driveway by simply holding the steering wheel perfectly still when she was going backward. If it brought her straight in, it should take her straight out, she'd reasoned. When she passed the rose bush on the driver's side of the driveway, it was time to stop and see if any other cars were in the vicinity, about to pass behind her on the street.

Edgar, startled by the sudden departure, sat frozen in his seat. He gripped the front edge of the seat cushion with one hand and the window crank on the door with the other. He looked straight forward, apparently not willing to face whatever might be behind them.

They made it to the street with no more excitement, other than getting just a tad too close to the mailbox.

"It'll be okay," she said. "It's used to my driving."

Edgar relaxed a little after the car started down the street. "Is that what you meant when you said that your car sometimes doesn't do quite what you want it to?"

"The worst part is sometimes I tell it to stop and it doesn't listen," Marcella said as she stared straight down the brick-paved Main Street, running wide open at fifteen miles per hour. "I'm still getting used to this car. Remember my other car suffered a meeting with a tractor.

With a wrinkled brow, Edgar said, "I see."

"It wasn't my fault, though. My car was parked."

CHAPTER 29

Heads turned and chatter quieted when Marcella and Edgar stepped through the front door at Lucy's Diner. Every table was full except one in the rear of the building, next to the one the ladies of the Rosebud Circle used for their Tuesday morning meetings.

Marcella led Edgar to the open table, walking as though nothing were different. They'd hardly seated themselves when Marcella felt a light hug.

"It's good to have you back home. Sweet tea?"

"Edgar, this is Stella. She's the owner here," Marcella said.

Edgar half rose from his chair. "Edgar Garrison. Nice to meet you."

"Oh, Honey, it's awfully polite of you, but you really don't have to stand up to introduce yourself." She leaned over and in a loud chuckling whisper, said, "You probably got about half the coveralls in this room in trouble with their wives. Most of them probably just thought you'd changed your mind about sitting down."

"I'll take sweet tea," Marcella said.

"Unsweetened for me, please. No lemon," Edgar said.

Edgar followed Marcella's lead and ordered roast beef, tossed salad, cooked cabbage, and green beans.

A young man stopped by the table. "Miss Peabody, glad you made it back home safely. Did you have a good time?"

"We had a great time. It was the best trip I've ever taken," Marcella said.

Marcella placed her hand on Edgar's arm. "This is Jeremiah Downs. He's the new preacher at the church across the street."

Marcella and Edgar finished their meals and the obligatory conversations with a dozen other people, then left.

Outside, Edgar asked, "Do you think I can figure out how to drive this car?"

"Oh, I'd say you probably can. Eva Jo does alright with it."

Edgar helped Marcella into the passenger side, then settled himself into the driver's seat. After acquainting himself with the location of the controls, he calmly and smoothly drove it home.

~

Marcella and Edgar had a good night of sleep. She had happy dreams about Edgar that she would keep to herself. He slept soundly through his first night in Morgan Crossroads.

Marcella had gotten up before Edgar and after leaving him a note to say where she had gone and that she'd be right back, she drove around the corner and down Main to Haley's Grocery. She picked up eggs, bacon, fruit, cereal, and milk.

Lorraine Haley, the owner, rang up Marcella's purchase. She smiled a toothy smile and said, "Cooking for two this morning. That must be fun."

Lorraine was 39 years old and had not found a suitable husband. After her father died, she had taken over the store and had worked there seven days a week since then. Though she had dreamed of it, there had been no time in her life for romance.

"Honey, it will be my first time, too. That is if you don't count Eva Jo or one of her grandkids."

"I bet you're looking forward to it, though, aren't you?"

"I certainly am. I just hope I don't get nervous and burn the bacon," Marcella said, laughing.

"You won't. It will be a perfectly fine breakfast, I'm sure."

Marcella suddenly slapped her hand across her chest.

"Are you okay, Marcella?"

"You know, it just dawned on me that I've never eaten breakfast with Edgar. I sure hope he likes bacon and eggs. All men like that, don't they?"

"I've never known one that didn't. I'd bet he'd eat anything you cooked for him."

"Honey, I surely do hope so."

By the time Edgar had showered and shaved, the smell of coffee and breakfast filled the house. He stopped when he reached the kitchen door and took in the sight of Marcella standing there with her back to him, working. There were biscuits already on the table, along with sliced strawberries and a bowl of cantaloupe chunks.

"The house smells wonderful," he said.

Marcella turned with a plate of bacon. He kissed her lightly on the cheek.

"How do you like your eggs?" she asked as she nervously set the bacon plate on the table.

"Just cook mine however you cook yours. They'll be fine," he said. "Can I help you with anything?"

She pointed to the coffee pot. "The cups are in the cupboard just above the pot."

He poured two cups of coffee while she scrambled eggs, then they settled at the table.

"Do you have plans today?" he asked.

"Normally the Rosebud Circle has breakfast at Lucy's Cafe, but Stella has an early appointment with the doctor. We're meeting at ten this morning. Will you be okay for an hour or two?"

"Sure. That might work out great. I thought I might wander down to the General Store and get to know Henry a little better. I could do that while you meet with your friends. Do you suppose I could drop you off, then borrow your car for an hour or so?"

Marcella said, "I certainly don't mind. That is, if you aren't afraid of it."

"I can probably tame it enough to make it for an hour."

"You'll like Henry. He might have some ways that seem somewhat backward to you, but he's a good man who would do anything he could to help another person. He reminds me of Papa in that way."

"He seemed somewhat hesitant yesterday."

"He'll be okay. I think he and Jesse got off to a slow start and he's just trying to figure out what's going on."

"I'm trying to figure out why Henry would care so much about what happens between you and me."

"Henry's father and my mother were brother and sister. Henry was born just a year or two after I was and ever since he was old enough to act tough, he has taken on the position of my body guard."

"So that's it," Edgar said.

"He just won't stand by and watch me get hurt, if he can help it. You two will be good friends before you know it, though. He trusts you."

CHAPTER 30

The Rosebud Circle was already humming along when Marcella arrived. The women drank coffee and nibbled on pie while they handled the more trivial gossip. In short order, the discussion moved from whether that good-looking new owner of the hardware store in Porterville was married to the particulars of Marcella's and Edgar's relationship.

"I've just got to ask. Did you and Eva Jo sneak off to Texas so you and Edgar could elope?" Gertrude said.

Marcella sat red-faced and speechless.

"Gertrude Gleaves, you know Marcella better than that," Eva Jo said as she stabbed her fork into a piece of pecan pie.

No one in the Rosebud Circle said a word, surprised first at Gertrude's forward way of asking what they all wanted to know and second, at Eva Jo's raised voice.

"We went out there to find me a husband, but there weren't any ornery enough to put up with me," Eva Jo said. "So relax. Marcella's not married ... yet, and neither am I."

"Eva Jo, I could smack you," Polly Brown said.

"So could I," said Dora Mae, laughing.

"Tell us about Edgar," Stella said.

Every lady around the table leaned in to hear Marcella tell her story. She told them how they had met in college and how she had waited on Edgar without knowing that he had done the same for her. In answer to their questions, she told them about their meals out and about going to the lake and having a picnic, but left out the part about the financial success he had enjoyed.

"You ladies should've been with us on the trip out there. There are some luggage handlers and taxi drivers scattered out between here and there that will be telling their grandchildren stories about these two crazy old women on a Greyhound bus," Eva Jo said.

"Call yourself crazy if you want to, but I was perfectly dignified," Marcella said, playfully pointing her nose in the air.

"Well, are you going to get married?" Polly asked. "You may as well, because every lady that's come into my shop has already decided you are."

Marcella stiffened her back, took a deep breath and let it out quickly. "Yes, we are." She brought her left hand from under the table and laid it out, complete with the ring from Edgar for all to see.

Oohs, aahs, and other audible expressions started with Lorainne and Jewell, then spread around the Rosebud Circle table. Apparently, it was like a contagious ailment for it spread to nearly every table in Lucy's Café. People gathered from every occupied table in the building to view the spectacle that Marcella had heretofore successfully kept hidden. The stranger from the table by the front door that had stopped in when Henry recommended he follow his gasoline purchase with a meatloaf dinner even came and left his compliments.

THEN CAME EDGAR

Applause broke out around that table and at several other tables scattered around where the diners had been eavesdropping.

"What will you wear?" Bernie asked. "I wouldn't worry about wearing white. It's boring, I think."

"Well just don't wear black," Gertrude said. "That might give folks an odd feeling.

"I know," Mary Beth said with her hand in the air. "Big bright floral prints—red and blue and yellow flowers. And I can make up corsages and flowers for the church to match her dress.

Marcella said, "I have an idea what I might wear, but I want to talk it over with Edgar first. We really haven't discussed it much."

"Okay, here's the big question." Dora Mae said. "When are you tying the knot?"

"You'd better think about that," Eva Jo said. "It might be kinda hard to fit it in the church schedule. You know you'll have to work around the bingo games and garden club meetings, and you can't have it on any fifth Sunday because then you'll have to compete with the community singing and dinner on the ground."

"We'll find a date. And who says we have to marry in the church?" Marcella asked.

"Good point," Stella said.

The front door opened and heads turned that direction.

"Your ride is here," Polly said.

~

When they were back in the car, Marcella recounted the story of the Rosebud Circle meeting to Edgar.

He smiled. "Looks as though we started something."

"Oh, don't worry about them. They just need something new to talk about from time to time."

"Do you have time to take a little ride?" Edgar asked.

"Sure. Where would you like to go?"

"I want to show you something."

"Oooh, I like this. A secret," Marcella said.

Edgar drove the car past Brown's General Store and slowed in front of the house that Fred Starnes had built. He drove between the stone pillars and down the driveway to the front of the house.

He turned off the engine, but stayed in the car. "What do you think about this house?"

"I love it. I always have."

"Have you ever seen inside it?"

"No, I've only daydreamed about it. A lot of people didn't like it when Fred built it, said it was too much for this area. I think it's beautiful."

Edgar walked around and opened Marcella's door. "Would you like to walk through it?"

She hurried out of the car. "Where did you get a key to it?"

"From Henry," Edgar said. "Fred Starnes left a key with him in case anyone was interested in buying it."

"How did you know that?"

"A little bird told me," Edgar said with a wink.

When they walked in, Marcella was taken aback, floored that such a house existed in Morgan Crossroads.

"I can't believe this," she said.

"Look familiar?" Edgar asked.

"It looks so much like your house," she said.

"Just a smaller version. This house is about half the size of mine."

They strolled through the house, looking in closets and cabinets.

Marcella rubbed her hand across the stone countertop. "This is beautiful. Feel of it," she said, tugging Edgar's hand toward the polished granite.

"I like it," he said.

"Are you planning to buy it?" she asked.

"I will if you like it. They're asking a fair price for it."

"How much is that?"

"Low seven figures."

"For a house in Morgan Crossroads? A million dollars?" she asked, stunned.

"It has some acreage with it, too. This house in the neighborhood where I live in Austin would cost probably three times that."

"I've never lived anywhere but the house I live in now, except for the time I was in college. And I inherited it, so I have no realistic idea of what houses are worth now."

"This one is worth the price, but only if you'll live in it with me after we marry."

"I can hardly believe it," she said. "Of course, I'd live here with you. I have no idea what I'd do with my house, but I've actually dreamed of living here ... in this very house."

"Then, do I sign the papers?"

"Sign them," Marcella said. She tugged on his shoulders, lowering him so that she could kiss him on the cheek.

"I'll call my agent and have the papers signed within a few days."

Edgar watched her take a slow walk through the house again. He smiled when she stopped to touch the stone mantles, to see the marble foyer and the artistic lighting fixtures.

"Look at this kitchen, will you? Mine would fit in here

four times." She looked at Edgar and pointed toward the center island. "And look at this. It's bigger than all of my counter tops combined. I hope you can cook, Edgar. I can't possibly use that entire kitchen by myself."

"You'll do fine," he said. "Just use the parts you need."

In the garden out back, he joined her on a heavy wooden bench that was shaded by a large pergola. A wall of bamboo eight feet tall guarded one side of a stone-lined pond where brilliantly colored koi swam leisurely between water lilies. She let her head rest on his arm when he wrapped it around her shoulder. He held her there, loving her even more deeply than he had known he could.

CHAPTER 31

On Sunday, two weeks later, Jeremiah Downs read an announcement to his parishioners at Morgan Chapel.

"Edgar Garrison and Marcella Peabody wish to announce their union in holy matrimony on Saturday, July 15th. The ceremony will be at Mason's meadow, weather permitting, with a reception following here at the church hall. The entire community is invited and will be welcome at both the ceremony and the reception."

Uproarious applause erupted half-way through the announcement, complete with whoops and hollers from Grumpy, Cecil, Eva Jo's grandson and several others. Whether the service was dismissed or just fell apart, the result was the same. When the applause died down, chatter, sniffling and nose blowing took over as the dominant sounds.

"It's about time," Gertrude Gleaves said. "We've been trying to figure out when it was going to happen ever since you came home."

"Miss Marcella, Granny said that man with the silver hair

is your boyfriend," Jewell Crabtree's five-year-old granddaughter said.

"Yes, he is," Marcella said.

"Can he be my boyfriend, too?" the little girl asked.

"He might be just a touch too old for you," Marcella said, as she ran her fingers through the little girl's long brown hair.

"She's a keeper," Henry said to Edgar.

Edgar looked around the sanctuary until he spotted Marcella. "I just hope I can do her justice."

"I obviously don't know anything about keeping her happy from the husband end of things, but I can tell you that she's always been easy to please for the people around here."

"You might want to do most of the driving," Grumpy added with a hand cupped around one side of his mouth.

Edgar glanced at Grumpy and grinned. "I'll keep that in mind."

"Can I be your maid of honor?"

"Who's the best man?"

The questions came from every direction and most of them were met with indecisive or indirect answers.

The next day Henry drove Edgar to the airport in Huntsville.

"I guess you probably figured out by now that I'm pretty protective of Marcella," Henry said. "Maybe a tad too much."

"I caught on to that one right away," Edgar said, smiling.

"I've always looked after her. Even when we were little, I watched out for her at school. She's never had a mother around, her father died years ago, and there haven't been any kids to look after her. So I sorta took over that duty."

"I'm glad that you've been there for her. I wish I had had the nerve to come look her up myself years ago. I just took it from her father that she was already taken, that someone else had scooped her up."

"Well, sir, you'll be the first. You must have made a serious impression on her back in your college years. That lady has lived here in Morgan Crossroads for her entire life and not one of us ever knew about you. As far as I know anything about it, she never one time considered dating anybody else."

Both men sat silent for a moment, both glancing at a passing train.

"Sometimes I feel like a fool. She was down here waiting on me, and I was out in Texas waiting on her. Strange, don't you think?" Edgar said.

"Maybe. Maybe not. People do things and don't have a clue why they did them."

"I guess I owe that boy of mine a thank you."

"Jesse? I've got to tell you, I didn't know quite what I thought of him when he came sliding into town. He had that dog with him. Have you seen that dog? Beatinest thing I ever saw. One eye goes this way." He gestured with pointed fingers. "The other one goes that way."

"Jesse may look a little strange to some people. But that guy's got a heart in him," Edgar said. "He's a gentle soul. I've seen him do things for people—generous things—that make me wonder how or why he did them."

"At first, I kept my eye on him, but I reckon he's okay in my book now," Henry said. "Marcella is a good judge of character most of the time, and I'd said she pegged him about right."

"He's his own man, and I like that about him. I'm awfully proud of him. I'm proud of Gloria, too. She's his sister. She's got three boys that can be a handful, but I like having them around. They have a way of brightening my day."

"You going to bring them back with you?" Henry asked.

"Oh, they'll be at the wedding, I'm sure. None of them would miss it, if it meant they had to walk all the way there," Edgar said.

Henry stopped along the sidewalk at the airport terminal. He turned to Edgar and said, "You may think I'm out of line to say this, but I'm going to say it anyway. In a few weeks, you'll be marrying Marcella."

Edgar felt a wave of nervousness—the kind that made his skin tingle and his heart rate increase. As discretely as he could, he slowly and deeply inhaled and exhaled until the feeling subsided.

"All I ask is that you treat her like the diamond she is," Henry said.

With a handshake, Edgar breathed a light breath. He said, "You have my word, Henry. You have my word," then left the car in search of his flight back to Austin.

There were loose ends to tie up in Texas before he could make a move to Morgan Crossroads. With the aid of his real estate agent, Edgar had sold his home in Austin to an oilman who had asked several years earlier to be notified if the house ever went on the market for sale. The same agent had also taken care of the details involved in buying the Starnes home in Morgan Crossroads.

There were banking matters to take care of, time to spend with Gloria and her kids, and a list of other things to do.

CHAPTER 32

"Eva Jo?" Marcella knocked on the front door. "Are you home, Eva Jo?"

No answer.

"Open the door and go on in." Eva Jo stood at the front corner of the house with the knuckles of each hand planted on her hips.

"Eva Jo!" Marcella slapped her hand to her chest. "You almost gave me a heart attack."

Eva Jo followed Marcella into the front room. "You usually call before you come. What are you sneaking out here for?"

"Are you any good at baking wedding cakes?" Marcella asked.

"My kids all say I bake a mean pecan pie. Will that work?"

"I'm serious, Eva Jo. I need somebody to bake a wedding cake for me."

"Well, didn't Gertrude Gleaves bake the cake when that Johnson boy got married?"

"I love Gertrude like she was my sister, but ...." Marcella sighed. "Did you see that cake?"

"Come to think about it, I can't say I remember much about it," Eva Jo said, her eyebrows scrunched.

Marcella glanced toward the ceiling. "Forgive me, Lord." She leaned toward Eva Jo and lowered her voice. "That's the problem. She baked those kids a yellow sheet cake with white frosting. She said that was what they wanted, but … but, if that is Gertrude's version of a wedding cake, I'm going to need someone else to bake it."

"You wouldn't have to worry about it falling when you carry it in the church hall," Eva Jo said.

"Seriously, Eva Jo, can you see the little plastic man and woman thing standing in the middle of a sheet cake?"

Eva Jo laughed. "Maybe they're an old man and woman and they couldn't climb all the way to the top of a …."

"I hadn't thought about the cake until now," Marcella said as she wrung her fingers together.

"All of my kids had their cakes baked somewhere else, or they eloped to the Justice of the Peace and didn't need one," Eva Jo said. "But I suppose I could try to whip one up for you. What kind of cake do you want? And how many people are you planning to feed from it?"

"I just want a pretty white cake with yellow roses around the top of each layer."

"Each layer? Exactly how many layers is this cake going to have, anyhow?" Eva Jo asked.

"Three, I guess. Or maybe four would be better."

Eva Jo blew out a puff of breath through swollen cheeks. "And then you want this little plastic couple sitting on top of that?"

"I saw a cake in a wedding magazine where the little bride and groom were edible, like candy or something," Marcella said.

"Where are you going find an edible bride and groom?" Eva Jo asked, concern creeping across her face.

"Don't you think it would be nice if they were edible?"

"I'm not so ...."

"I'm going to see if I can find some," Marcella said in a chipper tone.

"Okay, Marcella. Let's see if I've got this straight. You're going to have a couple of candy bars shaped like geriatric wedding characters on top of your cake so that you can eat them after the wedding. My question is, who eats the man and who eats the woman, and how's that a good way to start a marriage, you two chewing on each other?"

Marcella seemed stunned by Eva Jo's question. Rather than think it through to a logical conclusion, she said, "Maybe we'll just find a plastic one somewhere."

"You know I'm not Sears and Roebuck. My stuff don't come with a guarantee, but I'll do my best."

"You just let me know your price and I'll be happy to pay you for it," Marcella said.

"You'll do no such thing. Not in this lifetime, you won't."

"You can at least let me pay for the ingredients and pans or whatever else you need."

"We can argue about that later. Find me a picture of a cake like you want and I'll see if I can get into the miracle making business."

∼

By the time Marcella arrived at Lucy's Cafe, the rear table where the Rosebud Circle met was already aflame with chatter about her, Edgar, and their impending marriage. The gossip had really heated up when word got out that the household moving truck now parked in the lot next to Brown's General Store was filled with furniture that belonged to Edgar Garrison. The truck had arrived a day early, Dora Mae Crawford had found out, and the driver would have to wait until the next day to unload.

"How are they going to fit all of that into Marcella's little house?" Gertrude Gleaves asked.

"Somebody's going to have a yard sale. A big one," one of the Pearle twins said.

"I bet he'll have some nice stuff to sell," Stella chimed in.

"Who's having a yard sale?" Marcella said as she approached the table.

"Edgar," Polly Brown said. "We figure that there's no way he can fit all of his stuff into your house, so he's going to have to have a big yard sale."

"How in the world would he be able to fit enough stuff to fill a truck that large into your house with the things you already have in there?" Lorraine Haley asked.

"What makes you think he's moving in with me?"

"Henry said the driver told him the house he was delivering to was only a couple of blocks from the light," Polly said. "That sounds like he must be taking it to your house."

"Well, he's not moving into my house," Marcella said.

The table went cold, as if Marcella had sucked all the air out of the room.

"Do you mean the wedding's off?" Jewell Crabtree asked, almost in tears.

"What happened?" Lorainne asked.

"Nothing happened," Marcella said. "Edgar will be here tomorrow to show the moving people where to put his stuff in his house, not mine. He bought the house that Fred Starnes built."

And the gossip instantly roared to a spectacular volume

as it flew around the table, almost bowling Marcella over in the process.

"Can you imagine what that house must have cost?"

"If he can afford a house like that, Lord knows what he must have done for a living."

"I'd like to see what he's moving out of."

"I knew when I saw him, that he had some money. Did you see those trousers he had on?"

"Yes, I did. And they weren't from ...."

"Ladies!" Marcella shouted. "Edgar made some good choices over the years and he was able to afford the Starnes house. He bought it and sold his house in Texas. He'll be here tomorrow to move in. And yes, those were nice trousers."

"Stella, what kind of cake are we having this week?" Gertrude asked.

"My favorite. Jewell brought her pineapple upside down cake. You all make room for it," someone else said.

Stella brought the cake out, along with a pot of coffee. For the next hour, the conversation moved from subject to subject until they had discussed what color the bride's maids would be wearing, whether Marcella would be selling her house, why the county had changed the school bus route for the upcoming year, the rumor that postage stamps would be going up a penny, and a dozen other things.

Eva Jo asked how one would go about moving a wedding cake. No one knew, but several offered ways that it should not be done. The cake at Gertrude's second wedding had landed top side down in the gravel driveway when the board her sons were carrying it on had tipped over.

"Isn't the reception going to be in the church hall? Just bake it in the kitchen there, then you won't have to worry about dropping it," Polly suggested.

"The problem then would be how to keep the bingo

people out of it. You know those old men wouldn't take a second thought about tearing into it," Eva Jo said.

"Cancel bingo for that week. Problem solved," Dora Mae said.

"Whoever makes that suggestion had better be wearing a suit of armor," Polly said.

"Either that, or a real quick set of legs," Jewell said, laughing.

Stella said, "I'm not so sure I'd trust that old oven at the church. Your cake might fall all over itself. It would look more like a stack of pancakes than a wedding cake."

CHAPTER 33

The rain started just after midnight. For more than two hours, lightning bolts forked and jerked their way across the sky. Stone Creek overflowed its banks and flooded farm and pastureland from one end of the valley to the other.

For more than four hours, the traffic light was dark, as was most of Morgan Crossroads. Then the electricity came back on and the sun rose into a crisp blue sky. It shone on several trees that had blown over, and it shone on one particular furniture moving truck that was now sunk to its axles in the muddy lot next door to Brown's General Store.

Henry Brown stood on the porch of the store with the truck's driver. They were both amazed how far the tires had sunk into the mud, or that the ground had even become so saturated in one night of rain. The driver had gone to bed in the sleeper on his truck and had slept through most of the storm. It was not until he stepped out of the truck and sunk in mud past his ankles that he realized how unfortunate his choice of parking spots had been.

"I don't believe you'll ever drive outta there under your own power," Henry said.

"No sir, that won't happen. I'm not even going to try. The only thing that would happen is that I'd just be more stuck than I am now," the driver said.

"I'll see if I can get you some help," Henry said, straightening the bib of his overalls. He went inside and phoned Grumpy's Garage.

Henry explained the situation the driver had found himself in, then said, "We've gotta get this guy going." Henry lowered his voice. "He's got Edgar Garrison's furniture." He nodded his head. "Yeah, we've gotta get him outta this mess before Edgar gets here."

"I'll be there as soon as I can," Grumpy said. "Where's Marcella? We can't let her see her future furniture sitting in a mud hole."

Ten minutes later Grumpy drove up in his most powerful tow truck—an old red Mack that had previously seen more than thirty years of service as a pump truck with the Porterville volunteer fire department. He had removed its firefighting components and turned it into a tow truck.

After a couple of times walking around the stuck moving van, Grumpy crossed his arms, furrowed his brow, and said, "I don't know about this one, Henry."

"You don't think you can pull me out?" the driver said.

"Do we need to find somebody with a tractor to help you?" Henry asked Grumpy.

"If you just had one axle stuck, I could snatch you outta there in no time. But this," Grumpy said with his arms crossed.

Henry went inside the store and phoned Ollie to explain the situation. Ollie asked questions about why the truck was in Morgan Crossroads in the first place, why the driver had chosen Henry's land to park on instead of the truck stop down on the main highway, and a few more whys.

When Henry explained to him that the truck was in town to deliver Edgar Garrison's belongings to his newly purchased house, the former Starnes home, Ollie became excited as if he were being asked to help a celebrity out of a bind.

"No, I don't think that little Farmall tractor will help much," Henry said. "Better crank up that John Deere and bring it."

"Okay. I'll be there in a little bit," Ollie said.

Together, Ollie and Grumpy pulled the sixty-five foot long truck out of the mud onto the solid gravel part of the parking lot. The two of them, along with Henry and the driver, surveyed the truck, bright and shiny orange, except for the wheels and tires, which were the color of chocolate pudding. They collectively decided that it might not be such a great idea to drive it up the fancy driveway to Edgar's house without first washing off the mud.

Henry found a garden hose and the four of them had the mud washed off an hour before the ivory-colored BMW pulled up carrying two familiar men, a lady, and three anxious young boys.

∽

Marcella had watched the sun rise across the hills behind her house. In her back yard, an elm tree lay on the ground, its split trunk exposing forty years of growth. A clothesline where she frequently hung bed linens to dry had yanked one of its normally upright poles to the ground under the weight of the fallen tree. Six fifteen, the clock over the refrigerator said.

With too much else on her mind to bother with a felled tree, she went into the living room and sat in her chair. She took Papa's photo from the table and held it in her lap. "I do so wish you could witness what's going on, Papa. In two weeks, I'll become a bride for the first time in my life." Marcella chuckled lightly. "I almost waited too long, don't you think? Seventy-something years old and I'm just now marrying my teen heart throb. But, you'd like him, I'm sure. Edgar, that is. He's a lot like you. He's tall. He's intelligent and successful. Other than you, he is the most generous man I believe I've ever met. But most of all, he loves me. And when I'm near him, my world lights up. Something about Edgar lets me know that he would turn this world upside down just to take care of me."

Marcella braced herself against the chair arms to stand and walked to the window, still holding Papa's photo. She pulled the curtains to one side and looked toward the traffic light. "He'll be here soon. He's coming with Jesse and Gloria and her children. His furniture arrived yesterday and today I get to help him decide where it all goes. That's going to be so much fun. Do you know that I've never moved into a new house? There was that college dorm room, but that doesn't count."

The phone rang in the kitchen. On the way to answer it, she set Papa gently back in place on the table beside the chair.

"Marcella, you better get your working duds on," Eva Jo said.

"I'm always ready to work."

"I had to go pick up a loaf of bread at the General Store," Eva Jo said.

"You went out shopping at this hour?" Marcella asked.

"Can't make toast without bread and I needed that to go with these pear preserves."

"I guess I should think about eating pretty soon, myself," Marcella said.

"Henry and Grumpy and somebody else were standing there staring at that big orange truck full of your new furniture. The guy had it cranked up and running like he was about to go somewhere with it."

"Are you going to come help us move in?"

"Marcella Peabody, now you know I could not possibly let this day go by without being there. This is the biggest thing to happen in Morgan Crossroads since they put the light in," Eva Jo said. "Well, maybe when the pantyhose factory burned down, but that still wasn't as important as this."

The pantyhose factory had been a hub of activity in the early seventies, but that ended when a worker tried to weld a piece back onto a machine and accidentally burned the entire plant to the ground. Volunteer firefighters came from Porterville and three other communities, but even with all their resources combined, the fire was bigger and stronger than they were.

"When's Edgar supposed to be here?" Eva Jo asked.

Outside, a car door slammed shut, then another and another. "They're here," Marcella said and hung up the phone.

By the time Marcella reached the front door, Gloria's sons, Brian, Christopher, and Joshua had already taken over the porch swing. Jesse followed Gloria and Edgar up the sidewalk.

Marcella opened the door as quickly as her arthritis would allow. She swallowed away the choked up feeling she had when she saw her future family gathered in front of her house. There was a joy that she wasn't sure she'd ever felt, a joy whose time had come.

Gloria and Jesse gave Marcella generous but gentle hugs. Edgar hugged her and bent down to plant a light kiss on her forehead.

"Have you had breakfast yet?" Marcella asked.

"We're fine," Gloria said.

"We stopped after we checked out of the hotel. The boys wanted McDonalds," Edgar said.

"Have you been to the house, yet?" Marcella asked.

"No, but we did drive by Henry's store to see if the furniture truck was there."

"It's big and orange," Joshua said with his arms stretched out as far as he could.

"Mom said you're going to be our new granny," Christopher said. "Are you?"

Not quite being used to that idea, Marcella stammered a bit, grinned, and said, "Well ... I guess .... Yes, I will be."

"There will be plenty of time to sort out all of that," Jesse said as he ruffled Christopher's hair.

Marcella invited them into the house. After they'd all found seats, she offered them drinks. "I've got sweet tea, milk, and there's probably some orange juice."

"Keep your seat, Marcella. I'll get it," Jesse said. Gloria joined him as he disappeared into the kitchen. After rambling through the cupboards where Jesse thought he'd remembered the glasses being, they returned with tea for Edgar and Marcella and juice for the boys.

"How will you get all that furniture into the house?" Marcella asked. "You and Jesse can't do all that work by yourself. Do I need to see if I can find some men to help?"

Edgar assured her that there would be no need for that.

"The moving company furnishes people to do that. They should be here shortly."

"All you and Dad have to do is direct traffic," Jesse said.

"Sir, would you put that right over there?" Gloria said playfully, wagging her finger across the room. "Sir, that goes in the last room on the left. Or is it the first room on the right?"

CHAPTER 34

*H*enry, Grumpy, and Ollie walked the length of the winding driveway with the truck driver, examining the curves and the ornamental grasses along the edges, and determined that it would be possible to back the trailer from the road to the front door. Between a good dose of skillful driving and several minutes of hand motions and hollering by the three self-appointed navigators, Edgar's furniture arrived at his front door with the soggy lawn still intact.

Jesse, Gloria, and the boys crowded into the back seat of Edgar's car so that Marcella could have the front passenger seat. When they arrived at the house, Eva Jo was standing next to her pickup truck on the shoulder of the road.

"You missed a good show," Eva Jo said to Marcella.

"What show?"

"You should've seen that poor truck driver finagling that truck backward down that driveway," Eva Jo said, pointing across the lawn. "I don't know which was the most trouble for him, that crooked drive or those three characters that were trying to guide him."

"I'd say our furniture was in good hands if that man can drive like that," Edgar said, smiling.

A van turned into the driveway delivering five muscular young men to unload the truck.

"Looks like some football team is missing about half of their players," Eva Jo said. "I wonder if they'd like to bale some hay when they get through here."

"You haven't seen the inside of that truck," Jesse said. "They'll have a little less pep in their step by the time they're finished."

The moving men had worked without a break for more than two hours when Marcella and Eva Jo suggested they stop for lunch. Eva Jo had slipped away and packed lunch for everyone present. She laid out a variety of sandwiches, chips, and fruit on the patio table in the back garden. Henry parked a large cooler filled with soft drinks and water on the ground. Marcella sliced a peanut butter layer cake that Polly had made for the occasion.

After an hour off for lunch, the work resumed.

The final item, Edgar's recliner, was set in place facing the stone fireplace less than five hours later. With Edgar's and Marcella's guidance, the men had carefully hauled in boxes of dishes, a huge antique mahogany desk with a leather inlay top, and a billiard table, along with Edgar's complete library.

"Did you bring all of your furniture?" Marcella asked. "I thought you had more than this."

"Some of it I sold. Gloria and Jesse took part of it. We had to leave room for your things, you know," Edgar said.

After the moving truck had gone, Jesse and Gloria searched through stacks of boxes until they found towels and wash cloths for the bathrooms and linens for the beds. Fred Starnes had left the window coverings, most of which had been custom made.

Edgar rummaged through several boxes until he located the coffee maker and coffee. "Now, if I could just find the cups."

"Look in that box," Gloria said, pointing across the room.

"We're going to need a few things from the grocery store," Jesse said. "What's the name of that little market?"

"Haley's," Marcella said. "Do you remember where it is, down Main past my street on the right?"

Edgar tossed his car keys to Jesse. "Why don't you take the boys with you? They could stand to get out of here for a few minutes, I think."

"What are we going to do about dinner?" Gloria asked.

"Lucy's will be open for another couple of hours," Marcella said. "How does that sound?"

"Perfect. Are you coming for dinner, Eva Jo?" Edgar said.

"I'd better be getting back," Eva Jo said. "I've got some milking to do, and if I don't get that grass mowed, it's gonna overtake everything out there. I'm just about worn out, watching those guys haul that furniture in here."

"Thank you for the lunch," Marcella said.

"Yeah, thanks. That was really nice of you," Gloria said.

"Well, I couldn't sit here and watch you go hungry." Eva Jo said. "I reckon I'll see you tomorrow."

Gloria watched Eva Jo walk to her rusty old pickup truck. "I like her. But I really am glad you two didn't try to drive that truck to Texas."

Marcella said, laughing. "Honey, just wait until you ride in it. You'll really be glad then."

~

The only available table at Lucy's Cafe that could seat seven people was by the front window.

Stella came with water for everyone. She rested her hand on Marcella's shoulder. "Who are all these fine looking people?" she asked.

"You know Edgar," Marcella said. "And these are his children, Gloria and Jesse," she said with her face glowing.

"She's going to be our granny," Christopher said, pointing toward Marcella.

"Is that true, Marcella?" Stella asked.

"I will be, indeed. Who knew I'd have three fine looking grandchildren?"

Stella pointed playfully at the boys. "Well, you found yourselves a good one. They don't come any better than this young lady."

"She's not young. I'm young," Joshua said.

Over the laughter, Stella said she'd be back to take their orders and left to take care of another table.

The two oldest boys asked for cheeseburgers. The youngest ordered a grilled cheese. All three of them made quick work of their meals, finishing long before the adults made their way around their salads, roast beef, and vegetables.

After finishing their meals, Marcella whispered in Edgar's ear, "Hey, handsome, would you mind driving a girl like me home?"

"Okay guys, don't you think it's time to call it a night?" Edgar asked.

Gloria and the boys walked out and waited on the front porch.

Jesse stopped to pay. "Thanks, Stella. It was great."

Edgar drove Marcella to her house and after escorting her to the front door, gave her a gentle kiss on the cheek.

"Grandpa kissed her," Christopher said with his volume turned up.

"No, he didn't," Brian said.

"Yes, he did. I saw him."

Gloria settled the discussion by siding with Christopher. "I think that was sweet. Don't you, Jesse?"

"Yuk," said Brian.

"Get used to it big man," Jesse said. "That's what people who are about to be married do."

"Well, I'm never getting married, then," Brian said.

When he was certain that Marcella was safely inside, Edgar took his family to his new home where he would spend his first night as a genuine resident of Morgan Crossroads, Alabama. Jesse and Gloria dressed the beds while Edgar dug in boxes and luggage for pajamas and a book to read.

The boys cast their votes for a night of camping out. Gloria vetoed their vote and made pallets on the floor instead.

∽

Just after ten o'clock the next morning, Marcella rang the doorbell at her future home. Edgar welcomed her inside where a beehive of activity had been going for two or three hours.

"Look at this," Marcella said, taking in the changes. "Look how much you've done, already."

"Dad was up at the crack of dawn straightening the kitchen," Gloria said.

"Some of it I saved until you could tell me where you'd like it to go," Edgar said.

"Until I could tell you?" Marcella said. "I hadn't given it any thought."

Jesse said, "It's going to be your kitchen, you know."

"Where would you like this wall hanging?" Gloria asked. "Here?" she said, holding it against the wall. "Or over here," she said, moving it a few feet over.

"I think right there is the perfect spot for it," Marcella said, pointing to the last option.

Marcella followed Jesse, Gloria, and Edgar around the house, giving them her opinion about different decorating and furniture placement suggestions.

"Edgar, I'd like to show you something. Do you have time to take a short drive with me?" Marcella asked.

"Sure. Let me find my keys."

"You can drive my car. You probably wouldn't want to take your car where we're going," she said.

Once situated in Marcella's Chevy, she said, "Go right out of your driveway, then right at the light."

"Where are we going?" Edgar asked as they left Morgan Crossroads, driving toward Porterville.

"Since it's such a beautiful day, I thought it would be a perfect time to drive out to Mason's meadow and see where we will be married."

Past the charred stone chimney in the pasture that she used for a landmark, Marcella pointed out the turn.

The car dipped and jumped and bounced up the dirt road. Thankfully the brunt of the recent storm had bypassed this place.

"Are you sure this is the right way?" Edgar asked.

"Yes, I'm sure. The people who own it promised me that they'd have this road smoothed out by our wedding day," Marcella said.

When they reached the meadow and got out of the car, Edgar said exactly what Marcella had hoped he would. "This is beautiful."

"It is. Listen," she said.

"All I hear is that creek running and some birds singing."

"Exactly. Can you think of a more beautiful place to have our wedding?" Marcella asked.

To their left, a twig snapped in the thicket.

"A deer," she said. "No, look. Two of them."

"This will be perfect." Surveying the layout of the meadow, Edgar said, "The minister could stand there, in that low spot and the guests could stand there, up that gentle slope."

"Everyone would have good visibility and should be able to hear the ceremony," Marcella said.

They sat on part of the fallen sycamore tree near the center of the meadow.

"How are you coming with the arrangements?" Edgar asked.

"I think I've covered just about everything," Marcella said. "Eva Jo is going to bake the cake. Mary Beth is doing the flowers. I've ordered my dress and shoes, and Eva Jo's dress is coming from a bridal shop in Huntsville. The lady came out a few days ago with her catalog and measured her. Oh, and Henry is giving me away. Would that be okay with you?"

"Sure, choose whoever you wish. Henry has looked after you all these years, and it seems that he'd be the perfect person for the job."

"What about suits for the men?" Marcella asked. "Would you like tuxedos, or would you prefer business suits?"

"Personally, I'm not crazy about tuxedos, but I'll wear one if you want me to."

"Okay, business suits for the men. They do need to match, though, don't you think?"

"What about the music?" Edgar asked.

"Have you heard Jesse impersonate professional singers?"

"Yes, but it's been a long time."

"He has such a beautiful voice and I thought he'd do a great job singing *Love Me Tender*. Do you remember how Elvis sang that song?" Marcella asked.

"Of course I do, and I think the song would be perfect," he said. "I don't know if he would agree to do it, though. He's never sung much in front of an audience."

"Well, I haven't asked him yet, but it wouldn't hurt. I thought the people might enjoy it. You know, a little surprise tucked in there for them."

"What about the wedding march? How are you planning to have instrumental music out here?" Edgar asked.

"What do you think about leaving that part out? There is no aisle to walk down, no huge chapel doors to enter through. I thought we might just begin by standing in front of the minister."

"Good idea," Edgar said. "I say let the birds sing the wedding march." Just then, he spotted three deer crossing the creek. He pointed to them without raising his hand and whispered, "Look. They could stand as witnesses." He moved closer to Marcella and held her against his shoulder.

"What about you? Who have you chosen for your best man?"

"Since you want Jesse to sing, he's out of the running. This may not be a great idea, but what would you think I had all three of the grandkids to stand up as my best men?"

"That'd be unusual, but probably no more unusual than a wedding in Mason's meadow. But it's our wedding, and if you want the kids to be your best men, then you shall have them, I say," Marcella said, patting Edgar on the knee.

"Good. I think they'd enjoy that," Edgar said.

"Have I left anything out?" Marcella asked.

"No, I don't think so," he said. "But I've been thinking about the honeymoon."

She bolted straight up. "The honeymoon. I hadn't even thought about that. And the wedding is just two weeks away. Oh my! How did I forget that?"

Edgar took her hand and gently squeezed it. "Maybe that little detail is my department. I wonder how you'd like to take your honeymoon in Paris. Would you like that?"

"Paris? Paris, France? Of course I'd like that. Are you serious that you would take me to Paris for our honeymoon?" A grin spread across her face.

"Absolutely. I'm glad you like the idea because I've already bought the flight tickets and reserved a suite at a hotel there."

Marcella kissed Edgar on the cheek. "You know I won't be worth thirteen cents now, don't you? I'm getting married for the first time in my life, and now I have to plan a wardrobe for a trip to Paris. How much fun do you think one girl can bear?"

They laughed and walked back to the car, their arms around each other.

CHAPTER 35

"It was the awfullest thing you've ever seen," Eva Jo said in an animated way. "One minute, I've got what looks like a wedding cake on the table. The next minute, there's four little plastic feet sticking straight up from the floor. The little bride and groom are buried head first in white cake and icing."

Eva Jo had called Marcella to tell her that there had been a slight hiccup in the wedding cake making process. "No, I don't know what happened. It just slid off the table somehow."

"Well, what are you going to do?" asked Marcella.

"All I can do is try again. The bottom two layers stayed put. It was the top one that got loose."

"Well, we won't need it until the day after tomorrow. Will that be enough time?" Marcella asked.

"Here's the problem," Eva Jo said. "The little plastic guy kinda broke his neck in the fall. Do you have an extra one?"

"Well, no, I don't. And there's not enough time to order another one."

"I thought I might be able to glue him back together, but he's in a little bit too bad a shape for that," Eva Jo said.

"I'll see if I can get Henry or Jesse to run into Huntsville for another one. Surely somebody has one."

"Sorry, Marcella."

"That's alright, Honey. We'll work it out."

Eva Jo propped her fists on her hips and stared at the white blob on the floor. She shook her head. *Why'd you do that?*

⁓

Edgar and Jesse drove to the men's wear shop in Huntsville, armed with a written reminder of the directions Henry had given them a few days earlier. Marcella had seen a navy blue suit in Edgar's closet, decided she liked it just as it was, and suggested they just order a similar one for Jesse.

Jesse tried on the suit to see how accurately it had been altered to fit his tall frame. "Perfect," he told the fitter.

Edgar pulled two fabric samples from his pocket. He told the fitter, "We will also need matching shirts this color," holding up one of the samples. "And silk ties this color," holding up the other sample. The fitter showed them to a display with more shirts than either of them cared to investigate. Single needle tailoring. Double needle tailoring. One hundred percent cotton. Cotton blend. Button cuff or French cuff. After a half hour of inspecting one style, then another, Edgar paid for two cotton shirts with single needle tailoring and French cuffs. He bought four ties, all the same solid color, but two had a design woven into them and the other two had no design. He would let Marcella have the last say on which was the better choice.

Before they left the shop, Jesse asked the fitter if he

might know where they could find a wedding supply store. "We need to find someone who sells wedding cake decorations."

The fitter could not think of one, but a customer who happened to overhear the question said, "There is a bakery that specializes in wedding cakes. She pointed to the right. Just go down this street to the third light and turn left. It's right there on the corner. If you don't need the whole cake, she'd probably sell you just what you need. Her name is Marie. Tell her Liz said, 'Hey.'"

Jesse got behind the wheel and followed the woman's directions straight to the bakery. Inside, Edgar looked around at the presumably plastic sample cakes and enlarged photos of real ones. Nice work.

In a minute Marie appeared and he explained to her that they only needed the little man and woman for the top of the cake.

"What kind of couple do you need?" Marie asked.

"What kind of couple? Actually, I hadn't thought about that. Tell me what you mean and maybe I can answer you," Edgar said.

"You know, is the couple young or older, of a certain ethnicity or different ones, different genders or the same? If you can tell me that, I can probably come up with the perfect little cake topper for you."

Edgar asked Jesse, "How did choosing two little people for a wedding cake become so complicated?"

Jesse told Marie that Edgar was the groom. "The bride is also a senior citizen, same race."

"Great. Now, I see that you have wonderful gray hair. How about the bride? Is she also gray-haired?" Marie asked.

"No," Edgar said, slightly short in his tone. "Her hair is a beautiful vibrant red."

"Good. Just one more question. Would you like them facing each other, or side by side?"

Edgar looked at Marie with a blank expression.

Jesse said, "Either one would be fine. Just show us whatever you have."

Marie excused herself, disappeared through a curtain-covered doorway, and returned with three packages. She held up two of the packages. "I have them separate, so that you could have them facing or side by side. Or ...." She held up the third package. "I have them ballroom dancing."

"That one," Edgar said, pointing to a tiny gray-haired groom and a red-haired bride seemingly lost in each other's arms with the bride's dress swirling around her. He paid for the little dancing couple and headed for the door.

"Oh, I almost forgot," Jesse said. "Liz said, 'Hey.'"

Marie smiled. "Thanks. Do you know Liz?"

"No, ma'am."

Back in the car, Jesse punched into his GPS the address of the jeweler where Edgar and Marcella had ordered their rings. They had left the rings there to be sized and were told they would be ready for pickup today.

At the jeweler, Edgar's ring was ready. Marcella's would be ready in about an hour. To pass the time, Edgar suggested they have lunch and return later to pick up both rings. The jeweler recommended a restaurant a few blocks down the street. "It's just down the street on right. You could walk from here. You can't miss it."

The men settled into a comfortable booth in the quietest part of the restaurant. Both ordered prime rib with a baked potato and mixed green salad.

After the server had brought the food and left the table, Edgar said, "Jesse, you and I haven't really talked about this marriage idea. I know that you are supporting Marcella and me in it, but I'm curious to know what you really think about me getting married at this time in my life."

"It's a huge change," said Jesse. "I never thought I'd see you sell your house and leave everything you had accomplished behind."

"Does that bother you?"

"No, not on any level that matters much. Did you and Marcella ever discuss the differences in the life she lives and the one you've been used to?" Jesse asked.

Edgar took a swallow of iced tea. "Yes. She was concerned that I might find it hard to get used to her simpler way of living."

"Things do move slower down here," Jesse said.

"Much slower," Edgar said in a drawn out way. "But I think that will be good for me."

"There don't seem to be too many affluent people in Morgan Crossroads," Jesse said.

"Maybe not in money, but some of them are very affluent in other ways, like respect within the community and wisdom. And common sense. I think it takes a lot of common sense to live a rural life," Edgar said.

"Do you intend to keep up with your holdings in Texas?"

Edgar said, "I got rid of most of them. You know that I sold the house. I also sold all of my real estate investments except for Gloria's house and one other."

"Let me guess," Jesse said. "You kept the diner."

"How did you know that?"

"It wasn't hard. It was the last place you saw Marcella when you were in college, and the first place you took her when she and Eva Jo went to Texas."

"You're right. I kept it for sentimental reasons, I suppose. The only change I made was that it is in both names now, mine and Marcella's," Edgar said.

"Actually, I think that's pretty cool in some way," Jesse said.

"Cool?"

"Yeah, cool." Jesse smiled.

"Gloria hasn't said anything about my moving either. She seems excited, but I have to wonder how she's feeling about it deep down," Edgar said.

"She's terribly excited and happy for you and Marcella. She cried when she found out you were getting married."

"She never told me that," Edgar said.

"She wouldn't," said Jesse.

"Is she nervous about being out in Texas without me there to help her?"

"Financially? Probably. But not in any other way that I can think of."

"Gloria has worked hard to take care of those boys. I haven't told her this yet, but I will tonight after the kids go to bed. I've set up a fund that will pay her utilities and a stipend for food, gas, and any other living expenses for her and the boys so that she can go back to culinary school full-time and finish. She has a knack for baking and I want to see her have her own business someday."

"She's going to be thrilled," Jesse said. "She was disappointed that she had to drop out before."

The server topped off their tea glasses. "Would you like to see our dessert menu?"

"No, we won't need any. Thank you, anyway," Jesse said.

"You can leave the check whenever you're ready," Edgar said.

"She's been concerned about trying to start college funds for the boys." Edgar said. "She doesn't know this, but each of them has had a trust fund almost from the day they were born that is large enough to fund housing, books, and tuition to the college of his choice, from admission to graduation."

"Wow, Dad. She's going to flip when she hears all of this. Thank you for doing that for her. She deserves it."

"Jesse, son, you have a good job and as far as I can see, you are doing very well for yourself. But you should know that I'm willing to help you, too. If you ever come up with a good idea that you need a little boost getting off the ground, I hope you'll let me know."

Jesse reached across the table and shook his dad's hand. "Thanks," Jesse said, tightening his grip slightly.

~

"Would you look at that? Where did you find a little Edgar and Marcella dancing like that?" Eva Jo held the cake topper up for a good look at it. "This is as good as it gets."

The repaired cake sat in the center of the kitchen table, fully decorated and waiting for the topper. "What do you think?" Eva Jo asked.

Jesse said, "This is not your first wedding cake, is it?"

"Oh, I had one at all three of my weddings, but none of them was this big. This is the first one I baked myself, though. Thing weighs about a ton," Eva Jo said with a cackle.

"How are you going to get it to the church?" Jesse asked.

"I don't know yet. I'm about half afraid it'll fall apart before I get there if I try to haul it in my pickup truck," Eva Jo said. "You know, it kinda shakes and rattles a little. Probably a little too much for a cake like this.

"No, that probably wouldn't be a good idea. How about I borrow Dad's car? It has a smooth ride and large doors to slide the cake in. I could drive and you could ride next to it to hold it still," Jesse said.

"Can you be here about nine tomorrow morning so we can get it up to the church hall?"

"Consider it done."

~

"What do you mean, have I bought my suit yet?" Henry bellowed into the phone.

"Henry, you simply cannot wear coveralls to the only wedding Marcella will ever have," Polly said.

"I don't know why. She's never seen me in anything else but coveralls. Why change now?"

"Tell me, Henry, can you name one thing bigger than this wedding that has ever happened in Morgan Crossroads? Ever?"

"I reckon not."

"The wedding is tomorrow, Henry. You can call Casey or Cecil or somebody." Polly Brown's voice rose and lowered like a tidal wave. "Lock the front door if you have to, but get yourself into Huntsville and buy a decent looking suit. And find some dress shoes, too. Those Wellingtons won't cut it."

Polly heard Henry mumble something into the phone. Something about cost.

"I don't know how much it will cost. What else are you going do with that money? Break into one of those coffee cans and take enough money to buy one, whatever it costs. Oh, and you're gonna need a dress shirt—a long-sleeved one. And a nice tie. You should take a few hundred at least, I'd say. And don't forget, you've got that shindig tonight, so you'd better get a move on."

"I don't want to wear a suit, Polly. The thing will choke me." Henry stared at the checkout counter, mindlessly moving the two-cent mints container from one spot to another, then back. He mumbled something else, tracing the beveled edge of the glass in the counter top with his finger.

"What was that?" Polly asked.

"I, I don't know how to tie one of them ties."

"I'm not backing down on this one, Henry Brown. If you show up at that wedding and think you are going to stand next to Marcella in coveralls—I don't even want to think about it. You're going to stand out like a pickle in a banana pudding. Now, we'll find somebody to help with that tie. I'll call Marcella and see if she thinks Jesse might be able to go with you. He knows about suits."

CHAPTER 36

*T*here would be no aisle to walk down and no special seating arrangements, so Marcella decided to forgo having a wedding rehearsal. In its place, though, Henry and Cecil Grey decided that there should be a community-wide celebration. Edgar and Marcella agreed, knowing that there would be no way around it, whether or not they said yes.

Eva Jo and Gertrude Gleaves had volunteered to oversee the post-wedding reception, but only with the understanding that the church hall would be off-limits for the community celebration the evening before. "There'll be plenty to do without having to mop floors, clean greasy fingerprints off the windows and haul out two tons of garbage," Eva Jo had said.

After tossing ideas around for a while, Cecil asked Stella if they might use Lucy's Cafe and its adjoining parking lot for a barbecue. She agreed to close the cafe for normal business and instead make it available for a place to serve potluck food for the cookout.

Henry, Cecil, Dora Mae, and Jewell set up their grills in

the parking lot. Dora Mae had stated proudly that she was the only champion barbecuer in the valley. Henry dismissed the idea, reminding everyone present that she could only say that because no one else from the valley had ever competed.

Eva Jo and Gertrude had agreed to allow tables and folding chairs from the church hall to be used for the community party. That is, provided they were thoroughly cleaned and returned as soon as the dinner was over. Grumpy enlisted Ollie, Jesse, and Eva Jo's grandson to help haul them and set them up in the parking lot.

"Make sure you put those tables upwind from the grills," Henry reminded them.

Inside, Stella and Polly lined up several tables for the covered dishes that would be coming. There were separate tables for vegetables, salads, and desserts, which they hoped would include Jewell's famous extra sticky pineapple upside down cake. Cecil and Henry had asked Lorraine Haley to order plenty of hamburgers, steaks, and ribs especially for the occasion.

People drove in for the dinner from one end of the valley to the other and beyond. Word had gotten out over in Porterville and even as far up as Huntland, across the state line in Tennessee. There were dozens of men and women who had sat in Marcella's school classrooms and descendants of families whose lives had forever changed in some way because of the generosity of Marcella's father. Many more came who had heard the story of Edgar's and Marcella's secret and long distance love for each other, some who had heard it on the gossip vine at the laundromat in Porterville and others who had heard it through the more prolific chatter machine more commonly known as the Women's Missionary League at the Methodist church down near the Huntsville highway.

Traffic was so heavy that Cecil, acting as the official voice of Morgan Crossroads, asked the Whipper County Sheriff Department to send out a patrol car or two to help see that people who parked alongside the roadway could walk to Lucy's safely.

Because of the deluge of casseroles, desserts, and other foods, the three original tables grew in number to twelve. Brown's General Store and Haley's Grocery chipped in and provided an assortment of chips, cups, and iced down bottled drinks.

Revelers far outnumbered chairs, so much so that as many sat on the grass around the edges of the lot as sat at tables. Some gathered lawn chairs from the trunks of their cars. Others sat on borrowed blankets, or even on the bare grass. None seemed to mind, wherever they sat.

Raucous applause broke out when Marcella and Edgar walked to their table with their plates. Marcella, stunned by the turnout, and Edgar, who had been totally unprepared for the community's show of affection, joined Gloria, Jesse, and the grandkids at the only fully adorned table—a large round one covered with a linen table cloth, a vase of red roses, linen napkins, silver flatware, and the Rosebud china that had only ever been used for Rosebud Circle gatherings.

After everyone had been served and the smoke from the grills had died down, Polly borrowed a large skillet from Stella and banged the bottom of it with a metal spatula to catch their attention. "Hey everybody. Can I have your attention?"

She looked over the crowd for Henry, but didn't see him. "Can somebody go grab Henry for me, wherever he is?"

Grumpy shot off around the corner of the building and returned in a few seconds with Henry in tow.

"Henry," Polly said. "Can you come help me with this?"

Henry went to Polly's side and took a white envelope from her. "Okay, people, hold it down just a minute or two." He invited Marcella and Edgar to join him and Polly.

"We're all here because you two are doing something that nobody around here ever imagined we'd see. You're getting married tomorrow and that's gonna probably be the biggest thing that any of us can remember ever happening around here."

Edgar tightened his arm around Marcella's waist a bit. Her face turned a darker shade of pink as she looked up into his eyes. They held their gaze, lost in each other, hardly breathing as the crowd fell silent.

Henry cleared his throat and adjusted the straps on his coveralls. "We all decided to do this so that everybody that wanted to might have chance to come around and congratulate you and help you celebrate just a little bit. A bunch of us here in Morgan Crossroads put our heads together and came up with a little something for a wedding gift for you two lovebirds."

He held the envelope in the air. "We got you two tickets for a week-long cruise on a ship down to the Bahamas. It's the closest thing we could find to the Love Boat."

Applause erupted and went on long enough to embarrass Marcella. She took the envelope from Henry and nudged Edgar.

"You were right, Henry," Edgar said. "This is a night I had hoped for for a very long time, but never thought I'd actually live to see. You've welcomed me and made me feel like I belong here.

"All of you have come together to make this the best week that I have ever lived. Tomorrow you will witness me taking the young lady that I first met more than fifty years ago in a library at The University of Texas to be my bride. You've looked on as two old hearts with new energy have come together. Marcella has waited on me and I have waited on her for all these years, and I mean that in every sense of the word. I thank you for being a part of our celebration."

Applause erupted across the crowd. Edgar raised his hand. "Marcella has something she'd like to say."

"I could repeat everything that Edgar just said, but I'll just add to it, instead. I know that most of you were a bit confused when Eva Jo and I came home from a little vacation to Texas with a good-looking man on my arm."

"You can say that again," Dora Mae said, starting a rash of laughter across the crowd.

"By now, you know more about that. I just want to say that I never told anybody because I always carried hope in my heart that Edgar and I would meet again. In some way I thought that if I went around talking about the two of us, I might somehow jinx us and mess up the whole idea. Apparently I did something right. I never told, and here he is."

The crowd erupted again with applause, but quieted quickly.

Marcella continued. "And along with a husband, I'm getting a wonderful son, a beautiful and talented daughter, and three good looking grandchildren. I can't ask for any more than that. Now, over the past few days, along with getting ready for the wedding, we've moved most of my belongings to Edgar's house. So, effective right after the wedding, I will be Marcella Garrison and I will no longer live where you've always come to visit me. Tomorrow night we will have our first night together in our new home. The following day, Jesse, Gloria, and the boys will fly back to Texas and Edgar and I will zip off to Paris, France for our honeymoon."

Shrill whistles and yells echoed across the crowd.

Marcella straightened herself. Through a smile that she could hardly contain, she said "Tomorrow, the dream of my life comes true. If it is any better than this, I'm not sure I'll be able to handle it. And thank you so much for the cruise. Whose idea was that anyway?"

More than a dozen people raised their hands across the crowd, pointing at each other.

"It was Polly's idea."

"Jewell thought of the cruise."

"I think Cecil came up with it first."

On through the crowd it went, each person trying to out-yell the other.

"Well, whoever was involved, you probably know that this will be my very first cruise. And we'll take it right after we get back from my very first trip to Paris."

It was as if someone had blown the roof out of the sky. Edgar and Marcella could do nothing but absorb the roar of thunderous applause and ear-splitting whistles.

CHAPTER 37

By six o'clock Saturday morning, Polly's House of Beauty was a hive of activity. The aroma of Polly's freshly brewed coffee and Gertrude Gleaves' homemade cinnamon rolls overpowered the smell of hairspray and nail polish. There was a palpable air of excitement, like the state fair or the circus was coming to Morgan Crossroads.

Jewell Crabtree was under the hair dryer, and Linda Cruz was almost finished with Stella's nails.

"I didn't know you could do nails," Stella said.

"It's been a while, but I went through a nail technician program at a cosmetology school and got my license. That was before I made up my mind to become a pharmacist. It helped pay my way through college," Linda said.

"Thanks for stepping in for me, Linda," Polly shouted over the roar of the dryer and the gossip wheel that was spinning furiously. "Do you think you could do Lorraine for me?"

Linda motioned Lorraine to the manicure table and set into removing her old polish.

"Time's up," Polly said as she stopped the dryer for Jewell. "Let's get this hair finished."

"Do you know what Marcella is wearing for the wedding?" Jewell asked.

"Haven't heard," Polly said.

"I heard she was talking about trying to wear a gown," Dora Mae Crawford said.

"How does she think she can manage a gown out there in that meadow?" Jewell asked.

"What about shoes? Surely she's not planning to wear any kind of crazy heels out there," Polly said.

"I think Edgar might put the squash on that idea," Dora Mae said, nodding.

"I asked Eva Jo what Marcella was planning to wear and she tried to act like she didn't have a clue," Stella said.

"All I have to say about it is I hope Marcella doesn't try to go out there looking like the Queen of Sheba," Dora Mae said. "I can just see her now. She'll be falling all over herself, trying to keep her ankles straight in those heels and holding her gown up so she doesn't hang it on a tree stump or something."

Polly said, "I have a feeling Marcella will be a site to behold. In a good way, I mean. She'll be beautiful. You wait and see. I'm doing her hair at twelve."

"At twelve. The wedding's at two, isn't it?" Jewell asked.

"That's cutting it close, I'd say," Stella said.

"She wanted her hair to be the last thing she did before she put her dress on," Polly said.

"When is Eva Jo doing her hair? She's the maid of honor, I think." Jewell said.

"She usually does her own hair, except for cutting it," Polly said. "She's coming in at eleven, though—after she takes the cake to the church hall."

"Has anybody seen the dress Eva Jo's wearing?" Dora Mae asked.

Jewell stood and looked into the large wall mirror, patting all over her head, but moving not a hair. "I haven't heard about it if they have, but I know the bridal shop in Huntsville made one for her."

"I'm sure Eva Jo will be very pretty," Gertrude Gleaves said. "You wait and see."

"I wonder if that dress was what was in that big old box that I saw the UPS man carrying to her front door," Dora Mae said.

Polly looked at Dora Mae. How does one woman manage to see every single thing that happens in this place?

~

"I sure hope I do this right," Edgar said while sliding his tie into place.

"Do what right? Your tie?" Jesse asked.

"No, no. I hope I do this marriage thing right."

"I bet you do a spectacular job of it."

"I wish I could be that sure of myself," Edgar said.

"What's the deal with these last minute jitters, Dad? Haven't you been mentally practicing for this moment for several decades?"

"Sure I have. But in reality, I have more than seventy years' experience in the art of bachelorhood."

"Look at it this way," Jesse said. "So has Marcella. She's also been single for that long."

"Exactly. When two young people marry, they have their entire lives to grow together, to hopefully become one tight little unit. We both grew, Marcella and myself, but we did our growing along straight lines that never had another chance to intersect," Edgar said. "Thanks to my foolishness."

"Well now, they have intersected," Jesse said. "That's what counts today."

"A thousand times I've wished I'd never left Marcella behind. I've stood in my back yard looking out over Lake Travis many times, wondering how I could've made such a foolish decision." Edgar's eyes locked with Jesse's. "I've wondered why I was so fearful of finding Marcella."

For a minute, the ticking clock on the wall was the loudest sound in the room.

"Well now, you've found each other," Jesse said. He placed his hand on his dad's shoulder and nudged him toward the door. "Come on, we have a wedding to do."

∽

Marcella selected an antique Lalique perfume bottle from her dresser and gave the atomizer one gentle squeeze. Eva Jo sat on Marcella's bed and watched.

"You know you are going to cause that poor man's knees to fall right out from under him, don't you?" Eva Jo said.

"Do you think I can do this?" Marcella asked, turning around on her dressing stool.

"Of course you can. Honey, if there is a woman in Morgan Crossroads that can pull this off, it's you."

"I'm serious, Eva Jo." Marcella looked around the room, her hands following her eyes. "Take a good look at this house. I was born here and except for college, I've never lived anywhere else."

"And?" Eva Jo asked.

"It's so ordinary and I love it. But by tonight this house

will be where I used to live. I'll be living in a house that, compared to this one, is a mansion."

"You are going to adjust like a kid to new bicycle."

"But ...." Marcella locked her fingers together in her lap. "Life itself will change just as much. How am I going to learn to be the wife of a lawyer?"

"Ex-lawyer," Eva Jo said. "You are going to learn to be the wife of a man who used to be a lawyer, but retired just in time to be your husband. Look at it that way, why don't you?"

"I hadn't thought of it like that."

"And here's something else for you. Look how much Edgar's life is about to change. He gets up in the morning, runs through the shower, and takes three minutes to pick out a full suit of clothes for the day. You know, he's got a handful of shirts, a few suits, and a pair of green golf shorts that I saw Gloria hang in his closet. I can't wait to see him wear those over to see Henry," Eva Jo said, trying not to laugh.

"That doesn't sound like that much of a change," Marcella said.

"Oh, that's not going to be the hard part for him," Eva Jo said. "That poor man is going to wake up every morning to see you standing in front of a closet with more clothes in it than a Macy's store. And when he gets over that, he's going to have to face that army of perfume bottles and make up and nail polish and have you told him that you have your very own shoe department?"

"Should I leave some of them here?" Marcella asked.

"I don't know, but if we don't get going, Edgar's going to be standing out there in the middle of that meadow wondering if you fell off the planet."

"Would you look at that?" Marcella asked.

Ahead, cars lined both sides of the highway. Sheriff's Department officers stood by, directing some cars into the pasture next to the old charred chimney across the road from Mason's meadow.

After a few seconds of discussion, Eva Jo and Marcella had decided that Eva Jo's rusty old truck would probably be just a little too much for their new dresses and shoes to bear. Eva Jo drove them to the meadow in Marcella's car.

When Tommy Jordan, the officer, saw the car and the two familiar faces shining through the windshield, he directed them up the road toward the meadow. "Hey, there, Eva Jo. Miss Peabody. Ollie Smith came out here yesterday and graded the lane so you'd have a nice smooth ride up to the meadow."

"Have you seen Edgar?" Marcella asked.

Tommy's brow furrowed while he thought for a minute.

"Big fancy car," Eva Jo said.

"Oh, sure. A nice looking man with some little boys and a couple other people. BMW, I think."

"That's them. Thanks."

At the top of the lane, the meadow came into view on the left.

"Can you believe this?" Marcella asked.

At the low end of the meadow, beside the creek a small lectern stood between two tables that were covered with lace and topped with white and yellow lilies. There were two rows of folding chairs, borrowed from the church hall. From there the meadow sloped gently, like a natural amphitheater, to the fence. People were tightly packed across the entire meadow, some standing, others with lawn chairs.

Gloria hurried to Marcella's car as soon as she saw it stop.

"Everybody's here," she said. "Dad's in his car waiting and pretending not to watch for you."

Marcella smiled. "How is he?"

"He's fine," Gloria said. "I don't think I've ever seen him so nervous about anything. It's actually kinda fun to watch him, like suddenly, he's twenty and bringing his girlfriend home to show her off."

"Is Jeremiah here?" Eva Jo asked.

"Who?"

"The preacher," Marcella said.

"Oh, sure, he's here and anxious to get started," Gloria said.

"Is that Henry?" Marcella asked, pointing toward the rear of the crowd. "I hardly recognized him."

In place of denim overalls, Henry wore a nicely tailored navy blue suit, white shirt, and a patterned tie complete with a perfectly proportioned knot that Jesse had tied for him.

He spotted Marcella and Eva Jo and hurried to help them out of the car.

"Henry! You look like a completely different man," Marcella said.

He tugged at the knot.

Eva Jo swatted at his hand. "Quit. You'll get it all out of whack."

He snatched his hand back. "I don't know if that's good or bad, but it's your wedding day, so I bought a suit. Besides that, Polly made me."

Marcella and Eva Jo both laughed.

"That's the first time in the history of mankind that Henry Brown ever did what his wife told him to do," Eva Jo said.

"Well, thank you, Henry," Marcella said, giving him a slight hug.

Jesse walked Edgar to his spot in front of the lectern. Gloria nudged the boys, all in matching suits and ties, into position next to Edgar. Jewell Crabtree prodded her granddaughter into place with her basket of flowers.

When Jeremiah signaled, Edgar turned to watch the processional. Eva Jo walked slowly along the edge of the crowd and across the front to the lectern, followed closely by the flower girl, who haphazardly scattered lavender rose petals along the path.

Henry offered his arm to Marcella and escorted her gently to the lectern. All over the meadow, whispers and muffled comments peppered the air.

"Look at that dress," one said.

"She's gorgeous," said someone else.

Marcella walked beside Henry in an elegantly simple off-white silhouette dress, covered by a lace and pearl overlay with three quarter sleeves.

"Look at the back of her dress," Polly whispered loudly to Jewell Crabtree. "She looks so petite."

Her dress was banded at the waist with a long gold sash that followed her feminine figure down the back, stopping at the scalloped lace that formed the hem.

"And no heels," Jewell whispered back to Polly.

Marcella had considered the terrain and chose a pair of muted gold flats.

Eva Jo wore a similar dress, but with solid sleeves and without the lace overlay.

"I told you Eva Jo was going to be beautiful. Look at her," Gertrude Gleaves said to Dora Mae, pointing at Eva Jo.

"She hasn't dressed up like that since the school prom," Stella said behind a cupped hand.

Henry kissed Marcella on the cheek and sat beside Polly.

In the trees beyond the creek, chickadees and mocking

birds sang. Overhead, a perfectly clear azure sky covered them. From behind the crowd, a hawk flew past, swooped across the creek, then lit on a fence post, as if just in time for the festivities.

Marcella stood next to Edgar and watched as Jesse rose and walked to the left end of the flower-covered table. Expecting a talk of some kind, the audience sounded a collective gasp when the six-foot eight-inch tattooed literature professor with a ponytail halfway down his back broke into a near perfect Elvis impersonation of Love Me Tender, complete with a hiked up lip at the end.

So much for solemnity. The entire meadow came alive with laughter and applause. Eva Jo snickered.

"Watch Marcella and Edgar," Polly said to Henry through a laugh.

Marcella's and Edgar's shoulders were jumping as they both fought to hold back their own laughter.

Jeremiah approached the lectern. "What am I supposed to do now?" he asked the audience. "I had this all memorized and now it's gone," he said, smiling.

After a minute or two some semblance of order returned to the meadow and the preacher tried again. He successfully recalled where he'd put his notes and made it through the wedding vows.

"Edgar, do you take this woman, Marcella, to be your wedded wife, so long as you both shall live?"

"I do," Edgar said softly but directly to Marcella.

"Marcella, do you ...?"

"Absolutely!" she said, without waiting for the remaining questions.

Startled at the sudden outburst from the normally reserved little lady, Jeremiah stammered and asked, "Well, then, who has the rings?"

Henry stepped forward.

The ceremony completed when Jeremiah said to Edgar, "You may kiss the bride."

Edgar bent and wrapped his arms gently around Marcella and kissed her softly and passionately.

"Yuk!" Christopher shouted, just before Gloria could clamp her hand across her son's mouth.

"Reception's at the church hall," Henry yelled to the crowd. "Get there as soon as you can."

∼

Eva Jo's wedding cake, including the dancing couple on top, had survived the ride to the church hall in fine fashion. Jesse had carried the cake in the back seat of Edgar's car, with Eva Jo sitting next to it to minimize any jostling that it might endure along the way.

Mary Beth had turned out her best work when she designed the floral arrangements. Vases of beautiful white and yellow lilies accented the table, which was covered with satin and lace tablecloths.

On either end of the table, punch bowls sat at the ready, manned by Dora Mae on one end and Gertrude Gleaves on the other.

Grumpy had offered his karaoke machine, which the women put to good use playing big band music from the 40s and 50s.

To eliminate any possibility of a riotous attack on the cake, Marcella and Edgar cut their ritualistic pieces early and fed each other.

Marcella and Edgar had the first dance to *When A Man Loves A Woman*. Then, Jesse invited Eva Jo to dance with him to *On Blueberry Hill*. Gloria tried to dance to a more upbeat tune with Christopher, Brian, and Joshua, but that soon fell apart and the boys opted instead to go outside and chase each other around the yard.

After an hour of laughter, food, and gossip, Edgar tapped his spoon against his glass and asked for everyone's attention. Marcella joined him.

Henry stepped in to help quell the applause.

"There is one other thing that I almost forgot," Marcella said. She turned her back to the crowd and tossed her bouquet over her shoulder as heartily as she could. Women all over the church hall grabbed for it. Lorraine Haley touched it with her fingertips, but just hard enough to deflect it straight into Linda Cruz's hands.

Linda let out a slight scream. "Oh, no!" she said, laughing. "I don't even have a boyfriend. Now what?"

In the middle of the excitement over the potential of another wedding in Morgan Crossroads, the Garrisons and their family drove away and left the cleanup to those friends who had asked for the honor.

∼

By evening, Marcella and her new family had settled in. The boys, exhausted, fell asleep early.

Gloria and Jesse retired to their rooms, worn out and needing rest for the trip home tomorrow.

Edgar excused himself and went to take a shower.

Marcella had moved her Queen Anne chair and antique side table from her old house to the new one and had arranged them in front of the fireplace. Edgar's recliner had been relegated to his office and in its place sat the heavy chair that Marcella had bought for Edgar years earlier. She sat in her chair and looked at the table. In the center of it sat

Papa, just as he had for decades. She walked to the fireplace mantle, took the silver-framed picture of Edgar, and returned to her chair. She held Edgar's photo in her lap and gently picked up Papa from the table. She focused intently on the fading image. "You're disappearing."

She placed Edgar's photo in the center of the antique table, and took Papa down the hall to her bedroom, where she tucked him safely away in the back of her keepsake drawer. "Thank you, Papa."

Then, from the corner of her eye she noticed the bed turned down and on her pillow, a single long stem red rose decorated with a delicate gold lace ribbon tied in a bow.

ABOUT THE AUTHOR

Tom Buford is an author of fun fiction for the entire family. He and his bride have been married more than 44 years and make their home in rural Tennessee.

You can learn more about Tom and his writing on his website at:

tombuford.com

Be sure to register for Tom's mailing list to keep up to date with Marcella, Eva Jo, Dora Mae, and the rest of Morgan Crossroads.

If you enjoyed *Then Came Edgar*, please consider returning to the online store where you bought it and leave a review.

twitter.com/tombufordauthor

goodreads.com/TomBuford

pinterest.com/tombufordauthor

ALSO BY TOM BUFORD

Living With Fibromyalgia Patients: 79 Ways You Can Make Their Lives Better

CPSIA information can be obtained
at www.ICGtesting.com
Printed in the USA
LVHW092037071118
596327LV00001B/2/P

9 780970 810359